Shattered Tempests
Order and Chaos: Book 3
Jessica Dall

Shattered Tempests
Order and Chaos™
Red Adept Publishing, LLC
104 Bugenfield Court
Garner, NC 27529
http://RedAdeptPublishing.com/

First Print Edition: March 2019
Cover Art by Streetlight Graphics

Chapter One

Palmer's skull throbbed, energy pulsing between his eyes. He released the blue-tinged blurred vision and took a breath as his eyelids opened. Since Brier had regained consciousness a month earlier, Palmer's powers had been working about as well as they ever had, so he had to assume that whatever new thing was blocking him couldn't be good—especially when what he did see foretold more war and destruction.

"Damned visions," Palmer mumbled. He should have studied more when Goebel had first tried to train them a year before. Being able to block out the onslaught of information floating in the ether had seemed much more helpful at the time—it fixed all the odd problems Palmer had struggled with as a child before he even knew he had powers—but it didn't help him and Brier now. Not with something dangerous hovering far too close to them.

Irritation still working its way through him, Palmer stood, glancing across the little square house Brier and he had settled into. At least he hadn't woken her. Though she'd been better since they moved the ghosts of previous incarnations out of her head and into the ring she wore, she still didn't sleep well.

Moving as quietly as he could manage, he stepped past the cracked red plaster of the ancient doorframe and onto the lopsided street. Between the delicate pink light starting along the low mountains on the eastern horizon and the warm spring breeze, the city of ruins looked peacefully inviting. If only he could overlook the dread hovering over them all and enjoy the view.

A sudden buzz of activity registered in Palmer's mind, taking him out of his thoughts. He turned, searching the line of mostly demolished connected houses as he walked toward it. With Brier and him being half the population of Venchia, save a few doomsday cultists who still remained to worship Brier, Palmer had to assume what it was. Nico Adessi was having trouble sleeping. Again.

Around the next corner, Nico was pacing across the half house he had claimed—jumping in and out of sight behind the jagged wall that separated the space from the road. Palmer watched the man, debating whether he should try to divine what Nico was doing. *That would be practice, at least.* Instead, he walked up to the missing chunk of wall that likely had once been the doorway.

"You're up early."

Nico spun, hand going to his hip. Palmer glanced at the dagger strapped there and raised an eyebrow. Gods knew who Nico Adessi thought was going to attack him.

Nico's hand slid back down to his side as he recovered. "What are you doing here?"

"Got the feeling something was happening."

"Of course you did," Nico mumbled, running a hand through his blond hair—which was only just starting to look unkempt, somehow, after all the time they'd been living away from civilization. Even in the middle of nowhere, Adessis managed to look refined. Palmer had to wonder if that was *Nico's* power.

Palmer looked deeper into the half house and frowned at the full pack resting against the far wall. "Are you headed somewhere?"

"Shouldn't you know?" Nico turned away, going back to gathering the few things still left on the cracked foundation.

"People prefer being asked most of the time." Palmer didn't feel the need to bring up the headache he already had from just a blurry vision.

Nico rolled a blanket and stuffed it into his pack then tightened the drawstring. "I'm going hunting."

"Didn't you go yesterday?"

"I'm going again."

Palmer glanced at the pack. "Carrying everything you own with you?"

Nico's jaw twitched slightly, but he turned back to Palmer. "I take it the general hasn't had a change of heart about sending us troops this morning?"

Palmer shook his head. He hadn't had high hopes about General Gully agreeing to send any of his men from Latysia to help them strengthen Venchia when Brier had first suggested dispatching Cerise to make the request. After getting a very clear vision of Gully's reaction to the request—*I will not be ordered about by a little girl playing war!*—Palmer didn't have much faith that even trickster goddess Cerise—as duplicitous as she could be—would be able to pull soldiers away from the general.

"Then it seems we need to find an army somewhere else, if you're still intent on staying here."

Brier's the one who wanted to stay here... Palmer vaguely wondered if she was regretting that choice after a month of sitting around in empty ruins. "You're going to find an army?"

"Someone needs to."

"And you didn't think this was something that should be discussed?"

Nico rolled his eyes and pulled his pack over his shoulder. "Who else is going to go? You? The half man?" He motioned in the general direction of where they had left Goebel—still unconscious from being hit with whatever weakened version of Brier's powers had been sent his way a month before. "I can head north. There are pilgrimages with temples run by people already dedicating their lives to the gods. We might as well try to put them to good use."

Palmer had to admit it wasn't a bad idea. They certainly needed a new plan. *Still...* "You were going to leave without telling anyone?"

"You wouldn't have been able to figure out where I'd gone?" Nico shot him a challenging look.

"Brier?" Palmer asked, letting her name carry the weight of whatever her and Nico's relationship was after fourteen years.

Nico's body went stiff, and his nostrils flared as he released a breath. "If you hadn't noticed, we haven't much been on speaking terms lately."

"Not because she doesn't want to be."

He scoffed. "What does that mean?"

She knows you slept with her while she was possessed and that you know she doesn't remember, and she is waiting for you to come clean. Palmer tried to think of a way to say that without revealing that *he* had told Brier about it or getting her upset that he'd gotten in the middle of the standoff she and Nico were having. He shook his head. "She knows you're keeping something from her. I think she's waiting for you to talk first."

Nico's face went hard, and he turned to grab the rest of the weapons he kept in his half house. "I'll be back. It shouldn't take more than a week or two to reach the temples nearby."

"You have to tell her."

Nico shoved his longbow over his free shoulder. He'd been practicing with it nearly nonstop over the past month. "Is that a fact?"

"You don't think she deserves to know?"

"She never has to."

"It—"

"You've already won, all right?" Nico said. "So save me the morality play."

"What?"

Nico scoffed. "Do you really need me to say it?"

Palmer furrowed his eyebrows.

"She hasn't wanted to be with me since she came back with you. I'm not an idiot. And that's the great cosmic plan—you two all cuddled up together—isn't it? So I'm done. Leaving. You've won."

Palmer tried to think of something to say. "I—"

"You can tell her goodbye for me, if you think it will matter." Nico's eyes slid away from Palmer as he patted the weapons on him as if he needed to make sure he hadn't forgotten any of them.

"You really think it might not matter?"

The slightest twitch in Nico's expression said he knew what he was doing, but he shook his head and brushed past Palmer through the opening. "Expect me back in a couple of weeks." He hesitated for a beat. "Take care of her."

"You should say goodbye."

"Perhaps." Nico turned down the hill toward the easiest place to cross the river and headed north.

Palmer watched him go, not sure he was ready to handle what would happen when Brier did wake up to find that Nico Adessi had left the city. She still hadn't recovered from them not being able to find Rosette.

BRIER SET THE BOOK down on the floor of the little white room that had been turned into the new Augarian library, not entirely able to shake the thought that doing so would have given her head-librarian late father a fit. If sitting on the floor helped Rosette pay attention as Brier continued to try teaching the little girl to read, it would have to do.

"Try from the top."

"Books are stupid." Rosette pouted, little arms crossed tightly over the fine dress Brier had sewn to fit the seven-year-old.

"They're wonderful after you learn to read them." Brier took a seat across from her.

"Reading is stupid."

"Plenty of people would be thrilled to have the chance to learn to read. Not many little girls get to."

Rosette said something, but the words came out garbled.

"What, piccola*?" Brier looked up, but something was wrong. Rosette still sat there, but her little form flickered in and out, bathed in a deep red glow.*

Brier's heart rate spiked. "Rosie?"

The white room pulsed red and purple, holes opening up in the beautiful walls as Rosette continued to speak.

"Ros—"

"Kill them all."

Brier started awake, the final words rattling around her brain in a voice that was much too deep to have been Rosette's. Breathing too heavily, Brier propped herself up on her elbows and looked around. "Palmer?"

The little house was empty.

Releasing a tense breath, Brier lay back down on the pallet of blankets and pillows they had found amongst the stockpiled supplies in town. She'd been far too unappreciative of the feather mattress she slept on in the Augarian Palace. Then again, she'd lived with much worse over the past year, including sleeping on the bare ground in the middle of winter when she, Palmer, and Rosette had walked the entire way back to Latysia. Her stomach twisted. *Rosette.*

She sat up in a huff, pushing the hair that had escaped her braid overnight out of her face more roughly than was called for. It was likely better that Palmer had already left for the morning. The darker her nightmares became, the less she felt the need to share. And no matter what she could tell him of her dreams, he hadn't been able to get a sense of where Rosette had gone—if she was even still alive.

Making him search more was becoming not much better than self-flagellation.

A face appeared at the doorway, and Brier barely managed to stifle a groan. Since Peony had woken from her own quick possession, she'd been hovering around like a lost puppy, all but whimpering for Palmer's attention by the hour. With all the other problems they had in Venchia, the last thing Brier needed was a simpering, useless woman wandering around, lovesick over a man who was entirely clueless.

But Palmer had insisted that Peony needed to stay. "She's the only other one with a former incarnation in her mind who we can talk to, Bri," he'd said. "We might need her to get Marina and Clover gone for good."

Brier rubbed the ring on her right hand. The object still contained a pair of specters who had previously been in her mind. Unable to keep the disdain out of her voice as she looked at the woman in the doorway, she said, "Yes?"

"Oh... I..." Peony said. "I'm sorry. I was just... I..."

Brier felt Palmer's approach a second before he appeared just behind Peony's shoulder.

"Morning." He looked between Peony and Brier before settling on Peony as she twisted to face him. "Everything all right?"

"Yes!" Peony's dark-tan skin flushed red. "I just... well, my head... it hurts? I..."

Brier rolled her eyes, feeling her powers attempt to flare through her fingers as her temper wore thin. Palmer glanced at her over Peony's head as the woman rambled about whatever flimsy excuse she had for coming. Placing his hand on Peony's elbow, he maneuvered her farther from the door—whether because of the expression on Brier's face or the shift of energy in the air, Brier didn't know.

"Why don't you try eating something and see if that helps?" he said. "I'll check on you in a few minutes."

Peony offered a jumble of words Brier couldn't force herself to try to make sense of then finally shuffled away.

Palmer stepped through the cracked doorway, studying Brier for a moment before speaking. "Are *you* all right?"

"Fine." Brier huffed. "That woman grates on my nerves."

"You might get along if you stopped glaring at her long enough for her to speak."

"We're not going to get along as long as you live here with me rather than with her."

Palmer's eyebrows furrowed.

"*Rosette* knew that woman was infatuated with you a month ago, Palmer Tash. Try to catch up." Brier stood sharply and shook out the thin shift she'd been pretending was a dress for the past months for lack of anything better to wear.

Palmer blinked, not seeming to know what to say, though Brier wasn't sure if that was because of how harsh her tone had been or because she had invoked Rosette's name so callously. Since the last time they had failed to find any sign of the girl, they'd stopped talking about her entirely.

She forced herself to relax and changed the subject. "Where'd you get to this morning?"

Palmer didn't look any more comfortable with the change in topic. He started slowly, "I was talking to Adessi."

Brier narrowed her eyes, trying to read his face. She had certainly missed something while she'd been unconscious, the two men having gone from loathing each other to having some sort of companionable relationship. But Palmer and Nico still weren't friendly enough to just get together to chat, which meant they'd likely been talking about her.

"About what?"

"About what to do since Gully isn't sending any of his men from Latysia," Palmer said, picking up speed, his voice too tense to sound nonchalant. "He... we thought it would be a good idea for him to go north to see if he could find anyone willing to fight for us that way. There are some temples where we might find people willing to fight for a god."

Brier crossed her arms. "Nico wants to go off wandering the countryside, looking for holy men to be soldiers?"

"Or anyone else willing to be a soldier, I imagine." Palmer scratched the back of his neck.

"Cerise can't do that when she gets back?" Brier shook her head, imagining the shape-shifter had to be on her way back already if Gully had been as vehemently against sending soldiers as Palmer had made it sound. "She can travel faster than any of us as a bird."

"Well, we don't know when she'll be back... and if something's already headed this way"—Palmer sounded as if he were trying to come up with an argument as he spoke—"waiting wouldn't be a great idea..."

Brier frowned. "I take it you two have already decided on this, then? You don't seem to be asking my opinion."

"Well." Palmer slowly dropped his hand from his neck. "He's already left."

Brier froze, the knot in her stomach saying her body understood the words before her mind did. "What?"

"He left a little after dawn. With the good weather, there wasn't really a reason to waste time—"

"You two discussed it this morning?"

Palmer nodded. "We—"

"How early were you up"—she tilted her head—"if you came up with this new plan, watched him leave, and got back here with the sun barely up?"

"We..." Palmer faltered. "It was early."

Brier released a breath, knowing both men too well to not understand what had happened. It was how Nico functioned, after all.

As soon as he was done with someone, he entirely disappeared. That was that. The person might as well be dead for all he cared. She just never had thought he would be done with *her*.

"He wasn't possibly on his way out of town this morning already, was he, when you ran into him?"

"No." Palmer shook his head, his tone saying he'd found a technical truth.

"So he hadn't already decided he was going before you showed up, and you're not trying to spare my feelings."

Palmer started some other argument, as bad a liar as he was, then trailed off and released a breath. "He'll be back in a couple of weeks."

"You're sure of that?"

"He wouldn't disappear forever without a word."

Brier gave a humorless laugh. "Really? Because I'm certain there are more than his share of women in the world who would attest that disappearing forever is just like something he would do."

"He chased down kidnappers to save you," Palmer said.

"You're going to fight all his battles for him now?"

"I know he cares about you. And I'd like to think he'd tell you the same about me, were things reversed."

"You'd never leave without saying goodbye."

Palmer moved up to her. "He'll be back. Trust me."

She pressed her lips tightly together, but provoking more of a fight would do no one any good. She shook her head and moved to the two clay jugs by the door. "I suppose it's my turn to get water today."

"Bri—"

"Get me something to eat if you do go after the girl with the hunger headache." She picked up the jugs by their handles.

"I had a headache this morning. If it's some connection with me and Clover and—" He cut off at the hard look she threw him. He gave a tight smile. "I'll see what's there."

"Thanks." She gave Palmer one last look, tipping the corners of her mouth upward to try to soften her tone after the fact. She could only hope it didn't look as much like a grimace as it felt.

Chapter Two

Brier set the second jug on the riverbank and rolled her shoulders. She always forgot just how heavy the full jugs were. She looked back at the lazy, clear river running around the boulders that made the bottom of the hill Venchia had been built on.

"How do you possibly weigh so much?" she mumbled at the water and bent to wring out the hem of her shift.

Even with all the supplies they'd found stockpiled in the ruins, there didn't seem to be a single piece of fabric that wasn't the haircloth the cultists in the town had all worn. Brier supposed that was what she got for being the goddess of destruction. All the men worshipping her were too busy doing penance for their guilty souls to have anything that actually made life worth living in town. She was getting close to welcoming the end of the world as well, having to live like the cultists.

An odd shimmer of black reflected on the water, and Brier stepped back in surprise. She tested her hands for energy, half-worried her dark thoughts had tried to materialize. But no, it wasn't her. Her eyes followed the glint out toward the countryside on the other side of the river and reached a pale haze circling a cropping of rocks a hundred yards or so out of town. A knot in her stomach told her she knew exactly what the shimmer was. Death was circling—just as it had the day she'd seen Sage Visentin die. Just who was out there, though, she couldn't say. She had seen others die since the old Seer without the black haze coming over them. She wasn't sure she wanted ed to know who was important enough to have death circle as it was, waiting.

Trying to keep her mind from jumping to any awful conclusions, she moved the jugs to a spot in line with the last row of ruined buildings then pulled her shift up so she could wade across what looked like the shallowest part of the river. Slick mud and smooth river rocks made balancing difficult, but somehow, Brier made it across to the opposite bank without falling. Dropping her shift again, she wiped her feet on the long grass and jogged to where the haze was circling.

The smell of rot hit her before she could get close enough to see. Gagging, she changed up her breathing out of instinct. Gods, did she not miss smelling that. After thirteen summers of being plagued with the smell as some odd vestige of her unknown powers, she had very much appreciated the respite she'd gained since her training at Ruhegipfel. Now that she knew what it was, she could only hope it would never come back. She'd have to ask Goebel about it, whenever they could bring his mind back to the world of the living. She realized she'd been too caught up in everything new to ask about him.

Stomach once again under control, Brier started forward, trying to breathe as little as possible as the air grew more and more putrid—enough so that Brier had to question if she'd gotten it wrong and the death was lingering over someone who had already passed. A lump lay under a ratty blanket, curled up so tightly to the pile of rocks next to it that it nearly looked like a part of them.

Brier slowed to a stop a few yards back. "Hello?"

The lump might have twitched. Or it could have been the wind. Brier inched forward, not entirely willing to touch whatever was under the blanket. She finally got close enough that she could nudge the shape with her toe. Her foot hit what felt like bony spine, and the shape groaned in a weak, but undoubtedly male, tone.

Brier took a surprised step back. So he wasn't dead. She glanced up at the gathering black, pushing it back slightly for good measure, even though it didn't seem to be pressing down yet. Carefully, she leaned forward and pinched part of the blanket to pull it back. A shock of sweat-soaked blond hair came into view, plastered to a pasty skull.

Recognition hit, and the name escaped her lips. "Leone?"

Leone Adessi—Nico's cousin and the orchestrator of her kidnapping, the man who had brought her to Venchia, from what Palmer had told her—didn't seem to recognize his own name. His eyelids fluttered, but his pale eyes never fully opened. Brier placed a hand on his forehead and felt the grimy stickiness of sweat coating a searing fever. She pulled the blanket off him. He'd burn to death under the wool. A fresh wave of rot rose up with the gust of air from the blanket, and the death above them strained against Brier's hold. Brier clamped the energy back as bile climbed to her throat, burning as badly as the rot in her nostrils. A bandage was wrapped tightly around Leone's upper thigh, shining and angry with a sickly mix of red, brown, and yellow seeping out from under it. Whatever had happened to him, she'd found the source of the smell. His leg was slowly rotting away while the rest of him was still clinging to life.

"Palmer," she murmured. Palmer would be able to help. She could ward death off for a little while, but he could properly heal people. Sprinting back toward the river, she didn't let herself wonder if Palmer would even want to help after everything he'd told her Leone Adessi had done. If she let someone else die...

Brier couldn't bring herself to finish that thought. She'd been the cause of so much death already, and she couldn't stand by and let more people fall because of her. She likely wouldn't ever be able to tip the cosmic scales back in her favor, but it was something.

PALMER RUBBED HIS TEMPLES as he worked his way through the maze of ruins toward the storehouse they'd found in town. Brier's reaction had been as good as Palmer could have hoped, even if she had instantly seen through him. *Like always.* He either had to not tell her things at all—which always went over well when she eventually found out—or tell the truth. And telling the truth was difficult since upsetting her could lead to natural disasters—ones that Palmer wasn't strong enough to stop.

She is more powerful than you. Goebel's words, spoken before he'd become a shell of a man, echoed in Palmer's mind. *And these disasters she's causing, they'll continue to happen as long as that's true.*

He shook his head to clear it as the smell of something cooking caught Palmer halfway down the hill. Something fatty, savory enough to make his stomach growl. As the only good cook in town, Peony was most likely at the little fire pit in the open square near the storehouse, cooking something Nico had brought in from the previous day's hunting trip. Now it made sense why Nico had been out so long, not coming back until well into the afternoon. He was stocking up for them as best he could before he left. Maybe pointing out to Brier that he'd taken the time to see them well supplied would make her feel a little better.

The open square was built along one of the plateaus of the town. Palmer turned the final corner into the area just as Peony pulled a strip of meat off the wood coals. He stopped a few yards away so he wouldn't make her jump. "Smells great."

Peony glanced up, eyes wide for a moment before she offered a small smile. "Thank you. There's plenty if you like."

Taking the time to notice the flush rising up Peony's neck, Palmer had to wonder if Brier had been right about Peony's interest in him. Brier certainly understood women better than he did. He smiled back, trying to look friendly but not *too* friendly just in case. "Sounds great. I'll have to bring some back for Brier."

Peony's face darkened, and she turned back to the fire. "Of course."

He didn't want to question what that *Of course* meant. "How's your head?"

"It still hurts a little," she murmured, keeping her eyes forward.

"Would you like me to see what I can do?"

"It's fine if you don't have time."

"If I didn't have the time, I wouldn't be standing here." Palmer tried to keep his tone joking, which at least worked well enough to get her to look at him again. He stepped forward. "It's all right if I touch your head?"

She nodded quickly, the flush starting to work its way up to her ears.

Ignoring her blushing, Palmer placed a hand over her dark hair and willed the gold healing light to gather in his palm. It struggled a little, fighting past some remnant of his own power inside her skull that Clover had left. He managed to force it through. "I think your body's still dealing with what the possession did is all." He waited for the energy to die back down on its own before he lifted his hand. "Are you having any other problems?"

"Other than headaches?" She tilted her head back to look up at him.

He nodded. "I know I had plenty of issues before I had control of my powers—unknowingly having the universe in my mind and all."

She shook her head. "I'm all right, I think. Though my dreams..."

Palmer froze. "Dreams? About what?"

"I don't know." Peony's round face screwed up. "They're just dark. And... awful."

Frowning, Palmer tried to work out a question that would help determine if *dark and awful* was something important to them or truly just a bad dream. A buzz of energy caught him before he could speak. He turned as Brier appeared at the other end of the little square, flushed, panting, and soaking wet. She came out of her sprint and doubled slightly.

Chest tight, he moved toward her. "What's wrong? Is someone coming?"

She forced words out around gulps of air. "Need you. Help."

"With what?" He glanced over Brier's shoulder to the empty street to make sure no one was chasing her then focused back on her. "You're soaked."

"Slipped in the river." She managed to catch her breath enough to straighten, and Palmer frowned. They needed to find her a proper dress before anyone else showed up. Entirely wet on one side, her shift was practically see-through and was sticking to her. She caught his hand before he could shake off that thought. "Come on."

"Bri—" He jerked forward as she pulled. Losing faith that he'd get an answer out of her, Palmer started trying to divine what had happened then felt Peony still watching. He had the wherewithal to send the woman an apologetic look over his shoulder.

She hadn't gotten off her knees from where he had first found her by the fire pit, but Peony's face was pinched. Palmer made a note in his mind to follow up with her again once he had helped with whatever crisis Brier had found. He already had a bad habit of letting Peony slip through the cracks with everything else pulling at his attention. If her dreams were something he needed to know about—

Brier took a tight corner and nearly wrenched his arm from its socket.

"Bri... gods." Palmer pulled back hard enough to finally force her to slow. "Talk to me. What's happened?"

Her lips pursed as though she didn't really want to say, but she at least slowed to a more reasonable pace as she urged him forward. "Someone's hurt. You need to help."

He rolled his shoulder as they continued toward the river. "Someone?" There weren't many *someone*s in town now. "A cultist?"

She mumbled something.

"Bri." He came to a full stop, planting his feet. He wasn't a large man, but he was larger than Brier. She wouldn't be able to move him unless her panic reached earthquake levels. "I can't help if you don't tell me what's going on."

Her face scrunched up, but she answered, "Leo Adessi. He's dying."

Palmer stared at her, the words not fully making sense. "Leone Adessi? The man who *kidnapped* you? He's here?"

"He's hurt." Brier took a few steps back as though subconsciously urging him after her again. "Please."

"What do we care? Why is he even here?"

"Palmer, he's *dying*."

Palmer stopped himself from saying, *Good*. Even after everything that had happened, he hadn't quite shared Nico's willingness to kill the other Adessi, but Palmer couldn't say he'd be sad to see Leone go.

"Palmer..." She caught his gaze, her brown eyes pleading.

"He almost got you killed, Bri." Palmer shook his head. "He *did* get you killed, technically. He and Orris A—"

"Please." Her voice went soft. "Everyone's gone."

And it made sense. Any other day, Brier would at least have slowed down to think. On the day Nico had left, however, rationality wasn't likely. After what had happened over the past year, keeping the Adessi family away from her entirely was sounding like a better and better idea.

With a sigh, Palmer nodded. "Where is he?"

Brier took his hand once again and hurried them toward the river. After stripping off his boots, Palmer understood how Brier had ended up so wet if she'd tried to rush across the river. The water wasn't deep enough to serve as a proper defense from an army approaching from the north, but the slick riverbed would certainly slow down anyone coming to the ruins. They picked their way slowly over the slippery river stones. As soon as their feet were on grass, however, Brier was back to a near run, leading Palmer to an outcropping of rocks.

The smell hit Palmer in a wave, so heavy it felt like the air had grown thicker with the rot. "Dear gods." He brought his free arm up to cover his nose.

"Try to keep your breathing shallow." Brier moved to a lump pressed up against the rocks. "It's his leg, I think. And he's burning up."

Palmer moved hesitantly toward the lump, breathing as little as possible. His eyes hit the discolored bandage, and his stomach roiled. "Brier..."

"Can you help?" She looked up at him, eyes pleading.

He shook his head, honestly having no idea, though with her looking at him like that, he wasn't certain he could refuse to try. He forced himself to kneel. "Has he said anything?"

"No. I don't think he knew I was here."

"He might be too far gone, Bri."

"You've brought me back from the dead."

"But you're you," he said even as he steeled himself to deal with the seeping bandage. Not waiting for Brier's reply, he found the edge of the fabric and tugged. Leone groaned lightly but still didn't seem to register what was happening. Worryingly stiff, the bandage fought against being removed. Palmer pulled harder, and the fabric gave, taking the top layer of skin with it. Palmer jerked back at the sight of the gaping black wound, suddenly glad he hadn't yet had breakfast.

"Oh!" Brier's hands went over her nose and mouth. "What is that?"

"Nico shot him last month. Looks like the wound's putrefied."

"Shot..." Brier started a question before shaking her head. "Can you fix it?"

"I can try." Palmer saw a spot of pale skin that still looked mostly intact. Taking as deep a breath as he dared, he placed two fingers on the clear patch of skin and willed the healing energy back into his hand, severely wishing he were still dealing with Peony's headache. The gold glow grew, pooling under Palmer's touch as if it were just as hesitant to go near the rot as Palmer was. Closing his eyes so he wouldn't have to look any longer, Palmer gave a last push and felt the energy scatter out over the man in front of him. He hissed as a low burn started up his arm. Leone was too hurt. The power would begin to damage Palmer before he finished healing the man. He jerked back with a gasp. The smell in the air hit the back of his throat, sending him into a coughing fit.

"Are you all right?" Brier placed her hand on his back.

Palmer nodded, getting his breathing under control before he opened his eyes again. Leone still lay on the ground, his eyelids fluttering, but the red in his cheeks had lessened. Palmer swallowed then looked back at the man's thigh. Chunks of rotten flesh had splattered on the ground, closer to Palmer's feet than he cared for, but fresh pink skin showed where the rot had been, following a deep dip where the muscle of his thigh used to be.

Palmer rubbed his stinging hand. "It couldn't heal the dead part—I'm not sure he'll be able to walk again with his leg like that—but he's..."

Alive, Brier supplied, the word hanging somewhere between a personal thought and a shared statement between their minds. She placed the back of her hand on Leone's forehead. "He's still feverish."

Palmer's thumb paused in the middle of his palm. "I can't—"

"No." She shook her head, turning her worried expression from the man on the ground to Palmer. "Don't hurt yourself."

He looked at her concerned face and managed a smile. At least she seemed to be coming back from whatever hysteria had brought them down to the outcropping in the first place. He turned back to the barely conscious man on the ground. "I suppose we shouldn't leave him here now that he's not dying."

Brier pushed herself upright. "Do you think we can carry him? Or there might be something we could use as a stretcher—"

"I think I can manage," Palmer said. Leone Adessi, like his cousin, was nearly a foot taller than Palmer, but he looked mostly starved. As long as Brier helped keep the man's feet off the ground, Palmer could likely get him into town. Once they were there, though... Palmer tried to think of somewhere to put him. He glanced at the jagged rocks along one side of town, where Leone had paid Palmer and Nico a visit after they'd been captured and placed in the cells. "We can put him in the caves."

Brier frowned. "You think he needs to be locked up?"

"He did kidnap you, Bri."

She motioned toward the lump of a man in front of them, looking at Palmer as if he were insane to consider someone in that shape a threat.

"It will make me feel better." Palmer shifted Leone to get a hold of him under his arms. "Let's get this over with."

Chapter Three

Even if Palmer didn't like having Leone Adessi around, it was good for Brier to have something to focus on other than how empty the town had been since Nico Adessi's departure. He watched her go for the little bag she had been bringing with her to the caves every morning for the past three days, trying to judge her mood.

"He's getting better?"

Brier started out of her own thoughts long enough to look at him before she shrugged. So her mood hadn't gotten any better since when she'd awoken. "He was still delirious yesterday, but he's healing."

"Do you think you should be still going into the cell if he's getting better?"

Brier rolled her eyes and turned back to her bag. "Even if he were in any shape to do something, you realize I could dissolve his arm before he ever touched me, yes?"

"Just because you could doesn't mean you'd want to."

Though evidence of some thought passed over Brier's face, she pressed her lips together, keeping Palmer out of her head. "You're welcome to join me if you can pull yourself away from Peony and her headaches for an hour or two."

Palmer frowned, wondering if Brier was actually upset about the time he'd been spending with Peony or if her mood was simply bubbling over into general annoyance. He'd been trying to work through Peony's nightmares, which seemed more and more to be connected to Clover and the specters still trapped in Brier's ring.

"You know I've been trying to figure out how to get Clover and Marina—"

"Forget it." Brier shook her head as she turned for the door.

"Bri." He caught her wrist. "Slow down."

"You're giving her false hope, just so you realize." She pulled away. "The more time you spend with her, the more annoying gloating looks she's giving me."

"You barely see her." Palmer shook his head, refraining from blatantly telling Brier she was overreacting. He didn't need powers to know how well that would go over. "I doubt she's giving you—"

"The sooner you man up and tell her you aren't interested, the sooner she will move on. Or at least leave me the hell alone."

"Brier—"

"Unless I've entirely misread this"—she motioned between them—"and you'd rather be with that miserable woman. Then you should probably tell *me* you aren't interested and—"

"You know how I feel about you, Bri."

Brier made a face as if she didn't fully believe him—though she *had* to after everything that had happened—and swung her bag onto her shoulder. "Then deal with it, because I'm at the end of my rope, and bad things tend to happen when I'm there. I'm sure you remember."

Palmer held his tongue, having to assume that it was better to talk to Peony than have Brier focus her anger directly on the poor woman. As she swept out of the house, he finally gave into the urge to massage his temples. At least when Nico had been in town, Brier had focused on being upset with *him*. Now her displeasure was scattered to everyone else left in Venchia.

"Why can't everyone be happy for once?" Palmer grumbled, giving her time to make it down the street toward the caves before he went out as well. He stopped short, seeing Peony before he'd had the time to start looking. Lurking a few houses down, Peony appeared to have been waiting for him.

"What are you doing here?" As much as Palmer tried to soften his voice, it still came out sharp enough to make Peony flinch.

"I..." She swallowed. "You were late—later than the past couple of days—so I thought I'd come here." Her eyes drifted to the house he and Brier shared. "Were you fighting?"

Palmer forced himself to release a breath and ignored the question. "Did you have another dream?"

"Just the same one." She kept her eyes on the house for another moment before she looked back at him. "Though, I was thinking, maybe all of that would go away if we weren't here anymore."

"What?" Palmer frowned.

"Well"—Peony crossed one arm over the other as she continued in a rush—"I was looking through all the supplies and whatnot, and I was thinking what a shame it was that we didn't have any milk or eggs."

That obviously explains everything. Palmer continued to bite down his annoyance. "All right...?"

"It's almost my mother's birthday, you see, or what would have been her birthday, gods pity her soul, and every year we'd always make a cake. A cream cake. People would come to stay at the inn around then just to have some, you know—they loved it so much. Signore Fournier, the baker, he always joked that he was going to buy up all the eggs and milk every year at the beginning of summer so that we wouldn't be able to steal his business. He was actually a good—"

Palmer pressed his hand to his head. "Peony, does this have a point I'm missing?"

"Well, so, yes." She stumbled, taking a minute to find where she was before starting again. "I was thinking about the, um, eggs—"

"Eggs and milk, yes," Palmer supplied, trying to hurry her along.

"Yes, eggs and milk... so that got me thinking, there aren't eggs and milk here because we don't have any farms or anything, and no merchants come, but there have to be eggs and milk *somewhere*. Cittamuarta has beef. So I was thinking we could go somewhere that has those things—it doesn't have to be Cittamuarta—and we could get an inn there. Or even just a shop. You have some money, and I know how to bake and cook and all those other things we'd need. I used to help my mother with everything at our old inn. Then we wouldn't be stuck living out here, and maybe then the dreams would go away too. And then we'd be—"

Palmer held up a hand to stop her when it didn't seem like she'd be losing steam anytime soon. "I'm sorry. You want us all to move somewhere and start an inn?"

"Or a bakery. Or whatever else you think we could do. I'm sure I could run a bakery just as well as an inn, or I'd be happy to learn—"

"You realize there are people coming after Brier and me?" He shook his head.

"Her, not you. She could always stay..."

Palmer looked at her in a way he was sure would make her think she had grown a second head before he could catch himself. "You're suggesting just *us* leave?"

Peony finally faltered. Her voice turned meeker. "It would solve our problems, wouldn't it? All of this is really *her* issue, not yours. You don't kill any—"

"Her issues are my issues, Peony."

"But she's *awful*," Peony said then covered her mouth with her hand.

Palmer hesitated, trying to work out what he could say to that.

Peony started up in the silence. "I'm sorry. I didn't mean to say that, but... she can't make you happy. All you do is fight."

"She actually..." Palmer paused then tried to end the conversation before it spiraled entirely out of control. "Look, I don't know if I've given you the wrong idea about something, but I'm not leaving Brier here."

"I just…" Peony's voice went so quiet he could barely hear it. "I…" She turned around and hurried away with her chin tucked into her chest.

Palmer opened his mouth but refrained from calling after her. If Peony was anything like Brier, it would be better to leave her alone for a bit before he tried to reason with her. Once both Brier and Peony had had a chance to calm down, maybe he'd be able to go a few hours without someone in town being angry with him.

BRIER PINCHED THE BRIDGE of her nose as she left the last line of houses, trying to release the rest of her irritation before she made it to the caves someone had turned into a prison. For a man whose powers supposedly included some level of omniscience, Palmer missed things that were directly in front of his face on an alarming basis.

Ignoring that as well as she could, Brier made her way across the open expanse between the ruins and the boulders at the start of the caves, then she stepped through the rocky opening. The temperature dropped as she moved out of the bright sunlight and into the damp, earthy air trapped inside the cave. Slowly, her eyes adjusted to the dim space around her. Fishing the ring of keys out of her bag, Brier moved to the line of bars that had been built into the rock at the back of the cavern.

They key slipped into the hole easily and clicked—though she once again wondered why she even bothered. The worst of Leone's fever had passed, but the man had barely moved from the spot where she and Palmer had placed him days before. They likely could have set him in the center of town with a full arsenal, and he wouldn't have been able to hurt a soul. She didn't trouble herself to swing the door shut again.

Leone had twisted toward his good hip, as though he'd tried to turn on his side but hadn't fully managed to push himself over. She set down her bag and water jug then knelt next to him, gently rolling him onto his back.

"Chas?" He groaned out her nickname, his eyes struggling to focus on her face.

Brier sat back in surprise then offered a quick smile when she realized he was properly conscious. "Hey, there. Welcome back."

"What...?" The word seemed to catch in his throat as he coughed—a dry, croaking sound.

"Here." She turned for the rest of the pheasant broth Peony had made. It had long gone cold, but it was at least liquid and something to put in the man's stomach. From the way his abdomen had sunken in and his cheekbones protruded, Brier had to believe he hadn't properly eaten since the rest of his friends had fled Venchia a month before.

With her help, Leone lifted his head enough to be able to get the broth down—with much less trouble than she'd been having getting it down his throat when he was in the midst of some fever dream. His eyes lifted back to her face as she pulled the bottle away once again.

"Why?"

"Why what?" She eased him back down.

"Why..." He got the word out a little more easily, though his voice still scratched. "Why are you helping me?"

"Enough people have died." She shrugged it off more easily than she felt. "It's nice to be able to save someone for a change."

He studied her. "You think I'm worth saving?"

"I suppose you're lucky that I was unconscious through most of what happened." She sat back on her heels. "Last I remember, we were still friends."

Leone closed his eyes, as if talking was draining him too quickly. Or perhaps he was feeling guilty. "Am I a prisoner?"

Brier glanced at the bars of the cell. "Palmer insisted."

He nodded slightly, not opening his eyes again.

Why did you do it? The question lingered on Brier's tongue, but the man in front of her was in no shape to speak much longer, let alone answer the questions she still had about what had happened to take him from a friend to kidnapper. *Did you come back to Latysia just to take me to your uncle, or did that shift somewhere along the way?* Perhaps that was the other reason why she needed to save him. Alive, he could explain. Dead, he was just one more thing from her past that had been lost to her supposed divinity. She would just have to wait for her answers a while longer. She should go home and apologize to Palmer anyway. He could be an idiot, but he did always try his best. And she didn't even want to imagine what might happen if she lost him. She was barely hanging onto her own sanity as it was.

"I brought some solid food as well." Brier pulled out some nuts and other small foods she had found in the storehouse. "You should try to eat if you can. Regain your strength."

Leone's head moved up and down a fraction of an inch, just enough to be called a nod, but didn't answer. That was likely all she could expect from a man who hadn't known where he was—or even *who* he was—the day before.

After gathering her things, Brier stood and walked back to the cell door. Half of her still didn't want to bother with locking it, but if she was trying to stop fighting with Palmer, starting a fight over Leone wasn't the way to go. After locking the door, she took a deep breath, telling herself she would be able to keep her temper under control, for once, before she made things worse.

Chapter Four

The house was empty when Brier returned. Even with every-thing she had told herself, a low buzz of annoyance attempted to find purchase. She forced herself to take a deep breath through her nose and twisted the ring on her finger. That didn't help. Half the time, she was able to forget she was wearing the large green stone with red flecks, but so much had been piled onto that one piece of jewelry. She would have thrown it in the river if she could, or at least have given it back to Nico—it had been his mother's, after all—but as long as whatever remained of Clover and Marina was still inside it, she was stuck carrying it.

Feeling Palmer coming, Brier stepped farther inside then turned to face the door.

He paused at the threshold. "You're back already?"

She nodded. "He recognized who I was today."

Palmer's eyebrows rose. "Did that go... well?"

"He didn't try to attack me or anything, if that's the question."

He nodded, dropping his eyes as though he were worried to share whatever he was thinking.

Brier took another deep breath. "Can we not fight for a while?"

Palmer's dark eyes came back to hers. "I never want to fight with you, Bri."

"When was the last time you touched me?"

He blinked, obviously taken aback. "Just in general?"

She nodded.

"This morning, didn't I?"

Brier shook her head. "And I don't think yesterday either."

"I must have."

She shook her head again.

Palmer stepped closer and placed his hand on her cheek. Immediately, energy began to move from his palm into her, balancing something Brier hadn't entirely noticed was off.

She took a breath then placed her hand over his. "Do you love me, Palmer?"

"You know I do." He rubbed his thumb back and forth along her cheek.

Too tired to try to talk anymore, Brier leaned forward and brushed her lips against his. The familiar spark moved between them, and Brier had to wonder why they hadn't gone straight to that to solve any of the arguments they'd had over the past few days. She reminded herself that Palmer wasn't just clueless about women, but he also wasn't nearly as forward as the other men she had known in her life.

So she would have to be forward for the both of them. Catching her arms around his neck, Brier took a step back, trying to guide him toward her little pallet. He followed for a step then jerked back.

The sudden lack of contact made Brier's head spin. She tried to focus on him past the emptiness he left behind him. "What's wrong?"

"Peony," he said.

Brier's eyebrows flew toward her hairline. "Really? You're thinking about her *now* of—"

"No." Palmer shook his head. "No. Not because of... this." He motioned between them. "I think she's left."

"Left?" Brier frowned, still trying not to huff at the interruption.

Palmer's eyes flicked back and forth as they did when he was getting some vision that wasn't quite clear enough for him to make sense of. "Left town. Out through the pillars."

"Well, I can't say I'll miss her." Brier tried to keep the venom out of her voice as much as possible.

Palmer stepped away from Brier toward the door. "I have to go after her."

"*Why*? If she went past the pillars, she's headed south. She's likely going home. Back to Latysia and her little band of... whatever they were. Street thugs?"

Palmer's jaw twitched, as though she had touched on something else he didn't want to go into, but he just said, "It isn't safe for her to be wandering around the countryside alone."

"You haven't stopped anyone else from wandering off around the countryside alone."

Palmer lifted his eyebrows slightly, giving her a look that said she knew she wasn't talking about the same thing. "Adessi's armed and more than knows how to take care of himself."

"Who says she doesn't?" Brier returned. "She's a grown woman. If she wants to go—"

"She left because of me, Bri. I can't let something happen to her."

"Can't you just let this go for *once* and stay here with me?" Brier wrapped her arms around her middle, feeling too many of her ribs under the thin shift. Suddenly, she felt nothing like the powerful goddess of destruction she was supposed to be. She was just a frail little girl barely clinging onto the one or two threads of a fraying robe that was holding her out of the abyss.

"I'll be back before you know it. I just saw her. She can't have gotten far."

As one more straw began to slip, Brier couldn't stop the underlying anger she'd been feeling far too often of late. "If you leave now, I'm not promising *I'll* be here when you get back."

Palmer stared at her for a moment then called her bluff. "Where else would you go, Bri?"

Brier clenched her fists tightly enough that her nails bit into her palms. The desire not to have to find a new place to sleep was the only thing keeping her from blasting something apart as Palmer turned on his heel and rushed off down the street, intent on doing what he thought was right. As always. Palmer Tash was lucky she loved him, because she really hated him sometimes. And hate was far too easy to come by these days.

Chapter Five

Nico worked his way through the crowd toward the city walls of Ouene, far too aware of how he had to look after a month of living out in the middle of dusty old ruins and then days walking cross-country as he made his way northeast. The smaller priories closer to Venchia had looked as if they'd long been abandoned—whether from news of what had happened in Venchia or the proximity of the cult that had been nearby long before, Nico didn't know. Whatever the reason, Nico had given up after the second one—only partially because most were perched near the crests of mountains that were less than fun to climb—and turned toward the coast, looking for the city of Ouene and its temple to Isnotra, Goddess of Knowledge. He'd had to assume that rumors of a cult and residence goddess days away in the countryside wouldn't scare off the entire city.

Based on the mass of humanity he now found himself in, his assumption had been more than correct. The streets of the port city were stuffed to capacity, some of the smaller alleys leading between the colorful tight-packed houses entirely impassible. Nico didn't fight the crush slowly pushing him farther into town. With so many bodies around, he wasn't likely to draw attention, good or bad. Ideally, he'd be able to stay unnoticed long enough to wash and shave—and perhaps find a change of clothing—before he made his way to speak to the consiglio that ruled Ouene. He couldn't see the anchoresses known to serve the Temple of Isnotra being much of a fighting force, but Ouene as a whole certainly had soldiers—even if most would likely be trained more for sea battles than land.

After a final bottleneck at the end, the street Nico had been following opened into a wide market square. Surrounded by grander versions of same type of buildings Nico had passed so far—each four or five stories tall and painted pale shades of blue, pink, and purple under white trim work—the actual square marketplace was difficult to make out beyond flashes of cloth and color where stalls stood scattered around behind the mass of bodies. Nico stepped to the side, placing his back against a sky-blue wall to avoid the stream of people still making their way from the street behind him, and looked around. For as scared as the rest of the world had become in the past year, Ouene looked entirely unaffected. People laughed as they moved, haggling over goods, yelling in a slew of languages. And the mess of fashions... it was difficult to pick out who was Ouenen and who was foreign with the wide scattering of styles, only a few of which were anything like Latysian.

"Pastry, *sior?*"

Nico started, looking down at a little boy who had appeared from the shop on the ground floor of the building Nico rested against. The boy waited a second, holding his plate of wares toward Nico, then slipped into another language. He asked the question in at least two more tongues before Nico recognized the odd accent of the original question as Ouenen dialect. He nodded. Something other than the dried meat and nuts he'd been eating on his trip would be more than welcome. Finding his little-used purse, Nico fished out a coin and held it out to the boy.

The boy just smiled, handing Nico the warm pastry before turning to look for another customer.

"Boy?" Nico thought to call after him.

"Signore?" He turned back, easily slipping into pure Latysian at Nico's own accent.

Nico was too tired to be impressed. "The closest inn. Where is it?"

The boy pointed to another street leaving the market square. "Down Calle Mercà, signore. Though they're likely full up from the festival."

Nico tried to work out what month it was to narrow down what festival the boy could mean but gave up after a second, offering another copper coin for the information before he headed the way the boy had pointed.

The first three inns Nico passed turned him back out before he could properly ask for lodging, no matter how much he offered to pay, each time pointing him farther up the road, away from the market square. After the fourth refusal, Nico was about ready to build his own damned room in the middle of the street.

Looking at the quickly cooling pastry in his hand, he gave up trying to find a place to settle before eating, instead turning into a relatively empty alley that he hoped would keep him from being jostled long enough to take a few bites. Taking a place close to the wall blocking off the end of the space—likely the only reason people hadn't crammed themselves into that space—he studied the crescent-shaped folded dough, trying to figure out just what he had bought. The dough looked normal enough, but the filling, just visible though the three slices lining the top, didn't look or smell like anything he'd had before. He took a bite. The unfamiliar spices burned the roof of his mouth, making his eyes water. Still, he forced himself to swallow before looking at the thing again.

"Impressive." A young female voice made Nico start. "Most foreigners end up crying the first time they have one of those."

Nico frowned, studying the woman standing in a doorway across the alley from him. Her red hair hung loose around her pale face, and she couldn't have been much older than fifteen, though her odd clothing seemed meant to make her look older, with her skirt clinging tightly against her hips and her blouse draping immodestly low.

He didn't have to look at the sign hanging over the door to guess her profession.

"I'm Ella," she continued when he didn't answer.

"I didn't ask." He looked back at the crowd closer to the main street.

His dismissiveness only seemed to amuse her. "You're welcome to come in for a drink to go with your *alosa*, if you'd like."

"I'm not looking for a bordello, thanks." He took another bite of the pastry—an *alosa*—keeping it as small as he could without looking obvious.

"What are you looking for, then?"

"Nothing you can help me with." The pastry was actually rather good now that he was prepared for it.

"You never know. I'm very helpful."

"Ella, what are you doing out here?" A taller blond woman appeared at the threshold. With her hair pulled up in a bun and full skirts paired with a loose shirt and a man's waistcoat, she at least looked more respectable than the redhead.

"Bringing in business." Ella turned back to the blonde with a smile.

"I thought I told you to stay upstairs."

"It's dull upstairs."

The blonde dropped her voice. "Gisella Adessi, I swear to Isnotra, if you do not get inside, I'm sending you back to Mother's."

Nico's eyes jumped back up to the woman, his mind spinning as he tried to work out if he could have walked into some sort of trick.

The redhead huffed and turned back inside as the blonde looked at Nico. "I'm sorry..." she trailed off, taking a better look at him.

The new interest made Nico's skin prickle. He squared his shoulders, motioning after the redhead with his eyes. "Did you say her name was Adessi?"

"She doesn't work here," the blonde answered.

"That wasn't my question," Nico said. "I asked if you called her Adessi."

The blonde's eyes flicked over him. "Why? Are you family?"

"What would make you think that?"

"Because the oracle told me I'd be seeing my brother before the festival was over, and you look a *shocking* amount like the miniature I have of my father. I'm surprised Ella didn't see it."

Nico's hand brushed the handle of the dagger at his waist. He didn't fully believe the woman in front of him was going to attack him, but he'd been to enough brothels to know the women in them were rarely without some sort of security. And anyone who had managed what had to be the most elaborate trap in history... *Oracle*. The word registered. They had someone with visions working for them.

"My sisters don't live in Ouene. And they certainly aren't whores."

"We prefer *cortigiana*," the blonde said. "And I actually own the place. Gisella, of course, doesn't work. Mama sent her here when she remarried."

Nico stared at her, keeping his expression purposefully suspicious.

"You really think I could just know who some random man off the street was without someone telling me you were coming?"

"Stranger things have happened in the past year."

She shook her head and fished a locket out from below the neckline of her blouse. She held it out to him. "Here."

Scanning the little alley, Nico couldn't spot any place someone could be hiding, ready to jump him. Not unless someone was going to come flying out one of the windows of the tall building. He chanced a couple of steps closer and snatched the necklace from her. Nico snapped open the locket and glanced down at the little square portraits, one on each side. Though the red-haired woman in the rich blue dress on the right only had some lingering familiarity—and even that could be brushed off as her looking a fair deal like the red-head he'd just seen standing on the stoop—there was no denying that he knew the man on the left—his father, Orris, a quarter of a century younger, wearing an embroidered black jacket Nico remembered seeing tucked away in a trunk years before. Orris had worn that jacket at his wedding.

Nico looked back at the blonde. He had to admit there was a family resemblance he didn't want to see, much less recognize. "Where did you get this?"

"Mama didn't want it, so I took it with me." She shrugged.

"And that makes you...?"

"Caterina," she said. "Do you remember me at all? Or were you too young when you left?"

Nico shook his head, trying to push the insanity of finding his sisters at a *brothel* somewhere deep in his mind to deal with later. Or never. There was enough locked away in there that he never intended to think about again.

"I'm glad I could prove your oracle right." He held the locket back toward her by the chain. "But I'm in a bit of a rush. I don't really have time to catch up."

"Looking for an army, right?" Caterina took the locket.

Nico's eyes narrowed again before he could stop it.

"I told you, we have an oracle." Caterina flashed him a smile. "She told me I would find my brother before Védarente was over, and I should bring you to see our cousin Laura."

Nico's jaw clenched. So that was the festival he'd stumbled into. Védarente, the three-day celebration of Isnotra and truth and whatever those up north told themselves, allowed for general licentiousness for days on end. The Augarian had never approved of Védarente celebrations let alone hosted one.

Nico moved to the more pressing question. "Laura?"

"Lauretta," Caterina said. "She's an anchoress."

"An anchoress has an army for me?" Nico cocked an eyebrow.

"All I know is what I was told. You somehow find your way here, and I take you to Laura."

"Why not to the oracle?"

"The temple's closed during the festival. I imagine it's easier to see Laura."

"Isnotra's temple is closed during a festival for Isnotra?"

"The festival's more about being your true self, but explaining that is really more Laura's realm as well." She motioned behind her. "You're welcome to clean up here before we go, assuming coming inside won't offend your Latysian sensibilities."

"There are brothels in Latysia." *Or were, at least, before the city was destroyed.*

"Then please..." She stepped out of the doorway. "From what I hear, you're in a bit of a rush."

Nico glared. The suspicion that had served him so well in the past months pushed him to continue on his own. With the city in as much of a mess as it was, though, he wasn't sure he had much of a choice but to go along with the supposed oracle's plan. He'd just be sure to keep his weapons on him at all times. With a tense breath, he marched forward and into the bordello.

PROPERLY GROOMED FOR the first time in what felt like much too long, Nico had to admit he felt a little more like his old self. Still, the packed streets kept his nerves on edge. Too much was happening for him to fully keep an eye on the situation.

He tried to force his thoughts away from it, as much as he could at least. "If the temple is closed, how are we going to see an anchoress?"

Caterina kept looking forward, easily maneuvering through gaps in the crowd that didn't seem to be there the second before she shifted. "It's the one time of year the anchoresses are allowed to leave temple grounds. Laura always stays with Cousin Alfonso. We're almost there."

Nico opened his mouth to answer, but words failed him as he, Caterina, and Ella passed a final row of painted houses, and the bay Ouene had been built around opened up in front of them. Nico slowed, his mind struggling to take in the expanse. Along the curved coast, a row of stalls stood in front of docks filled with bobbing ships. With all the masts, it was actually difficult to make out the water until the bay opened to the ocean past two spindly arms of land that protected the harbor.

"Ella had the same look first time she saw the ocean." Caterina smiled, somehow holding her footing as people jockeyed around her.

"The view's better at Cousin Alfonso's." Ella nodded toward the left spindle wrapping around the bay and nudged Nico to get him moving.

As the ground began to rise again, leading toward the large houses that looked far too precariously placed on the strip of land around the bay, the crowds did begin to thin. Nico released a breath and let himself drop a few feet back from his sisters now that they weren't as likely to be separated. Blue continued to peek through grand houses along the coastline. Nico tried to keep himself from gawking, instead focusing on the arched doorways and tiled walls. Not quite the grand villas of Latysia, the coast-side homes were still generally impressive.

After walking nearly to the end of the point, where most of the coast had turned into cliffs, Caterina finally turned and moved up the slick stone steps of one of the last houses along the row. She quickly checked behind her for Nico and Ella before knocking on the warped wood door. Nico moved to the base of the stairs but didn't step any closer, not entirely trusting a house built so close to a sheer drop.

The door opened with a jerk, the wood not wanting to pull away from the swollen frame. A serious-looking dark-skinned man studied them before his mouth curled into a small smile. "Cat, Ella, to what do we owe the pleasure?"

"We've come looking for your sister, in fact." Caterina smiled back at the man—another cousin, most likely, though this one certainly didn't share a resemblance with most of the cousins Nico knew.

"Good timing. She just finished her prayers in the main room." The man took a step to the side to leave the door open.

"Wonderful." Caterina moved into what looked like a narrow hallway then turned back and motioned Nico forward. "I don't believe you've ever met our brother, have you, Vito?"

"Your brother?" The man, Vito, raised his thick eyebrows at Nico, his surprise saying he hadn't been made privy to the supposed oracle's prophesies.

"Nicodemo," Caterina said, sounding as if Nico's being there was the most natural thing in the world. "He's just come in from Latysia."

"Ah." The sidelong glance the man sent Nico said the city name meant more to him than Nico liked.

Nico brushed his hand over the lump that was the handle of his dagger, hidden behind his jacket, but he still followed Ella into the building, swinging the door shut behind him since the other three hadn't bothered.

After a few claustrophobic feet, the close-set corridor opened into a brightly lit room. Nico froze. Though the entire space was not much larger than his old bedroom at the Augarian, large windows on the far side that stretched from floor to ceiling—constructed of clearer glass than Nico had ever seen—made the smooth water of the bay appear to be part of the house. Nico's stomach tightened as he realized there didn't seem to be any land under that end of the house at all.

"Are we over the water?" The words escaped before he could tamp them down.

A female voice came from the corner. "There are stilts on this side of the house." A dark-haired woman Nico had originally missed in favor of the windows stood up from her position on a low couch. She smiled. "It's entirely safe, I assure you. This house has been here for nearly a century."

"Laura." Caterina strode forward. "So glad we caught you at home."

"Indeed. It's been far too long." She caught Caterina's hands as they kissed each other's cheeks.

Nico frowned but didn't speak. The woman standing with Caterina looked nothing like an anchoress. Not only missing the gray veil all anchoresses wore to cover their faces, she was dressed in the same skirts as Caterina, her thick black hair half pulled back in the style Ella seemed to favor.

The supposed anchoress performed the same hand holding and double kiss with Ella before she turned her dark eyes to Nico. "And who have you brought with you?"

"Our brother," Ella supplied, taking a seat on one of the other low chairs without being invited.

"Nicodemo," Caterina said, making Nico wonder if he should have mentioned he'd never gone by his full name. "Nicodemo, this is our cousin, Suora Lauretta."

"Feel free to call me just Lauretta." She smiled. "Or Laura if you prefer. I only get to be away from the temple once a year. It's nice to have a break from all the formality. You're from Latysia?"

Nico kept his body stiffly formal, not entirely willing to accept the woman as an anchoress but outwardly playing along with it. "Yes,

Suora. I've been told your oracle has been telling people to watch for me?"

The corners of Lauretta's mouth tipped up like she was trying to hide a smile, but that amusement still reached her eyes as she turned back to Caterina. "He is very Latysian, isn't he? So intensely serious."

"You should have seen him at the bordello."

Nico glanced back toward the doorway, debating whether he had made the wrong decision in coming after all.

"Would you like to have a seat, Nicodemo?" Lauretta motioned to the couch near her as though she knew he was considering leaving. "I'm glad Caterina managed to find you. Our oracle didn't give much to go on with all the crowds out there."

Nico didn't move, trying to determine what the strained tone he'd heard behind *our oracle* could mean. "I'm fine standing for now, thank you."

His resistance only seemed to amuse her further. "Would you like something to drink, then? I think we still have some of the *ch'a* that was made this afternoon, don't we, Vito? Along with those biscotti Ella likes?"

Ella perked up again from where she had flopped herself, nearly managing proper posture that looked entirely accidental. "The ones that Cousin Alfonso brought back?"

"Indeed," Lauretta said. "Would you all like to run to the kitchen? The staff's off, of course, and I'd love to have a chance to speak to your brother before we scare him off entirely."

With nothing more than a few nods, the other three wandered off to a second door along the far side of the room—which had to lead to the kitchen, Nico imagined. His fingers glanced over the lump of his dagger handle once again as the room emptied, and he tried to determine if the anchoress had some supernatural ability to command people—every other person he met these days seemed to have some power or other—but from what he could tell, everyone had simply decided to listen to her of their own volition. He returned to sizing up the woman across from him.

She waited for him to finish his inspection before she spoke again. "Would it make you more comfortable if I got my veil? I promise I am actually an anchoress."

"I didn't say you weren't," he said.

"No, you're just looking at me like you're trying to decide if I'm attempting to cheat you. I thought maybe the clothes were throwing you off. The Latysians I've met have tended not to like our informality here."

"If you've planned something elaborate enough to get me here in the first place, I imagine it would be odd for you to have forgotten to dress for your role," Nico said as though he were brushing it off, even as he watched her face for a reaction.

"So you do believe me, then?"

Nico wasn't certain he truly believed anyone after everything he'd seen. If she did have powers of some kind, she also could have assumed she'd be able to confound him before he noticed she wasn't dressed as an anchoress. He'd already proven to be at least somewhat immune to the other women with powers he'd met. No reason to think he wouldn't be immune to the supposed anchoress as well. All the same, he answered, "I'm still standing here, am I not?"

"So you trust me enough to not run for the door, but not enough to separate yourself from the exit by sitting." She tilted her head. "Good to know."

His eyes narrowed.

"I'm an anchoress to the Temple of Isnotra." She smiled at his expression. "I wouldn't be very good at my job if I couldn't read people."

"Is that so."

"People come to visit the oracle for any number of reasons, but most are afraid or are struggling with something in their lives. I've spent half a decade helping the people I can while they're waiting for their fortunes to be told. I'd say a fair share of people who come to the temple really need a sympathetic ear more than a prophecy. There are many who feel like they don't have anyone to talk to."

"Is that me, then?" He didn't bother to hide his sarcasm. "Someone who really just needs to talk?"

"For some of your problems, maybe." She looked him over in a way that was a little too probing for Nico's comfort. "You're a soldier?"

His jaw tensed. "What makes you say that?"

"You've made sure not to leave a strategically strong position since you've walked in, you have a—what is that, a dagger?—hidden but ready to pull if you need it, and while talking to me, you have yourself slightly angled to be able to see out of the corner of your eye if anyone else comes back through that door. That sort of alertness tends to come from someone who is no stranger to dangerous situations. Your shoulders are built up, which suggests practice with either archery or something heavy like an axe. And, well, that look on your face tends to appear on people who find life a little cheaper than most. You've likely killed someone? Many someones?"

Nico stared at her, keeping his face blank.

"Soldier seemed like a safe guess." Lauretta shrugged, seeming unperturbed by his lack of reply. Then she smiled. "That, and Delphi said you were looking for an army."

"Delphi?"

"Our oracle," Lauretta said. "That's her name."

"Of course." Nico slid his eyes over the woman slowly, making no attempt to hide that he was critiquing her. Infuriatingly, even that didn't seem to faze her. He lifted his gaze back to her brown-black eyes. She had to be a *very* distant cousin, if she was an Adessi with coloring so dark. "Did she get me one? Your oracle."

"She said she'd get you what you needed. What that means... well, she's an oracle. The only more annoying thing than someone *doing something for your own good* is someone doing that and always being right." Lauretta sounded seconds away from rolling her eyes. Finally, she stood, letting Nico see that she was actually quite tall for a woman. That was Adessi-like at least. She clapped her hands together. "Well, let's get you over to the temple so you can go save the world."

Chapter Six

Palmer looked over his shoulder. He hadn't felt like he'd been walking *that* long, but the ruins of Venchia were no longer in view behind him. How he hadn't found Peony yet, he didn't know. He could sense her out in front of him, and she could only have had a half-hour start on him at most, yet there hadn't been a sign of her as he made his way through the patch of hills running through the countryside. If Palmer didn't turn around soon, he wouldn't be able to make it back to Venchia before sunset—and if he didn't make it back before dark, Brier very likely would kill him when he did return—or at least turn Venchia into a smoking crater.

He briefly considered giving up—if Peony could avoid him, she could certainly make it somewhere safe by herself—but that nagging bit of conscience in the back of his skull wouldn't let him leave her out there by herself. He remembered the trouble he had faced when he and Nico had first come north. He just had to hope that Peony eventually would grow tired enough to have to take a break and he would then be able to close the gap between them.

Releasing a tense breath, Palmer forced his mind out, trying to get a clearer image of where Peony was in front of him. Something else caught the edge of his awareness—a nagging irritation. His powers themselves were annoyed that he wasn't fully perceiving it.

A second later, he heard horses. With nowhere to hide, Palmer dropped to the ground, hoping the tall grass would give some coverage. He scanned the crest of the hill to his right, and soon enough, a half dozen men on horseback appeared. He tried to divine where they had come from. Familiarity told him more than his powers did—he'd seen men dressed like that on his way north. They were from Elatita, the hill city run by a cult to love goddess Astarte—better known to Palmer and Nico as Carmella Huerta.

Palmer frowned. Either he had gone much farther south than he'd realized, or the Elatitans were expanding their territory, searching for bodies to replenish their plague-decimated city. Whichever it was, Palmer needed to stay out of sight. After the way he and Nico had left the last time—with at least one dead guard in their wake—Palmer couldn't imagine he'd be a very welcome guest should they find him.

One of the men said something to the other, gesturing away from Palmer. The horses turned, the horsemen moved far away enough that they were hidden by the landscape, and Palmer's shoulders relaxed a cautious inch. A distant scream made them tense again.

"Let me go!" Peony's voice carried over the hills.

Palmer cursed under his breath. He'd nearly caught up. His hands clenched then released as he debated what to do. He wasn't armed, and none of his powers—even if they were working perfectly—would help fight off a half dozen men. Brier could attack, but he could only help in the aftermath. His choices were to let the Elatitans have her and return to Venchia for the night or follow the rest of the way to Elatita with the hope that he would be able to sneak in and out without getting caught, risking his life in the process. He knew which one Brier would tell him to do. Just as he knew which one he would have to do if he wanted to be able to live with himself.

Cursing again, Palmer straightened enough to ease forward in the grass and turned toward Elatita.

BRIER STAYED AWAY FROM the house as long as she could bring herself to. Even as guilt for yelling set in, she couldn't help but nurse the anger a little longer. Nico had a wall around his emotions thicker than the ones that used to run around the Augarian, and Palmer was a gallant idiot, unable to keep himself from doing what he believed was right, no matter the consequences. She knew both men nearly better than she knew herself. She knew how they worked, and people didn't change. She couldn't be surprised that either had acted true to form. That didn't mean she couldn't at least make her thoughts on the matter *incredibly* obvious to the one man still around.

As the sun began to sink, though, Brier finally had to turn back up the hill. Unless she wanted to talk to either of the men in town who were too ill to hold a conversation or the cultists who worshiped her, she couldn't push Palmer away and not be *entirely* alone.

When she made it to their little house, however, it was empty. Brier pursed her lips then asked, "Palmer?" as though he could be hidden somewhere in the little square space. Unsurprisingly, no one answered.

A small knot of tension began to form in Brier's stomach. She had spent the entire day out wandering the ruins. Palmer *had* to be back.

Back doesn't mean here *exactly,* she told herself, trying to force the tension away. He was likely down at the storehouse or checking on Goebel. Brier hoped it was the first one. She avoided the unconscious man as much as possible—the sickly version of her powers that Marina had used on him made her skin crawl anytime she came close to the man. Palmer had managed to stop the rot well enough, leaving poor Goebel with everything above midthigh. She didn't need to see him.

Moving as quickly as she could without having to admit she was rushing, Brier headed back down the hill to the storehouse, but it was just as deserted as their house on the hill. She poked around all the same, trying to judge if anything had been taken, but she hadn't paid enough attention to the supplies to say what was or wasn't there.

Nico had been the one keeping an eye on all their rations. She hadn't needed to.

Pressing her lips together, Brier stepped back out into the main square and tried to see if their bond would let her narrow down where he might be, but other than the general feeling that he was somewhere, it gave her nothing. Brier released an annoyed breath through her nose.

"My, that was an angry nostril flare."

The voice behind her made Brier jump. She spun on her heel and found herself staring at Cerise's annoyingly beautiful face. "You're back."

"Nothing gets by you." Cerise smirked. "Can't say I come bearing good news, though. Should I fly a little higher up before I tell you? Get out of the rubble zone?"

"Palmer already said it was no good." Brier shook her head. "Have you seen him?"

"Him who? Kos?" Cerise lifted an eyebrow, still insisting on never using anyone's proper name in favor of her own creations.

Brier nodded. "When you were flying in. Did you see him?"

"Can't say I did. Impressive you could lose him, though, with how you two are joined at the hip."

"He went looking for Peony." Brier saw no reason to give Cerise yet more fodder for her taunts by mentioning any arguments. "Girl went wandering off outside town this morning. He should be back by now."

"Don't know what to tell you, Cay. Didn't see him. You'll have to go bother your other boyfriend for a while." Cerise examined her nails as though she could only bear to give Brier the smallest bit of attention.

"Nico's gone north. Looking for an army that way, since you had no luck with Gully." Brier went with the story Nico and Palmer had cooked up.

Cerise's unnervingly black eyes lifted without her moving her head. "Both Kos *and* Nicolas went off and left you alone? Interesting. I didn't think they trusted you enough to think you could lace your boot without one of them hovering ten paces back."

Brier narrowed her eyes, not dignifying that with a response.

"No, really." Cerise dropped her hand and finally looked straight at Brier. "It was getting to be a little sickening, both of them treating you like some little girl who needed protection from the big bad world. You are a *goddess*."

Brier continued to glare but pointed up. "Find him for me?"

"I don't know. You didn't say please."

Irritation from the entire day boiled up, and a low rumble started, moving out from Brier's feet through the ground.

"Touchy." Infuriatingly, Cerise's smirk only grew. "I like it."

"Go," Brier snapped.

"That's one way to get things done." Cerise made sure she got the last word with a smile before quickly shifting—a raven flapping away before Brier could think to say anything else.

Brier took a deep breath through her nose and released it slowly. She hadn't made anything shake in weeks. She needed to make up with Palmer quickly, or with Cerise back, Brier would very likely *actually* blow something up. Turning back into the storehouse, she looked for something to eat, trying to find a way to distract herself.

Cerise returned in what felt both much too soon and much too long, retaking her human form in the storehouse doorway. "Doesn't seem he's back."

Brier paused midbite, the knot in her stomach, which she'd managed to minimize, suddenly back with a vengeance. She forced a swallow, even though she hadn't nearly chewed the stale bread enough. She coughed. "What?"

"Circled the whole place." Cerise waved her hand in a lazy loop. "No sign of Kos. Or Peapod for that matter. Don't think they're back."

"That's not possible."

"I don't always tell the whole truth, but I don't lie, Cay. He's not here."

Brier stood sharply. "Can you look outside the city?"

"I just flew in from *outside the city*." Cerise shook her head. "Didn't see him anywhere nearby."

"Look again."

"Cay—"

"Look. Again."

Cerise's face darkened, annoyance finally making an appearance, but Brier's building panic wouldn't let her care.

"Sure." Cerise took a step back. "Not like I could use a rest or anything."

Even with the complaining, Cerise shifted back to her raven form and flapped off once again. Brier let the stale bread drop on the ground and walked outside to watch the bird soar off toward the south end of town.

"I'll be back before you know it." She heard the memory of Palmer's voice in her mind. It didn't make her feel any better. If he truly wasn't back, she could only imagine something terrible had happened.

THE SHADOWS WERE LONG, the sun nearly below the horizon by the time Palmer reached Elatita. The horsemen had long left him behind. Palmer tried to look at what few positives he had in the situation. At least the shadows would likely help him slip into the walled city without being seen—in bright sunlight, there would have been little chance of him making it up the slope to the gate without being spotted.

As Palmer reached the top of the hill, he realized he shouldn't have bothered ducking between the shadows. Unlike when Nico and he had first arrived, there were no men stationed to watch the gate. Palmer wasn't certain if he should take the empty guard posts as uncommonly good luck or something to be that much more worried about. Still sticking to the darkness, he slid into the city he had gone through far too much trouble to leave just over a month earlier.

A chill went through Palmer's body as though the temperature inside the city was cooler than a few feet back. He scanned the sad little buildings lining the street leading toward the center of town. Most had already been empty when he'd last seen them, remnants of what the city had been before plague, but they felt even emptier than before. There was something wrong with the city. Palmer just didn't know what.

Slowly, he made his way toward where he knew Carmella's temple was, about halfway through town. A loud bell pealed, making Palmer jump. He slid into one of the small alleys between two houses, praying that someone hadn't seen him and raised the alarm. But nothing happened. No one appeared. The street remained empty. As the ringing faded off into the twilight, Palmer took a chance and moved back onto the street toward the center of town.

"What are you doing?"

Palmer heard the first signs of life off in the distance. He inched up to the last line of houses before the town square.

"I forgot my knife," a second voice answered.

"It's past curfew. Get inside."

Palmer poked his head around the corner and saw a middle-aged man speaking to a younger one by the archery targets set up on one side of the open space.

"I'll be fine. I *feel* fine," the younger man—the second voice—said.

"You won't if you're caught out here." The older man put his hand behind the younger's shoulder blades and pushed him toward the houses. "Go."

Frowning, Palmer watched the men leave. So there was *certainly* something wrong. His eyes went to the little domed temple just off the square. Carmella would be able to fill him in more quickly than his half-working powers could.

Hoping everyone really was under curfew, Palmer took the chance and dashed across the open square to the temple. He made it to the door without being noticed and tried the latch. His good luck wasn't good enough to have that be unlocked. Opening locked doors was another Brier power. His visions were about the only helpful thing Palmer had, compared to Brier, and even those, he didn't really have.

Shaking off his annoyance, Palmer took his chances and knocked. After a minute, he attempted a second knock, a little less certain. Perhaps Carmella had left. That would likely explain everyone's skittishness. If they had lost their goddess—

The door opened just enough to show a dark eye. It widened in surprise then narrowed as the door opened wider. "You actually came back."

Palmer slid through the door as soon as there was enough space for him, nearly knocking Carmella over.

"Excuse you!" She frowned at him, the expression still managing to look more like a striking pout than a serious frown. That was Carmella Huerta: so beautiful that it was impossible for her to look unattractive even for a moment.

"Sorry," Palmer said quickly, making certain the door was shut again before he looked back at the woman. With Carmella's initial glow subsiding, Palmer could see that whatever was wrong with the town hovered around her as well. She'd grown thinner, her soft curves more angular, and there were dark circles under her honey-brown eyes. "What's happening here?"

Carmella arched an eyebrow.

"There's something wrong with the town."

"Oh, really? You think?"

Palmer hesitated at her tone of voice.

"Everything's been wrong since you left town. When you *killed* that guard."

Palmer winced at hearing it out loud. "Technically, that was Adessi."

"Of course." Carmella flopped back on one of the curved benches lining the wall of the temple, managing to make even that motion look graceful with her fine, gauzy dress fluttering behind her. She glanced at the door. "I see he's not with you. He get the girl?"

"What?"

"That would have been my guess for what was going to happen. I told you about those two. Brier and Nico... there's something strange between them. Always has been."

Palmer shook his head, less than eager to discuss any history Carmella, Nico, and Brier had between them. At least growing up as a ward of the Church rather than in the palace meant Palmer had escaped the drama happening on the other side of the Augarian. "What's happening *here*?"

Carmella stared at him then said with a huff, "I don't know. You left, and then bad things began to happen."

"Bad things?"

"People started disappearing at night. Turning up dead."

"Something's killing them?"

"That's what everyone thought until they really started looking at what happened to them."

Palmer waited for her to continue, lifting an eyebrow when it seemed she was actually pausing for effect. *Definitely the time for showmanship.* He refrained from rolling his eyes. "What happened to them?"

"*Something* isn't killing them. They're killing themselves."

Palmer frowned, turning the words over in his mind. "You don't think that could be solved with *not* holding people captive in the city anymore?"

"These aren't people upset about being here." Carmella shook her head, making her dark ringlets bounce around her shoulders. "They're Elatitans who have lived here all their lives. Ones who are perfectly fine one day, talking about training for the next, and then hang themselves deep on the deserted side of town. There's something happening—something *wrong*."

"And all this started happening after we left?"

"A day or two later." Carmella nodded.

"Did anything else change, other than us leaving?"

"And people suddenly *killing* themselves?"

"Yes, I got that part." Palmer tried to keep from sounding too annoyed when he was still relying on Carmella's help to get both Peony and him out of the city again. "Did anything else happen between our leaving and the deaths?"

Carmella shrugged, slumping back against the wall. "Normal trainings and rounds... more looking for people—you and Nic are lucky you didn't get picked up again. I can't think of anything else."

"Is there anything connecting the people who have died? Is it in one part of town?"

Carmella shook her head. "It happens most to people out after dark. That's why they enacted the curfew. But it can be anywhere, anyone. It doesn't matter how old or young the person is... if it's a native Elatitan or someone found... a man or woman..."

Suddenly, getting to Peony quickly seemed that much more important. Palmer shifted his weight. "Some of your men picked up a friend of mine earlier today."

Carmella's huffy look turned dark. "And here I thought you'd come to keep your promise."

"I said I'd come back when everything was over," Palmer argued. "It isn't. Peony just managed to—"

"Peony." Carmella straightened slightly, one eyebrow arching. "Your friend is a girl?"

Palmer suppressed a grimace. "Yes."

"Does Brier Chastain know? She doesn't like other girls much, from what I recall."

That might be an understatement. Palmer didn't feel the need to think about, much less share, the problems between Brier and Peony. He suspected Carmella would like hearing about that drama a little too much. "Can you help me get her back?"

Carmella stared at Palmer as though trying to read his face before she finally stood and took a few steps toward him. "How about a deal?"

"Another one?"

"Well, I'm not sure if you've actually completed our first one," she said. "But I'm willing to let that slide for now. The new deal is, you figure out what's wrong with my town, and I'll help you and your *not* Brier friend leave. Perhaps I'll join you, depending on what you find out about what's happening."

If he could get his powers working, it wouldn't be too difficult to figure out what the problem with Elatita was. Of course, that was a much bigger *if* than Palmer wanted to face at the moment. But then, powers or no, he didn't have many other choices than to agree with what Carmella Huerta wanted once again.

He glanced up at the dark windows lining the little circular room. "You said whatever is going on happens at night?"

Carmella nodded.

"I suppose I'd better start looking around, then."

"I'll be waiting here, then," Carmella said, sounding vaguely as though she were trying to mock his tone. "You likely have until day-break before someone spots you."

Palmer nodded once and turned for the door. *Dear gods, do I hate this city.*

Chapter Seven

Nico stared at the painted mask Lauretta held out to him, the deep red and black swirls curving along what he assumed was plaster, making it look like a deranged harlequin.

"*What* is that?" He let disdain drip from his tone.

"It's Védarente." Lauretta didn't waver, keeping the mask hovering between them. "You have to wear a mask."

"I'm fine, I assure you."

"You're already *obviously* Latysian." She dropped her dark eyes over his clothing. "Do you want to stick out even more than you already do?"

Nico didn't answer.

"I picked the one with the widest eyeholes, if that makes you feel any better. It won't hem in your vision. No one will be able to sneak up on you."

Nico didn't enjoy just how well Lauretta was able to get into his head. There was a reason he'd never liked anchoresses—even if this one was looking less like an anchoress by the minute. Though he'd made it more than clear that he had no intention of changing his clothing when all the women of the house had gone to dress for the festival, Lauretta had decided to go from the somewhat respectable skirt and waistcoat to clothing that he couldn't imagine even *unrespectable* women of Latysia would wear outside, consisting of red gauzy fabric, bare-midriff cut, and strappy sleeves.

"You can take it off once we're with the oracle." Lauretta jiggled the mask at him impatiently. "It's just while we're in the crowd."

Nico forced himself to take the wretched thing, the pale inside feeling more like smooth ceramic than plaster. With a deep breath, he placed it over his face and tied the ribbon behind his head. "Should I even ask why everyone wears masks to a *truth*-telling festival?"

"When are people more truthful than when no one knows who they are?" Lauretta picked up her own gold-tinged mask and tied it in place.

"Sounds like inviting trouble, if you ask me."

"Lucky we aren't asking you, then." Her half mask did nothing to hide her smile. "You can consider it a break, if nothing else. It must be exhausting trying to keep your face from moving all the time like you do. I mean, I knew Latysians were stoic, but you've elevated it to an art form." Before Nico could formulate a reply, Lauretta turned for the front door. "Come along. It's not far to the temple, but the crowds are only going to get worse the later it gets."

Worse? Nico couldn't imagine how anyone would be able to move on the streets if they were any thicker than he had seen during the day, but he didn't argue. He'd made his choice. It was time to see it play out.

Though the sun had set, the streets were still brightly lit, torches attached to the sides of buildings filling in the spaces between large bonfires that were being built. Nico supposed the torches were necessary. No one would have been able to maneuver on the street with a lantern in that crowd. Nico even had to wonder if the barely there dresses most Ouenen women wore were in part practical. He couldn't picture himself, or anyone else, allowing Brier out of her room in something similar, but she no doubt would have struggled in her full skirts. She certainly wouldn't have been able to slip through the mass of people as Lauretta did.

He suddenly realized he'd thought of Brier entirely naturally, just a vague passing thought without any of the sick feeling that had always risen with her name since her first disappearance. It made him miss a step.

"Are you all right?" Lauretta looked back.

Nico honestly wasn't certain. "Fine. Tripped."

Even in the dark behind the mask, Lauretta's eyes expressed doubt, but she didn't ask any more questions, simply motioning for him to keep following her around the curve of the bay.

The crowds were thicker than earlier, if that was even possible, but Lauretta managed to lead them through in no time at all, soon leaving the music and voices of the growing party and starting up the other spindly point of the bay leading to the temple. After the crush of the city, the emptiness around the crest of the point was nearly eerie, as if Nico and Lauretta had crossed an invisible line the rest of the city knew to avoid.

Lauretta seemed to notice Nico slowing before he was even aware of it. "The temple's closed, but not to me. You'll be fine as long as you stay close."

Something about her tone didn't make him feel much better, but Nico picked up his pace. Lifting the golden rope tied between the pillars lining the circular sanctuary, Lauretta ducked under and stepped onto the marble floor then held it for Nico to do the same.

"I can hold a rope for myself," Nico grumbled, following suit.

"Just being polite." Lauretta let it drop behind him. "Wasn't meant as an affront to your manly aptitude, I assure you."

Nico flashed her a hard look.

She actually rolled her eyes at him. "This way."

Nico stared after her as she swung around the rows of stone pews toward a hallway that curved along the side of the sanctuary. Not eager to be caught standing in an empty temple by himself, though, he had little choice but to follow. He caught up as the pillars marking the hallway from the sanctuary turned into solid wall. "Where—"

"Shh." Lauretta held up a hand, slowing her pace as they moved forward. She stretched her neck to look farther around the curve before ducking back and hugging the wall.

Nico copied her, hearing the soft whisper of slippers on stone somewhere out ahead of them. "I thought you were allowed to be here," he hissed.

"I am," she returned at the same whisper. "Suora Daniela just hates me. She's going to raise the whole temple if she sees you here."

"And she hates you because...?"

Lauretta glared at him but answered, "Delphi and I... have a complicated history. We grew up together. Suora Daniela thinks I get special treatment because of it."

"You grew up with an oracle?"

"Not as much fun as it sounds."

"Tell me about it," Nico mumbled, darker thoughts about Brier starting to form around the corners of his mind.

Lauretta sent him a questioning look.

"I grew up with a god," he said. She stared at him, but Nico saw no reason to add more than that if she was going to be so cryptic about everything she knew. He leaned away from the wall. "I think she's gone?"

Lauretta looked at him before she leaned out as well and nodded. "This way."

The hall began to slope downward, leading under the temple from what Nico could tell, though the curve made it difficult for him to fully get his bearings. The muscles in Nico's neck stiffened, not being able to see more than a few arms' lengths ahead of him not sitting well, but eventually, Lauretta turned off at one of the straight hallways and stopped at a latched door. She lifted her hand to knock.

"Come in," a woman's voice answered.

Lauretta huffed as though annoyed. "She's trying to impress you apparently," she said to Nico before she lifted the latch and stepped inside.

Nico's hands glanced over the weapons still on him, more for comfort than because he thought he'd need them, then he followed her. Though the room was large, most of the space was empty, just a simple bed on one side with a chest and a desk on the other. Sitting under the one window on the far wall—which was positioned far enough up to suggest Nico was right in assuming they'd gone underground—was a woman wearing a proper anchoress's attire, making her not much more than a lump of gray veils on a wooden chair.

"Delphi." Lauretta motioned toward the chair before going to undo her mask.

"I assumed." Nico took the signal to remove his as well.

"Nicodemo Adessi," the lump said in a steady voice. "We finally meet."

Nico cocked an eyebrow. "Is this the part where I'm supposed to be awed you know who I am? Because trust me, I've seen people do much more impressive things over the past year than divine my name."

"Of course you have." The oracle didn't sound flustered in the slightest. "That's why you're here."

Another brilliant deduction. Nico motioned toward Lauretta with his head. "Your anchoress, here, said you have an army for me."

The veils moved just enough to show that the oracle had glanced at Lauretta before she answered, "I have some soldiers, yes. Enough to get you where you need to go."

"Where I need to go?" Nico asked.

"Back to Latysia."

Nico scoffed. "Missed a bit on that one. I'm not going back to Latysia. There isn't much of a Latysia to go back to."

"No, you are."

Oracles... Nico hadn't liked any of the fortune-tellers he had met. Seers with their divine prophecies or street mountebanks promising love and riches to anyone willing to give them a coin. If he'd wanted vague and useless predictions of the future, he could have stayed with Palmer Tash.

"Listen, I've had a long… year. I need an army and to go to *Venchia*. Do you have one, or don't you?"

"You *will* go to Latysia," the oracle said. "Now or later. That is where the final battle will be."

Nico tried to convince himself to turn around before he wasted any more time, but he couldn't help asking, "Final battle?"

"Where the gods' war will finally end, and you will save the world."

"Me." Nico let sarcasm leach from his tone.

"The balance is all wrong this time. Kosmos does not have the power to fight her. You will be the one to stop Chaos's reign."

Nico actually laughed. "Oracle, Delphi, whatever your name is, I don't know what kind of vapors you've been using, but I think your visions got a little scrambled in the ether. Kosmos and Chaos, if that's what you want to call them, are fighting on the same side."

The veils moved as the oracle shook her head. "A second gods' war is coming. Chaos will sweep the land, and the world will end, unless you go to Latysia. You will be the one to stop her."

"Right. Thanks, then." *For wasting my time.* Nico turned back toward the door. "I'll be off."

Lauretta stepped in his way, her hands out to stop him. "Nicodemo, she's never wrong." Her eyes flicked to the pile of veils. "With her visions, at least."

Nico frowned. It was finally his turn to try to read Lauretta's expression. There was bitterness behind the second part of that statement that wasn't typical of an anchoress speaking of her oracle. Then again, if they had been childhood friends, they no doubt had more than enough time to work up their own conflict. Nico could understand that better than most, though he had to imagine he and Brier had Lauretta and Delphi beat for *complicated*.

Lauretta said, "Will you please listen to her?"

Nico stared at her for another moment before he finally turned back to the lump of veils. He arched an eyebrow, prompting her to speak.

"Do you know the story of the gods' war, Signore Adessi?" the oracle asked.

"From children's stories." Nico shook his head, mostly remembering doing everything he could to avoid sitting with the seers and hearing all the myths they spent their lives convincing themselves were true. "The gods started to fight about who should rule the pantheon. They all fought between themselves for... whatever people feel like saying—years, centuries, millennia. Janus won and became king of the gods."

"Not the Latysian story." The veils moved again as the oracle shook her head. "The real one. The one that nearly ended the world a million years before any of us were born."

Nico remained silent, waiting for her to continue.

"There is no king of the gods," the oracle said. "That is a Latysian invention—Janus, the name given to Kosmos when they decided to lift creation over destruction. There have always been two. The old ones. The rest of us exist because of creation *and* destruction. As soon as the balance begins to shift, we are all at risk. The last time Chaos became too strong, it was nearly the end of the world. Kosmos knew he wouldn't succeed, so he asked Isnotra for help."

Temple of Isnotra. Of course any story Nico was going to hear in that temple would tie back to her. Still, he waited for the oracle to continue.

"He couldn't defeat Chaos, so he asked for Isnotra to take her memories so he might place her inside something he would be able to defeat."

"A human," Nico supplied.

The oracle lowered her head an inch in assent. "Of course, Isnotra knew well enough that, while Kosmos could join any of them to a human, it still wouldn't be possible to kill a god so easily. Chaos would simply be reborn time and time again until, eventually, she would regain her memory and her power and they would be thrown straight back into war, and so Isnotra did the only thing she could think to do."

"And what is that?"

"Doom all of them to humanity. She took all of their memories, tricked Kosmos into turning them *all* human and scattering them across the land—far away from one another, where any damage they could do would be tempered by their very short, very human lifespans."

"But another war's coming, according to your visions," Nico said.

"The gods are finding each other again—drawn together, whether they realize it or not—and remembering who they are. It won't be long before we are all right back where we started."

Nico took in the entire tale, nodding slowly. "Good story, but there's one problem."

"And what is that?" the oracle asked.

"I know the current Chaos and Kosmos, and of all the things they're liable to do to one another"—he couldn't fully stop the grimace—"fighting to the death certainly isn't one."

"Things are changing."

"I doubt they'll change *that* much."

The oracle remained silent for several minutes before she finally stood. Nico stopped himself from raising an eyebrow. The woman had to be taller than Brier, but not by much. He imagined she sat in her meetings to hide just how miniscule the Oracle of Ouene really was.

Tiny women trying to run the world these days...

"You can believe what you wish, Signore Adessi," the oracle said. "There is no running from fate. The future will come to pass, whether you accept it, deny it, or fight against it. You may have your soldiers, but mark my words: you will go to Latysia, and you will be the one to end Chaos's reign. You're the only one who can kill her."

Nico's blood suddenly turned to ice in his veins. "*Kill* her?"

The oracle nodded.

"I'm not going to kill her."

The oracle didn't move.

"Even if I wanted to, I couldn't," he argued. "She could dissolve me before I took a step toward her."

"Those who are loved by the gods hold a bit of their power."

Now with the oracle speak. "What does that mean?"

"It means, Nicodemo Adessi, you are perhaps the most important man currently alive."

He stared at the veils then turned toward Lauretta.

The anchoress gave a quick shrug. "Try not to let it go to your head."

Chapter Eight

Taking a deep breath as though he half expected to end up underwater, Palmer slid back out the doorway and into the darkness. If anything, the chill he had felt upon first entering the city had only grown worse, making the air around him thick and heavy. He forced another breath, trying to push the chill far enough away for him to properly use his powers. The headache started nearly before the premonitions this time, but he forced through it, stretching his sight farther and farther out, searching for anything out of place—or at least more so than everything else in a town that was already coated with fear and death.

Fear. The thought registered as his mind caught on a dark spot a few blocks away. He hadn't felt something that dark since... *Rosette.* A flicker of hope tried to find purchase in his chest. When Rosette was scared, or angry, people were more likely to start vomiting blood than kill themselves, but she had supposedly told Brier a story about making someone's "mind break" what felt like a lifetime ago in Ruhegipfel. A constant dose of her powers could possibly drive someone mad. Palmer turned toward the spot. If the problem was, in fact, Rosette, that would certainly be the easiest ill to remedy. He and Peony would be out of Elatita by morning.

As Palmer moved forward, the temperature dropped until he could see his breath in the moonlight. He frowned. Of what he had seen of Rosette's powers, making summer into winter wasn't one of them. Still, he tried to keep hope alive. Pulling into himself as much as possible, Palmer crept forward, trying to catch sight of whatever was out in the dark.

"Look at what you have done." The hissed words floated toward him, breezy enough that Palmer could have believed the air itself had formed them. "Look. Look at what you have done to me."

In the distance, whimpering mixed in with the whispers. That, at least, sounded temporal.

"And here you are, living on, with me turned to dust."

An odd flash of light passed by a window, making Palmer pause. After checking behind him to make sure no one else was on the street, he moved toward it, hearing the whimpering grow louder.

"How can you bear it, Otto? Why do you try? Why haven't you just killed yourself already?"

Palmer pressed his back against the wall beside the window before leaning forward just enough to see through the glass. A man sat huddled in one corner, knees pulled up to his chest as he rocked, murmuring, "No, no, no, no," through his whimpers. The odd light flashed again, and Palmer looked up, finally seeing the black-gray mist that circled the man's head. It sparked then dimmed, ducking closer and closer to the man on the floor.

"You should," the hiss continued, reverberating through the air. "Kill yourself. Do it. Do it."

As the dark energy built, Palmer's entire body began to react against it. He glanced around the dim room as best as he could, then at the street around him, looking for someone, anyone, who could be casting that apparition. Palmer couldn't see anyone—and he didn't dare try to sense whoever it was through the darkness in the air. Not when that would pit him against something that felt so blatantly... evil.

"Do it!" The energy inside the house spiked, and Palmer's flew out to meet it—a net to fight it—before he could consider what he was doing. The flashing mist seemed to shriek, writhing against its confines, trying to break through before it finally shot up through the roof and to the far side of the house. Palmer sent a last glance toward the weeping man on the floor and took off after it.

The mist darted through the street, leading Palmer first toward the town wall then away again, moving quickly enough that Palmer's lungs began to burn as he tried to keep pace. After rounding another corner, Palmer found himself at a dead end. He panted, looking for where the mist had gone before the tingle on the back of his neck gave him the answer. He spun on his heel, hands glowing slightly as his body readied for an attack.

A red-haired boy, perhaps twelve or thirteen, stood at the entry to the alley, head tilted as he studied Palmer.

"Who are you?" Palmer asked as loudly as he dared in the silence.

The boy turned into mist, shooting to the other side of the alley, forcing Palmer to spin once again. He tilted his head the other way as he regained form. "Who are *you*?"

"I asked first," Palmer returned, far too aware of how childish the retort sounded in current circumstances.

The boy glanced down at Palmer's still-glowing hands, and his face broke into a wide smile. "No way..."

Palmer curled his hands into fists, forcing the glow back down, at least enough to hide it.

"No way." The boy stepped forward, the chill in the air dissipating in an instant. "Are you...?"

Palmer checked behind him. The exit was clear if he wanted to run. But he could protect himself, it seemed, if the boy dissolved again.

"You're Kosmos, aren't you?"

Palmer snapped his head forward again.

"You are!" The boy grabbed Palmer's hand and shook it vigorously. "Great to finally meet you. Did you come to see me? Is Chaos here, too?"

Palmer pulled his hand away, face contorting as he tried to work out what the hell was happening. "I'm sorry. Who are you?"

The boy pointed to himself, giving Palmer a look as though it should have been obvious. "Orcus, god of death. And I've been looking everywhere for you. Well, for Chaos really, but word is that you travel together."

"How would you know I'm Kosmos?"

The boy snorted. "No one else would have been able to stop me like that while I was ghosting. I mean, I've read all the myths. Well, heard them. Well, heard the ones I could get people to tell me." He took a breath in the midst of his rambling. "You're shorter than I pictured."

Palmer nodded slowly, still taking everything in. "I take it you're the one who's been causing all the deaths around here, then?"

"I had to do something to pass the time." He smiled, unsettlingly cheery for someone who'd just had a grown man whimpering on the floor. "I was considering wiping the town out in one go, but I've been trying to track you all down since I heard reports of that city down south going to pieces, and they tried to hold me hostage here, so I thought I'd make it a little more fun. It's likely driving whoever's in the temple crazy too."

"You think it's fun... driving people to kill themselves?"

The boy shrugged, looking past Palmer's shoulder. "Where's Chaos? You have no idea how long I've been waiting to meet him."

"Her," Palmer corrected on instinct.

The boy blinked. "Meet her, then. She wasn't out on the street too, was she? I didn't feel him—her—at least, and believe me, I've felt it every once in a while when she's gotten involved in some deaths. She did that not too long ago. Somewhere nearby."

Palmer started to answer then paused. "I'm sorry, do you go by Orcus?"

"Yes." The boy pursed his lips. "Or Gil, if I actually plan to deal with people before I kill them. That's not often these days."

Palmer's stomach twisted again, nothing about this boy sitting well with him.

"But Chaos..." Gil insisted when Palmer didn't continue. "*She's* certainly not the one in the temple."

"That's Carmella..." Palmer said cautiously. "Astarte."

"Figures." Gil snorted. "So where is she? Chaos?"

"A day or two north." Palmer didn't feel the need to be any more specific. "I actually came here looking for someone. Two some-ones. You haven't noticed anyone else like us around here, other than Carmella in the temple?"

"Other gods?" Gil seemed to consider it. "I don't think so. Which ones?"

Thinking about it, Palmer wasn't sure they'd ever given a name to what Rosette was. "She'd be a little girl. Able to make people sick?"

"Oh, Discordia?" Gil lifted his eyebrows. "No, I haven't felt her in a while, actually."

"You can feel her?"

"Anytime she kills someone. According to the myths, she's my sister, you know."

Whenever they did find Rosette, wherever she was, there was no way Palmer was letting this boy anywhere near her, let alone pretend-ing to be a brother.

"And the other one?" Gil asked.

"What?"

"You said two people."

"Oh, human," Palmer said. "She would have been brought in this afternoon."

Gil wrinkled his nose as though he couldn't understand why Palmer would be worried about a human, but he glanced at the dead end behind him. "You tell me what she looks like, and I can go check around. I've floated over to the girl's side of town now and again."

Palmer furrowed his eyebrows. "You want to help me?"

"The sooner we find this human, the sooner we all go wherever Chaos is, yeah?"

Palmer pressed his lips together, debating turning the boy away altogether. In the few minutes Palmer had known him, nothing had suggested that dealing with Orcus would lead to anything good. Especially if it meant bringing Brier a child who liked killing people for fun. But Gil was one of them, for better or worse, and taking him along would apparently hold up Palmer's end of the bargain with Carmella—even if it was a less fortuitous outcome than he'd been hoping for.

"If you get the woman I came for," Palmer said, "you can come with us."

"Like I said, give me a description, and I'll have her back here in ten minutes and us to the gate in the next five—assuming you can keep up."

First things first. "Bring her to the temple. I'll meet you there."

"Fine." Gil drew the word out as if going to the temple was the largest inconvenience in the world, but he dissolved into a cloud and shot off before Palmer could say anything else.

Well, one problem down. Palmer glanced up at the dark sky. If they could leave within the hour, he would be back in Venchia by midday the following day—afternoon at the latest. He'd still have an angry Brier to deal with, but he could certainly hope one day away from her wouldn't lead to any world shattering.

Turning on his heel, Palmer headed back to see Carmella. Perhaps he would be able to convince her to come as well, and they'd have the proper start of a pantheon. If nothing else, that would certainly be interesting.

NICO STARED OUT AT the mayhem taking place along the inner harbor, vaguely wondering what his life would have been like if he were one of those people down there. If his father hadn't taken him from Etrusa simply to spite his mother. If he had somehow ended up in Ouene with his sisters.

His sisters. Nico couldn't imagine he would have been in favor of either one starting a whorehouse, but he at least wouldn't have been caught up in the mess he had to call his life. Even if the world were still ending, it wouldn't be *his* problem. He could be down with the bonfires and half-naked women, having a grand old time.

He stiffened at the sound of footsteps behind him.

"Just me," Lauretta announced herself before he could turn. She stopped at the bench beside him. "May I?"

Nico motioned half-heartedly. The woman was going to sit whether or not he gave permission.

"Delphi wanted me to come out. She seems very intent on my taking care of you."

"I don't need anyone to take care of me."

"I'm sure *I* wouldn't be fine after hearing I had to kill someone. Someone who loves me."

"I've killed people before," he said, "and she doesn't love me."

"I told you, Delphi's visions are never wrong. You have a connection to Chaos." She smiled. "Physically, at the very least. Emotionally, more than likely."

"That's an entirely different story," Nico mumbled, not finding her response nearly as amusing as she seemed to.

"Would you like to talk about it?"

Not especially. "No offense to your vocation, Suora, but I didn't come here to have my fortune told *or* to talk about my feelings."

"Well, you already got one, and I'm here if you'd like the other."

Nico continued to watch the party out in front of him, hints of drums and pipes floating up toward them when the wind blew the right way. He vaguely wondered what people drank for Védarente. He imagined it had to be something good, or at least something that would let him get drunk fast. He hadn't been properly drunk in… well, since he and *possessed* Brier had ended up in bed together. At that thought, his stomach turned enough that he suddenly wasn't certain alcohol was a good idea.

"Are you all right?" Lauretta continued to watch him.

"Do you have to do that?" he snapped.

"Do what?"

"Stare at me."

She looked at him for too long before she finally turned to stare straight ahead. "Delphi has sent a message to Lais. You have your soldiers whenever you want them."

"Lais?" he asked.

"My cousin. Part of the capital guard."

"*Another* cousin?"

"My cousin, not yours. Other side of the family."

Nico released a breath. "How are we related, anyway?"

"Cat and I figured it out once. My mother is your father's fifth cousin? Fifth cousin once removed? Something like that."

"So barely, then."

"Still makes me Lauretta Adessi." She shrugged.

Nico frowned. "You said your *mother's* the Adessi?"

"In Ouene tradition, you take the better known of your family names. Adessi won out over Samara, since Samara… well, my father managed to marry well. Love match."

Nico snorted. "And how did that work out?"

"Very well, I'd say. I could only hope to be as happy as they were."

Nico harrumphed.

"You aren't a romantic, I take it?" Lauretta continued to sound annoyingly amused by his derision.

"My parents were a love match," Nico said. "Then my mother cuckolded him and ruined all of our lives."

Lauretta paused, looking as though she were thinking through what to say. "You can't always help whom you love."

"You can stop yourself from being reckless about it." *Since that's the trick, isn't it?* His mother had been reckless twice—first in marrying his father then in having a lover—and caused all of this. Then he'd been reckless and ruined what he'd managed to make of it. With Orris Adessi's and Catarina di Serafin's blood in their veins, was it really any wonder his sisters were running a brothel and his life was in shambles? They hadn't stood a chance.

"I don't know about that," Lauretta said lightly. "Mad things seem much saner when you're in the midst of love than when you look back at them after you've fallen out of it."

Nico shook his head. "What would an anchoress know about love?"

"More than you'd think." She sat forward, catching her hands in front of her. "I don't want to rush you, but Lais is waiting to hear from us. Do you need more time?"

Time was the one thing Nico certainly didn't have. And they *weren't* going back to Latysia, so it was all moot, anyway. He stood stiffly. "Which way?"

Lauretta motioned and started back down the trail toward the heart of the city.

Chapter Nine

"How much *farther*?"

Palmer sent a sidewise glance at Carmella, quickly beginning to regret bringing her along. Whereas Peony had been entirely silent since Palmer had decreed they were all returning to Venchia, and Gil seemed nearly giddy to be out and moving, Carmella was acting like a spoiled child, dragging her feet and complaining she was tired. He had to half wonder if she'd ever walked anywhere before.

"It's a few more hours at this pace."

"*Hours?*"

"We could walk faster." Palmer shot her a look.

Carmella pouted.

Gil turned back from his position a few yards ahead of them. "Is she always this annoying?"

"I beg your pardon?" Carmella puffed up.

"You have feet," Gil said. "Love goddess too good to use them?"

"Now listen here, you little brat—"

"*I'm* a brat?" Gil said.

"You killed off half my town!"

"Would have killed off all of it if—"

"I swear, if you two don't stop it, I'm leaving you right here," Palmer snapped.

Everyone went silent for one blissful minute before Gil mumbled, "You're not my dad."

Palmer pointed at him. "Do you want to go to Venchia or not?"

Gil said something under his breath that Palmer was certain was profane, but then the boy went quiet, so Palmer let it go. The four of them moved in silence, if a little more slowly than Palmer would have liked, making their way north. As they started up the next set of hills, something tickled the back of Palmer's mind. He frowned, trying to pick out what he was sensing.

"Is something wrong?" Peony asked softly.

Her unexpected voice shocked Palmer out of his thoughts. "What?"

"You look upset."

"No." Palmer finally slowed to a stop. "There's something out there."

Carmella snapped out of her pouting long enough to ask, "*Something*?"

"Want me to scout out ahead?" Gil turned around, placing his hands on his hips.

Palmer shook his head, moving up toward the crest of the hill. He scanned one way then the other, unable to shake the feeling that there was something out there, even if the countryside looked as empty as ever.

As he started to turn around, a blue shimmer caught the corner of his eye. He squinted, pointing. "There. There's something there."

Carmella moved up next to him. "I don't see anything."

"I'll go look." Gil dissolved and shot off before Palmer could tell him not to.

The dark cloud headed straight for the blue shimmer. And then it was gone. Palmer furrowed his brow.

"What happened?" Carmella asked.

Palmer motioned, starting toward the spot where Gil had disappeared. They'd nearly reached it when the black cloud shot back over their heads.

"Should probably run." Gil's voice breezed through the air, the cloud not slowing.

Palmer didn't have a chance to react before the shimmer parted. As if a veil had been lifted, rows and rows of tents came into view, the previously empty countryside suddenly filled with men.

"Osamli," Peony murmured, looking at the triangular flags at the top of the tents.

Palmer's stomach knotted. The Osamli controlled an entire empire far off beyond any city-state that had ever answered to the Augarian. How a sizable force had managed to make it so deep onto the peninsula without news spreading, Palmer didn't know. Any city by itself wouldn't stand a chance against an Osamli invasion. Pure distance had likely been Latysia's saving grace in avoiding conflict. If the Osamli were there, and Latysia at full strength wouldn't have been able to put off an invasion, what hope was there for any army Brier could amass in Venchia?

Dread coursing through him, Palmer took a step backward. He had to admit Gil had the right idea. "Run."

"Halt!" The call came from the tents.

Palmer grabbed both women by their arms and started back the way they had come.

Other shouts went up. They wouldn't be able to outrace anyone going uphill, so Palmer skirted the bottom, trying to make it to one of the gaps between the hills.

Carmella tripped, the light fabric of her dress tangling around her legs.

"Go," Palmer urged Peony before turning back to help Carmella.

Peony hesitated.

"Go!" Palmer motioned.

The loud crack of gunfire set Peony forward around a hill. "They're shooting at us?" She fought to hike up her dress.

"So it seems." Palmer struggled with Carmella's tangled skirts and finally ended up ripping the fabric entirely.

"Hey!" Carmella exclaimed as a long slit opened up in her dress.

"Run!" Palmer grabbed her by the wrist and turned.

Pain shot through Palmer's hip nearly before he heard the next shot. The bullet felt as though it ripped straight through to the bone. He fell. Clutching the wound, he felt warm blood smearing his palm, the damage too deep for even his powers to heal it quickly.

"Palmer." Carmella took a step forward then hesitated, looking uncertain.

Palmer started to tell her to go as well, but men had already circled them, a mix of swords and harquebuses pointed in their direction. A warm wave of energy started to build as Carmella pushed her powers out.

Men. Palmer glanced around the circle as he clamped his hand down harder on his hip, trying to hide the glow he could feel starting. *Carmella could be helpful.*

The men facing them began to lower their weapons, their eyes becoming glassy.

"I think you want to let us go," Carmella said gently. "Don't you?"

The man directly in front of her dropped his weapon altogether before a man behind Carmella shouted, "*Birnekli*!" He grabbed her shoulder.

"What?" Carmella jerked back.

The man brought a white-silver piece of metal down on Carmella's wrist, and it snapped into a cuff. Carmella sucked in a sharp breath, and the warm energy in the air disappeared.

Palmer tried to get to his feet without taking his hand from his hip. "What...?"

"My powers." Carmella flexed her hand, concern moving in waves over her beautiful face. "I can't..."

Another man grabbed Palmer, and cold metal slapped his wrist as well. The air left Palmer's lungs, and the tingle of energy still healing his wound gave way to burning pain. He blinked, trying to breathe through it as the fullness in his mind emptied into a vacuum. The combination made him double, leaving him winded and shaking.

"Palmer?" Carmella placed a hand on his back before the men of the circle began barking commands.

Though Palmer couldn't understand a word the men were saying, their sharp jabs to his back made it very clear what they wanted him and Carmella to do. Head still spinning, Palmer stumbled forward, heading for the magically appearing tents and gods knew what else.

BRIER'S FINGERS JITTERED along her knee, as much as she tried to control it, the nervous energy keeping her from remaining still. Palmer hadn't returned before nightfall, and now the sun was creeping toward midday with no sign that he was any closer to returning. She half wanted to send Cerise out to look for him again, but any good will Brier had with the woman seemed to be quickly fading. And Cerise was spending her time with Goebel, anyway. If there was anywhere in town Brier didn't want to go, it was to see Goebel.

Can you hear me? She tried once again to send out the thought on the off chance that Palmer had gotten close enough to hear her, but she might as well have been talking to herself.

Palmer. Nico. Rosette. One by one, everyone important left in her life was disappearing. She was half-ready to get up and leave the ruins as well. *If I had anywhere to go.* She frowned. Her father was dead. Nico was obviously done with her. Palmer and Rosette were gods knew where. Anywhere she went, she would be just as alone as she was in Venchia. Brier stood up sharply, quickly gathered her things, and headed for the one place in town she knew someone wouldn't be able to leave.

Leone still didn't look like much more than flesh and bones, his skin pasty and cheeks sunken so deeply that he might as well have been a skull sitting on top of soiled clothes, but he'd finally managed to sit up. He rested against the wall of the cave, staring off at nothing.

"You're looking better." Brier moved up to the cell and let herself inside.

Leone turned his head toward her and stared for a long enough time that Brier wondered if he fully realized she was there. "So I didn't hallucinate you."

"Doesn't seem you did." She sat down in front of him. "Have you been eating?"

"Not very hungry."

"You're thinner than I am, Leo, and that's saying something these days." Brier made a face. "You need to eat."

Leone's eyes moved over her. "You still look fine."

"Thank you for lying." Brier pulled out some food for him.

"You've always been pretty, Chas. It's part of why..."

Brier pulled her eyebrows together, giving him a questioning look.

"Part of why I couldn't believe it—when I first heard what you were."

Brier nodded slowly, trying to work out how she should take the statement. "How do you think I should look, then?"

Leone gave a weak shrug.

Brier studied the man in front of her. He was broken, crippled. Leone had never been quite as handsome as his cousin, his face slightly too long and eyes just a smidge too close together to be declared the more attractive of the two Adessi boys in the Augarian, but he'd certainly never been hard to look at. *What did you do to yourself?*

She sat back, lips pursed slightly. "Are you afraid of me, Leo?"

He searched her face right back. "Should I be?"

"I asked if you *are*."

He watched her for another long moment before he said, "I saw what you did to Latysia."

Brier frowned as her stomach tightened. "That was as much your uncle's doing as mine. The city wouldn't have come down if he hadn't tried to kill me."

"He was trying to fix you."

Brier gave a bitter laugh. "Is that what he told you?"

"He always cared about you."

"I'm not sure he ever cared about anyone as much as he did about himself."

"Catarina," Leone said. "By all accounts, he truly did love her. I mean, he carted enough of her things out here with him."

Brier frowned. "What?"

"You haven't found Uncle Orris's things?" Leone picked up some of the dried meat Brier had set in front of him and studied it as though he couldn't fully remember how to take a bite. "He somehow got a good dozen trunks out here with him. The one with Catarina di Serafin's things—I imagine he's had that since he left Etrusa. Not like he made a lot of trips back to see the adulteress."

"He could have just not wanted her to have whatever he took." That sounded more like the Orris Adessi she knew. That was why he'd taken his son with him, by all accounts. He'd certainly had no interest in being a father.

"He could have burned it all, if that were it. Or at least left it for you to... um, he could have left it at the Augarian. To be destroyed."

Brier wasn't certain she wanted to think of the person who'd tried to kill her—twice—as a lovesick man who'd let heartbreak warp him. She much preferred her monsters to stay monsters. *Per-*

haps that's why Leo can't deal with me. Chaos. The abyss. She could certainly understand the *idea* of her being some men's monster.

"I'm still me, you know," she said.

"What?"

"I'm still Brier. I'd like to believe I still am, at least."

"You just bring down cities now."

Brier released a long breath through her nose, the one sentence hitting some sore point inside her chest she hadn't been aware of. She opened her mouth to answer. A sharp pain moved through her before she could utter a syllable. With a soft cry, she doubled over, placing a hand on her chest. It felt like part of her soul was being sucked away.

"Chas?" Leone's arm went out as though he were going to catch her, but he must have either realized he couldn't move that much or been too frightened to actually touch her.

Brier forced her lungs to take in a new breath past the pain, and the emptiness she felt began to register. "Palmer."

"What?" Leone asked, his sunken eyes alarmed.

"I can't feel him."

"*Feel* him?"

"Palmer. I..." She tried to fight down the panic as a growing realization shot through her. "I could feel him out there. Now... nothing."

"What's that mean?"

Brier didn't want to consider the most likely possibility. She pushed her pack toward him as she scrambled to stand. "There's more food in there. Some other supplies."

"Chas," he called after her, but Brier was already back outside, needing to move if only to keep up with her racing thoughts.

A pained shout echoed through the ruins. Brier turned, trying to place where it had come from. With a caw, Cerise swooped down from above. She spoke in a rush before her entire body had turned human again. "Goebel's awake. Whatever Kos did, it's weakening."

"Can you feel him?" Brier curled her hand into a fist, pressing it into her chest as though that would fill the emptiness.

"Goebel?"

"Palmer," Brier said. "I don't feel him anymore."

Cerise's expression changed. The complete lack of the self-assured smirk on her face made the sudden emptiness in Brier's chest even more alarming. "At all? You don't feel him at all?"

Brier shook her head, feeling her braid whipping back and forth over her shoulders. "Does that mean he's...?" She couldn't bring herself to even speak the word *dead*.

Cerise's face remained far too grim, but she grabbed Brier's arm and pulled. "Come on."

Brier was too caught up in her thoughts to object. Taller than Brier—slightly taller than her normal height, it seemed—Cerise nearly pulled Brier off her feet as they ran. Somehow, Brier managed not to trip over the rough cobblestone—or her own feet—before they slowed down at the small house Goebel had been given. Though the shouting had stopped, Brier could hear the groaning before they reached the doorway. She swallowed, tasting bile at the back of her throat. Her body hadn't dealt with the sudden emptiness. She couldn't handle Goebel's pain *and* her bastardized powers as well.

She yanked her arm free. "I can't go in there."

Cerise spun toward Brier, her face contorting. "You have to do something."

"Do what? I'm not..." *Palmer.* She apparently couldn't even bring herself to say his name. "I can't heal anyone."

"It's your energy. Shoot it back. Suck it into that ring. Figure it out."

"But... I don't... I can't..." Brier gulped for air as her chest constricted, not able to take in enough breath no matter how quickly she tried to fight for it. "Cerise, he's... I can't feel..."

The slap resounded, leaving Brier's cheek stinging, before she realized Cerise had struck her. Brier cupped her cheek, mouth gaping open.

"You are a goddess," Cerise seethed, sounding more serious than Brier had ever heard the woman as she pointed a long finger straight at Brier's face. "You can fall apart and wonder what happened to your boyfriend later. Right now, you hold yourself together and do what you are here to do."

"I don't heal people!" Brier snapped, still holding her stinging cheek.

"Figure. It. Out." Cerise shoved Brier into the house, nearly sending Brier straight onto her face.

Annoyance made energy spark through Brier's body, the feeling stronger than ever. Whether that was from the sudden emptiness allowing the energy to echo inside her or from the sickly buzz of Marina's powers covering the room, Brier didn't know.

"Brier?" Goebel's strained voice stopped her before she could send some life-threatening jolt in Cerise's direction.

She turned toward the pallet set up in the corner of the room and saw Goebel's grimacing face. Whereas Leone had nearly wasted away in the past month, Goebel looked as though he'd simply woken after a long nap. If she could ignore his pain and keep her eyes away from the swirling purple energy slowly eating its way up his legs, Brier would almost have been able to pretend that he was the man who had left them months ago in Latysia.

She swallowed the lump in her throat. "How...?" She trailed off. Asking the man how he was feeling seemed cruel in present circumstances. "Cerise wanted me to help," she said, sending the woman standing in the doorway a dark look.

Cerise barely seemed to register it.

"Help?" Goebel repeated the word, sounding entirely confused.

Brier could hardly blame him. "I'm not sure how I can..." She forced the name out. "Palmer was stopping it. I can't feel him anymore. I don't know where... do you think he's dead?"

Brier's stomach dropped out, having said the words aloud, and Cerise gave an annoyed huff, but Goebel seemed to consider it, even past his gut-wrenching grimace. "You can't feel him?"

"Not at all," she whispered. "What does it mean?"

"I'm not sure, *schatzi*. I don't know of anyone who has trained both of you. How connected you are or aren't—" He cut off with a pained hiss.

Brier forced herself to look down. The swirling purple energy was sending out thin tendrils, climbing up the stubs that had once been Goebel's thighs toward his hips.

"Do something." Cerise pushed Brier forward.

Brier looked over her shoulder. "Touch me again, you're losing that hand."

Cerise arched an eyebrow.

Forcing another swallow past the lump in her throat, Brier took a few uncertain steps toward the pallet. "I don't..." She held a hand out toward his thigh.

Her palm moved over the energy, and it jumped. Brier gasped as the jolt moved through her hand and felt a heady rush as the *wrong* energy coursed upward, nearly beating out the shout she heard. Something jerked her back. Brier blinked, trying to clear her head. By the time she could see straight, Cerise was flexing her hand as though it stung and kneeling at Goebel's side.

"All she can do is make it end faster, Cerise," Goebel said, the blood draining from his face as he grimaced.

"You're *not* going to die," Cerise said. "That's final."

"If Palmer is gone, we don't have time to find a new Kosmos. Let her kill me."

Brier turned on her heel, running back out onto the street. Palmer gone. Someone taking his powers. Having to kill someone. One word after the next sliced like a knife. It was too much—all of it. She needed to get far away, needed to keep moving. Perhaps she could outrun all the awful thoughts fighting for a place in her mind.

Chapter Ten

The hefty fabric of the tent made the light inside oddly golden. Palmer didn't have time to marvel at the thick carpet that the camp apparently carried to place over the grass or the richness of the pillows there were to sit on. He focused on the cuffs on his wrists—one apparently dampening his powers, the other connected to a thick chain holding him to the post in the center of the space.

"Have a talent for getting captured, don't you?" Carmella grumbled, shaking her wrist enough to make her chain clank.

"Technically, no one in Elatita captured me." *This time.* Palmer pulled at the thinner cuff, trying to force it to release where one end overlapped the other. Though there was nothing but a shallow dip there, the two ends fit together so solidly that they might as well have been welded shut. He stopped pulling and looked at Carmella. "Can you get yours off?"

"You don't think I would have if I could?"

Palmer barely stopped himself from rolling his eyes at her snarky tone. "And your powers aren't working as well, I take it?"

"They would not with the *kirilbilzik* on." The thickly accented voice made Palmer jump. An older man with a thick head of gray hair maneuvered through the tent flap, carrying some sort of case. "They are not uncomfortable—that is my hope—but you understand we must be careful."

Palmer lifted his right wrist cautiously. "This is a... *kirilbilzik?*" He was certain he'd butchered the unfamiliar word.

"Yes." The man set down his case and opened it. "My invention. It... stops the powers but with no lasting problems. I am quite proud."

"Who are you?" Carmella asked the question Palmer realized he should have started with.

"Oh, I am sorry." The man straightened with a smile. "I am Dr. Guda. I have spent much of my life studying the *birnekli*."

"*Birnekli*?" Palmer got that one to sound a little closer to the man's pronunciation.

"People who are like you. With the powers."

"You mean gods?"

Dr. Guda's smiled disappeared, and his broad nose wrinkled as though he had smelled something unpleasant. "There is no God but the one God—the one who has given *birnekli* the powers."

Palmer glanced at Carmella, seeing his discomfort mirrored on her face, but neither of them replied. She must have shared his feeling that it wasn't a prudent idea to debate with the man who had apparently stripped them of their powers.

Having settled the matter of the nonexistence of gods, Dr. Guda smiled again and turned back to his case. "You will be moved soon, but first, I start with my samples."

"Samples?" Palmer shifted uncomfortably.

"For how I make my inventions." Dr. Guda straightened again, holding a pair of tweezers and a small glass container. "Hair first."

Before Palmer could squirm away, the doctor had plucked a hair off Palmer's head and placed it in the container.

"Hey!" Carmella exclaimed as he pulled out one of her long dark strands as well.

"You can tell me your powers?" Dr. Guda said, ignoring their protests, and placed Carmella's strand in a separate container. "It saves me much time."

Palmer shared another look with Carmella. Neither of them spoke.

"I say *please*?" He looked up as he shuffled through his case once again.

"What sort of inventions are you making?" Palmer replied instead.

"Ones that help humans and the empire." Dr. Guda came up with a short blade Palmer certainly didn't like the look of.

"The Osamli Empire?" Palmer watched it cautiously.

"Yes." Dr. Guda's smile widened as he turned back to Palmer. "Hold still, please. Will not hurt much."

Palmer wasn't sure he believed that, but chained as he was, he didn't have much choice but to sit and take what was coming. After grabbing Palmer's forearm with a deceptively strong grip, Dr. Guda straightened it then sliced the skin just below the crease of the elbow. Palmer hissed, still seeing no sign of healing as blood beaded along his skin. The doctor tilted Palmer's arm so the blood flowed into another vial.

"See? Is not so bad." Dr. Guda corked the vial before placing a bit of cloth over the cut. "Hold that." He cleaned off the knife and turned to Carmella.

Carmella scrambled back. "Don't you even think—"

Dr. Guda grabbed her arm.

"Let me go!" She tried to shake him off.

"You must be still, or I will have to give you something to relax."

"Carmella," Palmer warned. He didn't know what the doctor meant by *something to relax*, but he didn't want to find out.

She sent him an incredulous look. The doctor took the brief break in concentration to make his cut and collect her blood.

"Thanks to you." Dr. Guda looked extremely pleased. He added some other liquid to each of the blood vials then stored them back in his case. "If you will not speak, I will leave you now." He waited, probably to see if either of them had the desire to suddenly tell him what he wanted to know. Then he nodded and once again left the tent with his case.

"Why did you let him do that?" Carmella hissed as soon as they were alone once again.

"You'd rather find out what being given 'something to relax' means?"

Carmella glared but didn't continue to complain.

"Come on." Palmer turned his attention to the cuff connected to the chain. "We need to get out of here before they decide they need to run more *tests* on us."

"Best idea you've had all day." Carmella shifted onto her knees. "What do we do?"

Palmer looked at the thicker iron cuff, at the loop where it connected to the post behind them. How deep they had dug down to put in that post, Palmer didn't know. He had to imagine they would be able to pull it over if they dug out enough of the earth, but then the fabric of the tent would come down on top of them. Not exactly a stealthy getaway—or any kind of getaway if they ended up trapped in a sea of canvas before guards arrived. He moved his hand back and forth, finding much more leeway in the fit of the thick cuff than the thin one—the *kiril-whatever* Dr. Guda had called it—which fit like a second skin. Pulling, Palmer found he could almost work his hand through the hole. "How does yours fit?" He lifted his left hand. "Can you work your hand out?"

Carmella pulled, making a face as she tried to wiggle her hand free. She finally shook her head. "It's too small."

Palmer gritted his teeth. If he could just get his thumb in another fraction of an inch...

The flap of the tent moved again, and two men walked in, one dressed in the loose-fitting garb Palmer had seen the Osamli men wearing, the other in the shirt and trousers Palmer would more expect from a Latysian merchant. The first brought the second to the post and locked him to it as well. Without a word, the Osamli man turned around and left the tent. Palmer looked at Carmella, who sent him a look as though she expected him to speak to the remaining man.

Of course. Palmer cleared his throat. "Are you Latysian?"

The man looked up sharply, his dark hair moving back from his face. "Are you?"

"We are." Palmer nodded.

"Technically, I never lived *in* Latysia," Carmella said. "We had an estate in…"

Palmer cut her off with a sharp look before turning back to the man. "You?"

"From Cittamuarta, so not far from you," he said. "Or it wasn't until they got to it."

Palmer thought of the strong-walled city, still alive and teeming even after Latysia fell the last time he had seen it. "The Osamli attacked Cittamuarta?"

"Where they got me. Burnt it to the ground. But we aren't by Latysia?"

"We left Elatita this morning," Palmer said quickly. "I'm Palmer. This is Carmella."

"Vitale," he returned. "Most people call me Vito."

Palmer's eyes went to the thin cuff on Vito's right wrist. "And you're… like us?"

Vito eyed Palmer's cuff right back. "Heke. You?"

Cittamuarta had long been famous for its healing waters, stemming from the Temple of Heke, god of health. If they actually had Heke in the city, the city's waters working that way made all the more sense.

Palmer placed a hand on his chest. "Kosmos." Then he pointed. "Astarte."

"Good." Vito released a breath. "Glad to finally meet someone on the right side."

"Right side?" Palmer frowned.

"Supposedly, the doctor had his hands on Isnotra years ago, from what I've heard. That's how they got that veiling thing."

"Veiling thing?" Carmella finally spoke.

"Why you can't see them from a distance. Isnotra can apparently mess with someone's perception. Though I can't say I've met her. The only other one of us they have right now isn't on our side. Discordia, as far as I can figure."

The name sent a jolt through Palmer. "Discordia? Is she a little girl? Blond?"

"You've seen her?"

Either the veil or the cuffs would explain why Palmer hadn't been able to get any sense of where Rosette had gone. He just hoped nothing awful had happened to her while she'd been stuck in the camp. "She was in Venchia with me. We've been looking all over for her."

Vito's face reacted as though Palmer had just said something morally reprehensible. "What were you doing with someone like *her*?"

"Like *us* you mean?"

"She's not like us." Vito shook his head. "She's one of Chaos's lot. If they'd left us alone at all, I would have gotten rid of her before she could do any damage."

"She's a little girl." It was Palmer's turn to look at Vito as if the man were mad.

"She's one of Chaos's. She'd kill any of us."

"I assure you she wouldn't."

"She will once the war starts."

Palmer shook his head. "What war?"

Vito hesitated, raking his eyes over Palmer suspiciously. "I thought you said you were Kosmos."

"I am."

"Then you would know."

"My powers are a little tied up at the moment." Palmer lifted his right arm.

"But still, the *gods' war*?"

Palmer remembered the story well enough from his days as an acolyte. It still didn't seem like anything to base killing a little girl on. "That supposedly happened eons ago."

"But we're finding each other again. When he has his children and the trickster, Chaos will once again try to destroy the world."

"First, she's a *she*," Palmer said.

"Are you sure?" Carmella droned. "She spent enough time with the boys that—"

"Second"—Palmer decided to ignore any cattiness—"we're all working together here. We aren't trying to get rid of anyone."

Vito continued to watch Palmer suspiciously but said, "I suppose it doesn't matter as long as we're stuck here. I've been here two months. Still haven't figured out a way to get this thing off." He motioned toward the small cuff. "Let alone getting away from camp."

"We were just working that out," Palmer said, though the knowledge that the Osamli had managed to hold Rosette for a month without the little girl escaping, with as good as she was at slipping away from places, didn't bode well for the rest of them. Then again, if he could find Rosette and they could all figure out a plan together, that could be useful. "Do you know where they have Rosette? Discordia?"

Vito frowned but nodded. "The doctor's using her to make some new invention, from what I've heard."

That didn't sound good at all. "We need to get there, then."

"You're not likely to get anywhere they don't want you to be." Vito shook his head.

Palmer chewed on the inside of his cheek, a plan slowly coming together. Not a good one, by any stretch, but a plan. "We'll just have to get them to want us there, then."

Chapter Eleven

As the sun began to set, Brier found herself deep into the ruins near the empty space that used to be a grand palazzo before she and Marina had brought it down. After she had dissolved most of the rubble—and Orris Adessi's body, since Nico hadn't wanted to bury it—in their search for Rosette, Brier had entirely avoided the area. She certainly hadn't thought of searching any of the nearby buildings for anything Orris Adessi would have brought with him to the ruins.

Taking a deep breath, Brier clenched and released her hand, still feeling the buzz from when she had nearly touched Goebel. The headiness of Marina's energy joined with the gaping emptiness still in her chest made Brier unsteady, as though she'd had a little too much to drink—unfortunately, without any of the pleasant giddiness or relaxation drinking used to give her. She could only hope that Orris Adessi had brought wine along with news of anything else Leone had seen. She could use a glass. Or a bottle.

After looking around, Brier headed for the largest building still standing. She knew Orris Adessi far better than she wished she did. He would have looked for somewhere suitably grand to live, even in the ruins.

Unlike the smaller buildings up where Brier had been living, which were mostly one or two square rooms, the houses near the old palazzo seemed to have all once been grand villas, each built around an open center. Brier wound her way through rooms in various states of repair, looking for any signs of Latysian chests. Just as the light grew dim enough that Brier thought she would have to give up for the night, she noticed something glinting in a back room. Moving through the doorway, she spotted a stack of trunks, the gilding of one stacked below another catching the orange light coming through a western window.

Leone was right. Brier looked over the half dozen trunks. Even if she hadn't recognized them as Latysian, the painted wood certainly wouldn't have survived in its current state if the trunks hadn't recently arrived. She knelt in front of the closest. A large iron lock held the latch shut. With a wave of her hand, the bottom clattered to the ground, and the metal connecting it to the hooked shackle dissolved into nothing. She pulled the shackle out and flipped the lid open. Layers of men's clothing and personal effects filled it. Frowning, Brier shut the lid again. If she found a sewing kit, she likely would be able to make the fabric into something she could wear—it was rich, and ripping Orris Adessi's clothing apart at the seams would be gratifying—but it wouldn't help her at the moment.

She dissolved the locks on the next two trunks. A mix of gold and silver wares filled the second. Books were stacked in the third. Brier gritted her teeth. Though the light was too dim to read the titles, she had to believe they'd been taken from the Augarian library. Her father's library. *Her* library. The violation nearly felt as deep as Orris kidnapping her. Twice. She shut the lid with a thump, telling herself she would return in the morning when the light was better to see what was actually there. After looking at the other three chests, she finally went for the fanciest one, even though that meant dragging another off the top of it. With a grunt, she freed the ornate chest and got it open.

At the top, it held bedding. She picked up a delicately embroidered sheet and frowned. The fabric smelled dusty, as though it hadn't been used in years, though it had obviously been carefully kept. She set it aside, more and more convinced that it was a marriage chest. A few more layers down, she found a dress, which confirmed that assumption. In the fading light, she couldn't tell if the fabric was black or dark blue or green. No matter the color, it was a proper gown and made of something other than the rough fabric the cultists used. Quickly, Brier pulled it on, tying it as tightly as it could go. It was still slightly too big and entirely out of date with the ribbons at the shoulders, indicating that there were separate sleeves she would have to tie on, but just wearing a proper dress once again made her feel that much better. Come morning, perhaps she would even try to do something with her hair.

The orange sunlight quickly turning red as the sun sank below the horizon, Brier turned to the next chest to look inside. The row of dark bottles made her smile. *There we go.* She picked one up and pulled out the stopper. The warm, rich, entirely welcome smell of wine hit her nose, and she took a hearty drink. She nodded. For all his faults, Orris had always had good taste.

After a few more swigs, Brier pulled out two more bottles and stood. She had more than enough to get drunk, but she wasn't certain she trusted herself to drink alone. With few options for drinking companions left in town, she left the villa and headed uphill.

With not more than a touch of pink along the western horizon outside, inside the cave was pitch-black. Brier set down the bottles and called just enough energy so the purple glow let her find where the torch was attached to the wall. Though she had no clue how long it had been since the torch had been used, the pitch still caught, and a pool of firelight illuminated the rough stone walls. She picked up the bottles and turned toward the cell.

Leone blinked, looking as though she had woken him. "Chas?"

"Drink with me." She placed one of the bottles by his side then sat with a thump before uncorking her bottle to take a large gulp of wine expensive enough that any connoisseur would be horrified at how she was downing it.

Leone considered her, his sunken eyes looking even deeper in his skull in the flickering light. "You found Uncle Orris's things, then."

"And he always had wonderful taste in wine. Drink."

He pushed himself up to a sitting position, pulling his lame leg after him as he maneuvered to rest against the wall. "Why?"

"Because I've had an awful day, I want to get drunk, and I could really use a friend."

Leone hesitated. "I'm a friend?"

"You used to be," she said.

Leone watched her for another minute before he finally grabbed the bottle she had set next to him and pulled out the stopper. He took a drink and made a pleased face. "Very good."

"Told you." Brier tilted the bottle to drink. Based on how far she had to angle it, she'd nearly gone through half already. She could only hope the warm relaxation would hit soon—ideally, before any nausea made her slow down.

They drank in silence before Leone said, "You don't want Nic to know you found his father's things?"

"What?" Brier brought her eyes back to him, the room shifting enough with the motion that she had to admit the wine was hitting her.

"There's a reason you aren't drinking with him?"

"He's not here." She shrugged as though she didn't care, taking another long drink, trying to get it in before she'd be forced to slow down.

Leone's eyebrows pulled together as though he didn't understand the words coming out of her mouth. "But you're here."

"Can't get anything by you."

"He wouldn't just leave you here."

"Seems he would." Brier finally set the bottle down beside her. "But that's life. Everyone I care about is now missing, dead, or just plain left, so in grand Latysian tradition, tonight I drink."

"Are you already drunk?"

"Quickly getting there, thanks be. I've lost a good deal of my tolerance without you boys around to be a bad influence."

A hint of a smile threatened to emerge. "*We* were the bad influence."

"Who used to sneak in the liquor?" Brier kicked her legs out and rested back on her hands in a decidedly unladylike way. She pointed, her finger not quite finding Leone at first. "You kissed me once on one of those nights."

Leone's eyebrows rose. "If I remember correctly, *you* kissed *me*. And then passed out half on top of me. I thought Nico was going to throw me out the window."

The wine let Brier giggle. "He never was good at sharing."

"Understatement, I think." Leone tilted his bottle back at a steep angle. He was quickly catching up. He paused. "Are you *sure* he's gone?"

"You're welcome to go look for him"—she started giggling again—"but I think you'll find you don't have a leg to stand on."

He sent her a dark look. "Sure. Laugh at the cripple."

"You laugh or you cry these days." Brier picked up her bottle. "I'd rather laugh at the moment. Are you with me?"

"Who am I to argue with a goddess?" Leone mumbled.

Brier released a tense breath. "Could you just... pretend you don't know what I am, Leo? I'm still Brier. I've always been Brier." *I need to be Brier.*

Leone studied her, thoughts moving behind his eyes that Brier was glad she didn't understand. He shrugged. "I can try."

Brier had to accept that as enough. At least for the night.

NICO WATCHED THE CAMPFIRES start, a handful at a time, not able to stop himself from scanning the darkening horizon for any sign of people who might take notice. The oracle had managed to put together a somewhat respectable force of forty or so men. They wouldn't be nearly enough to stand up to an army, but Nico had to imagine they'd easily deal with any roving marauders. That still didn't mean he cared to draw more attention than was necessary.

A snap and the sound of galloping hooves made Nico jump. He twisted, frowning as he watched a horse starting away from the camp, the animal and its rider not much more than shadow in the waning light. Nico's hand went to the bow on his back on instinct, though he didn't pull it as he looked at the rest of the camp. If any of the other men found the sudden departure alarming, they didn't show it.

Then again, they were all Ouenen. Nico didn't have to wonder where their loyalties would lie if something was happening that *he* needed to worry about. Footsteps moved up the hill, and his eyes snapped to Lauretta moving toward him. He mentally groaned. *Who else?*

He still couldn't see any good coming from carting an anchoress along into battle, but no one seemed willing to listen to his opinion. With Lais, Lauretta's capital guard cousin, *also* a woman, it seemed Ouene had no issues throwing women into battle anyway, so what did the *stiff, serious Latysian* know?

"Delphi." Lauretta stopped in front of him, not offering any further explanation.

Nico bit down a harsher reply. "She sent out a rider?"

"That *was* Delphi," Lauretta said.

Nico's eyes snapped toward where he had last seen the rider. "She's leaving?"

"Apparently, it's what she's supposed to do." Lauretta's tone made it sound as though she were only just refraining from rolling her eyes. "I asked for her to actually explain for once, but of *course,* that would ruin everything."

"I hate oracles," Nico mumbled.

"Try living with one." Lauretta shook her head as she looked off after the figure.

Nico slid his eyes back toward the woman next to him. "If you don't like oracles, couldn't you find another temple to join?"

She released a heavy breath but shrugged. "You can love someone without liking them all the time."

Nico supposed that was true. Of course, that train of thought brought him far too close to things he'd rather forget. He forced the topic back to safer waters. "You didn't become an anchoress *just* to be with your friend?"

The long shadows morphed Lauretta's expression enough to hide what she was thinking. "I'm sure others have done crazier things when they were sixteen and in love."

Nico snorted. "You ran away to a temple because you were in love?"

"You disapprove?"

"Seems counterproductive, rather than just running off to marry or whatnot."

"Assuming I would have had any chance in changing Delphi's mind, sadly, that wouldn't have been an option. We aren't Latysia, but Ouene still wouldn't allow *that*."

Nico paused, feeling as though he had missed some important part of the conversation. "What?"

"*What* what?"

"Allow what?"

"Us marrying," Lauretta said, enunciating each word carefully, as though she thought Nico had gone a little slow.

"Us... as in, you and *Delphi*?"

"That's what we were talking about, wasn't it?"

Nico blinked, still feeling two steps behind. "She's a woman."

"Yes, she is."

"You... want to be with a woman."

"I *was* with a woman," Lauretta said, her voice turning bitter, "but apparently, that wasn't what was supposed to happen either. Have you ever had *the cosmos decrees it* as a reason you can't be with someone?"

Cosmos. That phrasing was just unfair. Nico stuck to more pressing matters. "That's something that happens in Ouene? Women are just... *with* women?"

"I imagine it's something that happens all over."

"Not in Latysia it didn't."

"You believe you know what *every* woman in Latysia did in her own bedroom?"

"*That* wasn't happening." Nico shook his head, not even quite certain *how* "that" would work.

"If you say so."

Nico wasn't certain if she sounded amused or annoyed, but either way, he moved on. He hadn't been friends with many women in Latysia—there hadn't been many who lived in the Augarian anyway—but Brier barely seemed to tolerate most of the other women she'd been around. He had a hard time believing she could convince herself she was in love with any of them. It had to be a phenomenon particular to Ouene—a strange town that created stranger people.

Nico started to ask another question before a shimmer of movement just south of them caught his attention. "Did you see that?"

"See what?" Lauretta turned to look where he was.

Glancing at the group slightly farther down the hill, Nico saw the rest of the men—and women—who had been introduced as the captains all still talking amongst themselves. Nico slipped his bow off his shoulder, taking a few steps away. "I'm going to look around."

"I'll come." Lauretta turned after him.

"I don't need company."

"I can help," she said.

Nico blew out a breath, having to assume arguing would just waste valuable time. He glanced over the shapeless dress Lauretta had changed into for traveling—an anchoress's garb without the veils. "Do you at least have a dagger or something?"

"You think I'll need one?"

Nico shook his head but pulled out the one at his hip and offered it to her. "Better to have one and not need it than need it and not have it."

As soon as she took it, Nico turned toward where he thought he'd seen the movement, figuring she would trail along without more invitation. At the edge of where they'd made camp, Nico didn't see anything out of the ordinary. Still, he couldn't shake the lingering feeling that he was missing something.

"Does it... feel odd to you?" Lauretta said.

Nico didn't respond. He scanned the area before he crouched. "Were any of our men up here?"

"I don't think so. Why?"

Nico touched the broken blades of grass. The ground wasn't quite soft enough to leave a proper footprint, but the shape was distinctly human sized. He straightened again, pulling an arrow, though he didn't yet string the bow. "Someone was up here."

"You're sure?"

"*Sure*? No. Instincts say so, though." He glanced over his shoulder. "This is about where I'd want to be if I were sizing up the camp."

Nico heard the telltale twang of a bow a second before a bolt hit the dirt much too close for comfort. *Crossbow.* His mind identified it even as his body went into motion, pulling an arrow back as he scanned for any sign of the shooter. That gave him at least a few minutes before another shot was loaded.

"There." Lauretta pointed.

Nico's eyes caught a faint shimmer of blue in the distance. Unthinking, he loosed the arrow. It flew a dozen yards then disappeared.

Nico lowered his bow in shock, even as he heard a *thunk* that said the invisible arrow had hit a target. A second later, the air itself shimmered, and a prone body flashed into view.

"What...?" Lauretta's question trailed off.

Nico pulled one of the other blades he wore and moved forward. For not having been able to see a target, he had to be a little impressed with himself for having made the shot. The arrow had gone straight into the man's chest. It had hit his lung, if the wet wheezing was anything to judge by.

The man looked up in the darkness, hissing something in a bitter tone, though Nico couldn't understand a word of it. Lauretta's voice behind him made Nico start as she answered in the man's language—though her voice still had the same gentle lilt as when she spoke Latysian.

Nico turned his head, raising an eyebrow questioningly.

"Osamli," she said by way of explanation. "He's Osamli."

"You speak it?"

"Well, my father was Osamli," she said, her eyes going to the man as he said something else.

Nico couldn't say he cared to know whatever the man felt the need to spit at them. "Ask him why he's here."

"He's going to die if we don't get him help."

"He's going to die faster if he doesn't talk." Nico shifted his grip on his blade. "Ask him."

Lauretta frowned at Nico as though she wanted to launch into some other lecture, but she kept quiet and listened as the man spoke.

"Well?" Nico asked.

"He said something rather rude about your mother."

"He has a good chance at being right about that. Not helpful, though." Nico stepped on the man's chest, applying enough pressure that he imagined it would quickly be difficult to breathe with a bleed going into a lung.

"Nicodemo!" Lauretta exclaimed as the man gave a soft shout.

"I don't have a lot of sympathy for people who shoot at me." Nico didn't move his foot. "Ask again."

Lauretta spoke again, her voice taking on a slightly higher pitch. When the man answered, she translated, "He said he's here for the glory of the one true God and the Osamli Empire."

Nico decided to ignore the talk of gods for the time being. "He's a far way from that. Where are the rest of his friends?"

"Friends?" Lauretta frowned.

"I doubt he wandered out here by himself."

Lauretta translated before making a face at the answer. "That was what he thinks we should do to ourselves."

This is going nowhere fast. Nico shook his head. By the way the man was starting to gurgle, he was going to be dead in the next few minutes—ten, fifteen tops.

Lauretta exhaled. "I don't think I've been sworn at quite this much in—"

Nico drove his blade down. *That* went straight into the man's heart.

"What are you doing?" Lauretta's voice rose another dozen pitches, coming out in an alarmed chirp.

"We can waste time getting cursed at, or we can move on." Nico pulled his blade free and crouched. "Get a light. He might have something useful on him."

"You just killed him!"

"He was dead anyway." Nico motioned at the arrow. "At least this has him complaining less."

Lauretta stared at him.

"Are you going to do something to help or not?" Nico started going through the man's clothing.

Without a word, Lauretta turned back toward the camp. Whether she was going for a light or simply storming off, Nico didn't know. There was just enough light along the horizon to examine the man. The loose tunic he wore covered a pouch that hung at his hip. Nico pulled it free and poured out the contents. Coins, a comb—those weren't helpful. Nico picked up a small scroll on the chance that Lauretta would be able to translate it once she got out of her strop. Apparently, Ouene either didn't make their executions public, or the woman had never gone to one. Nico thought of the niggling discomfort he'd felt the first time *he* had killed someone, though that moment was lost in that hazy mass of memories he'd avoided long enough to mostly forget. *Seeing* someone killed, though, hadn't been news since he was a child.

Not finding anything else of much interest on the body, Nico helped himself to the man's dagger and began to straighten. A glint of something in the man's hand made Nico pause. Though it was far too soon for the body to have gone stiff, the man's grip didn't want to release even as Nico pulled.

"Even dead, you have to be difficult," Nico mumbled, finally managing to work the object free. Made of pale metal, it looked a bit like a broach, the setting scalloped around some sort of stone in the center. The back, though, had a button rather than a pin that would allow it to be attached anywhere. Nico pressed it, but other than a soft click, nothing happened.

"Adessi?" The voice sounded like Captain Lais, so Lauretta apparently hadn't been able to bring herself to return.

"Over here." Nico still stared at the odd broach.

The lantern light swung in his direction. "Where?"

Is everyone *useless?* Nico slid the broach into his purse and stood. "Right here."

Lais actually jumped back, the lantern in her hand swinging back enough that it nearly hit her yellow-and-black tunic, the uniform of the capital guard. "How did you do that?"

"Do what?" Nico asked, quickly feeling a headache building as annoyance took hold.

"You just... appeared."

"I stood up."

"No. I was looking right there. You weren't there, then you were."

Nico began to say something biting about her skills of observation before the thought hit him. He pulled the broach back out, not yet clicking the button. "You can definitely see me?"

Lais nodded.

He pressed, noticing the slightest shimmer of blue in the air this time. "Now?"

The lantern lifted, fully illuminating the confused expression on Lais's dark-tan face. "I can hear you."

He released the button, and Lais's eyes met his once again.

"How are you...?"

"Get everyone together." Nico placed the device back in his purse and looked down at the body lying next to him. "I think we have a problem."

Chapter Twelve

"But really, have you thought this through? What will they do if they find out who you are?" Carmella hissed under her breath.

Palmer didn't bother to answer. He had no idea what interest the doctor would have in him once Palmer started talking about his powers. Palmer couldn't even say if the name Kosmos would mean anything to people who didn't believe in gods. For the moment, though, it was a moot point since none of the guards who had moved through during the day had been able to speak Latysian. That, or they simply weren't interested in conversing with prisoners.

When Palmer's silence continued, Carmella huffed. "I should have stayed in Elatita."

"So you could be locked in a temple instead?" Palmer glanced at her.

"At least *they* worshiped me."

Voices outside the tent saved Palmer from having to listen to the same griping that Carmella had been cycling back to all day. He might have been biased from everything Brier had told him about Carmella, but he couldn't say he was much enjoying his time with her. She seemed to have fully embraced all the negative traits he attributed to the women over on the palace side of the Augarian.

The voices went quiet, and Dr. Guda's familiar form ducked through the tent flap. Palmer straightened, his heart rate picking up. It had been one thing to come up with the plan. It was another to throw himself into the fire, especially when gods knew—or perhaps didn't, as it were—what the doctor was doing with the rest of his experimentations.

Dr. Guda stopped in front of Palmer, looking through a few sheets of paper. "You had a good day, yes?"

Palmer stared at the man. Assuming Dr. Guda didn't have a good enough command of Latysian to be sarcastic, Palmer guessed the doctor was attempting a greeting.

Dr. Guda lifted his eyes. When Palmer gave no response, the doctor said, "You have very interesting blood. Different than them." He motioned vaguely at Carmella and Vito. "I will like to do more testing."

"What sort of testing?"

"Nothing big now." Dr. Guda turned and said something Palmer didn't understand.

A guard came through the tent flap and unlocked the large shackle on Palmer's wrist before pulling his sword. Palmer didn't need to know the language to understand that it was a threat not to run.

"If you will come." Dr. Guda held out an arm kindly as though Palmer didn't have a blade pointed at him.

After sending wide-eyed Carmella what he hoped was a reassuring look, Palmer moved toward the tent flap. Outside of the little prison tent, the air was oddly light. Men sat around, talking and laughing. Some ate roasted meat, while others played games with dice or little stone pieces. For a force of men who shouldn't have been there in the first place, they all seemed shockingly at home.

Only a few tents from where they had been held, Dr. Guda turned into an even larger tent, and the guard gave Palmer little choice but to follow. Though from the outside its size had been clear, a number of white sheets had been hung around the inside space, making it difficult to see much of anything. Dr. Guda moved one of the sheets aside and said something in Osamli. The guard led Palmer to a bench before shackling his feet. With another word from the doctor, the guard disappeared once again.

Palmer finally spoke, scanning the tent. "Should I be worried?" A little table with instruments made of different metals stood next to a stand. A book was open on top of the wooden stand, but Palmer had to imagine that there was somewhere else the doctor kept his notes. Palmer certainly didn't see any of the vials the man had taken earlier.

"I would not be. There can be, what is it you say... discomfort with some things, but first we talk, yes?"

"Talk about what?" Palmer asked.

"You tell me your powers now? That will be less discomfort in long run."

Palmer tried to work out what to say. He'd been ready to pull out everything when he'd thought he would have to say something to get the doctor's attention. Now that he had it, and Rosette still wasn't in view, he needed to find some way to string the doctor's attention along while not having anything happen to him that would stop him from figuring out where Rosette was being kept.

"I can heal," Palmer said, starting with what seemed the safest. He lifted the hand with the smaller cuff. "At least when this isn't on."

The doctor frowned. "We have one healer. Your blood is not the same. You can do more?"

A man moved into the empty space between two of the sheets, speaking quickly as he made frantic movements toward some circular object. If it saved Palmer from answering, he was more than happy with it. Dr. Guda answered the man sharply, his face darker than anything Palmer had seen so far.

After another panicked flurry of movement from the man, Dr. Guda took a breath, placed on his calm smile once again, and looked at Palmer. "If you will give me one moment."

Palmer watched the doctor leave. With the soft, carpeted ground and hanging sheets obscuring everything, Palmer had a difficult time telling where the men had gone. Still, he wasn't going to get a much better chance to try to find something that would lead him to Rosette.

He stood, trying out the shackles on his ankles. The short chain between the cuffs would keep him from running—or really, walking any faster than at an awkward waddle—but he could move. Turning in the opposite direction from where the doctor had gone, Palmer pushed his way through the sheets to search for signs of Rosette or anything out of the ordinary.

The space next to where Palmer had just been wasn't much different from what he had already seen, though the leather straps attached to the bench didn't speak of anything good. Ignoring the unhappy churning in his stomach, Palmer continued forward. The next area seemed to be Dr. Guda's office, stocked with a small travel desk and stacks of books and papers. Palmer started to move on before his eyes fell on a set of vials sitting with a stack of papers. As if his hands had minds of their own, he reached out and grabbed a few that held blood so dark the red nearly looked purple and slipped them into his pocket.

Voices beyond the sea of white fabric made Palmer grimace. He glanced back toward where he had been left, but a soft humming deeper in the tent caught his attention. Following the sound as quickly as the shackling would allow, Palmer wound his way through the sheets toward one of the corners of the large tent. The closer he got, the more the hair at the back of his neck began to stand on end. The humming was actually mumbled singing, and the voice was dangerously familiar.

Pulling the last sheet out of the way, Palmer saw a metal cage large enough for perhaps a dog. It held a small blond girl. Palmer rushed forward, nearly tripping as the chain pulled too tight.

Half stepping, half falling, Palmer knelt in front of the cage. "Rosette."

The seven-year-old continued to sing under her breath as though Palmer weren't there, picking at the linen bandages wrapped tightly around her palms.

Palmer frowned. Staring at the cloth, he saw the dark spots in the center. If her palms weren't currently bleeding, they had been. "Rosie." He reached through the bars to touch her. "What—"

The shriek that sounded as soon as Palmer touched her was loud enough to make his ears ring.

"Rosie, Rosie," Palmer hissed. Even if he could have managed to quiet her, it was too late. Sheets shifted as men moved toward the corner. Palmer tried to get to his feet, but the shackles wouldn't let him outrace anyone.

One of the guards grabbed Palmer by the shoulder and hauled him to his feet.

"Rude to wander." Dr. Guda moved forward, pointing at Palmer sharply. "You must not do that or there are consequences."

Palmer didn't bother to ask what *consequences* the man meant. "What did you do to her?" He forced the words out through a clenched jaw.

Dr. Guda looked where Rosette was still thrashing in the cage, rattling the bars with her little hands. Shaking his head, he pulled a bottle out of the pocket of his tunic. "Her. She is very dangerous *birnekli*. Most dangerous we have." He poured some of whatever was in the bottle onto a rag. Surprisingly quickly, he had it over Rosette's mouth. Slowly, the thrashing stopped, then she went limp. The doctor straightened again. "She looks little, but you must not touch. She has her *kirilbilzik*, but she will still bite. More animal than child."

"She didn't use to be." Palmer clenched and unclenched his fists as he tried to fight down the rage he felt building—and with Rosette as much on a leash as he was, he had to imagine that her powers had nothing to do with it.

Dr. Guda tilted his head. "You have known her before?"

"She was a perfectly normal little girl." Words started coming out—wise or not, Palmer couldn't slow down enough to consider. "You did something to her. What did you—"

A second guard gripped Palmer's other arm.

"Let me go," Palmer snapped, trying to shake the man off—even if the guard was two heads taller.

"You will need to calm down," the doctor said, watching Palmer closely.

"Then tell me what you did to her!"

Dr. Guda said something to the guard to Palmer's right, passing off the rag he'd used on Rosette.

"Don't you—" Palmer didn't even get half a sentence out before the cloth clamped down over his nose and mouth. A sickly-sweet burning sensation flooded his senses, forcing its way up his nose and down his throat. He tried to speak, but too soon, his vision began to go. Even as he fought to stay conscious, too soon, his head went hazy, and everything disappeared.

"SO, THERE COULD BE gods know how many people with those things, watching us?" One of the guards Nico hadn't bothered to learn the name of pointed at the device.

"Apparently," another murmured.

"The good news is that it seems you have to be pressing down for it to work," Lais said, her voice strained. "It would be difficult to properly fight and hold onto one of those things."

That had to be why the man hadn't been trying to reload the crossbow before he was hit. Nico had given up on his, even though it had been much easier to aim, simply because it took so long to load. He wouldn't have been able to begin to crank a bolt into place while holding the not-broach in his hand. Though if the man had been bent while trying to reload, it likely would have saved his life. The shimmer as a target would have had Nico aiming much too high.

The only time invisibility would make you more of a target. Nico turned the device over in his hand. There certainly was something to be said for dumb luck.

"But could it even work?" the first guard said.

The tent went silent, and Nico realized everyone was looking at him. He cocked an eyebrow. "I'm supposed to know?"

"You've known gods, supposedly," Lais said.

"She lived with an oracle." Nico motioned dismissively at Lauretta. "Does that mean *she* should know?"

"Well," Lauretta said, "there are stories about Isnotra having the ability to hide things from view. Not to turn them invisible, so to speak, but to make it so no one could perceive what she wanted hidden."

"You're saying they have Isnotra's favor?" The guard's eyebrow's furrowed, his entire face scrunching up as though someone had stolen his favorite childhood toy.

The niggling feeling Nico had been trying to identify clicked into place. "Or they're using her power."

"How would someone do that?" the guard asked.

"The metal." Nico held up the device. "It can be used to hold onto powers." At least it had been used to hold onto the specter things between the time when Brier was possessed and when they were put in that ring. "Stones as well. If they somehow got that power in here."

"How do you know that?" The guard studied him across the circle.

"My father was trying to manage something similar," Nico said, clipping his tone short enough to signal that he didn't intend to answer questions. "It killed him, but if the Osamli got it right, it doesn't seem inconceivable."

The tent went silent. Before Nico could say something biting to get them to stop staring, Lais stood. "We'll have to double the watch. Tell the men to raise the alarm if they *hear* anything. Other than that, we'll have to pray that we're headed the opposite way of wherever that man's friends are and that they don't come looking for him until morning. What an Osamli force is even doing here... you'd think someone would have heard."

"If they all have those..." The guard pointed to the device.

Nico slipped it into the purse at his waist, having no intention of handing it over to anyone else in the camp. He stood. "I'll check the perimeter."

Lais started to say something. Nico didn't bother to listen. Ducking through the flap, he stepped out into the night.

Chapter Thirteen

Brier's head pounded, feeling as though someone were throwing bricks around inside her skull. She certainly didn't miss *that* part of drinking. Rubbing her temples, Brier forced her eyes open and looked around. There was daylight making its way into the little cave, but otherwise, everything looked the same. So she apparently hadn't wandered anywhere or done anything. She ran her thumb along the band of her ring and deemed the new moderate drunken behavior a success, even with her mouth feeling as though it had been packed with cotton.

"Dear gods," Leone groaned next to her, bringing his hands up to his face.

"Agreed." Brier forced out a long breath. "Always more fun the night before, huh?"

"I don't think I've had a headache like this in *years*."

"Old us would be ashamed."

Leone gave a weak laugh before it turned into a cough. He released another groan as it passed. "Gods." He hesitated. "Am I allowed to say that?"

Brier gave him a questioning look. "Say *gods*?"

"Well, since you... are?"

"I still say 'dear gods.' And I think it's called for." Brier forced herself up to sitting with another groan. "I'll go down to the river. Water should help. Possibly. I hope."

Leone nodded again, closing his eyes and rubbing his temples.

Once again, Brier didn't bother locking the cell. She barely felt able to walk, and she had two good legs. She doubted Leone would go anywhere. The bright sunlight outside the cave turned the thrown bricks in her brain to full-on boulders rolling around. Brier squinted with a grimace. At least the pain was a great distraction from the hollowness still gaping in her chest.

So as long as I can stay drunk for... the rest of my life, everything will be fine.

"Good morning." Cerise's much-too-loud voice drilled into Brier's head. "Looks like you had a fun night."

Her entire body cringing, Brier twisted slightly to send Cerise as withering a glare as she could manage. "What do you want?"

"I was waiting for you to sleep it off so Goebel could get some help."

The sour mood turned even worse. "I can't do anything for him."

"You can drain some of the energy. Like yesterday."

"That won't fix him." Brier shook her head.

"It'll buy us time," Cerise snapped, her beautiful face drawn, hints of dark circles under her eyes.

The nausea already churning in Brier's stomach twisted worse at the blatant worry on Cerise's normally smirking face, making one part of Brier want to do something with that awful energy still clinging to Goebel. The part of her that remembered the sting and was nursing her own awful pain and worry won out. "I won't."

Cerise seemed to swell in size. "Won't?"

"You'll have to figure something else out." Brier turned back toward the river.

"Do you know what he's done for you?" Cerise's voice rose, the noise joining the pain already in Brier's head.

"Kidnapped me?" Brier spun back to face her. "Put me in the middle of all this."

"He saved you." Cerise stalked forward, larger than she normally was, as though anger had made her forget her normal shape. "If you *knew* what he went through to help you—"

"Me? Trying to help *me*? You lot are no better than anyone else who knows what I am. Wanting to use me or control me or—" She cut off as Cerise grabbed her arm. "Let go!"

"Listen here, you ungrateful little *child*."

"Let *go*!" Brier didn't try to stop the angry purple energy that sparked over her skin.

If Cerise even felt it, she didn't show it. She shifted her grip, and easily lifted Brier off her feet. Anger pulsing through her, Brier gave into the near burn inside her chest and shot everything she had been feeling straight down. The energy hit hard, sending a cloud of rock showering down on them. Cerise lost her grip, and Brier stumbled back to her feet, nearly falling as the ground continued to shake and crack under her. Slowly, stillness returned, the roar of the ground falling silent and the dust settling. Brier spun back to face Cerise and found the older woman at the bottom of a jagged crater, looking dazed as she propped herself up on her elbows.

Oh gods. The instinct to beg an apology bubbled up in Brier's throat, but when she opened her mouth, all that came out was, "Do *not* grab me."

"Oh, you are *so* going to win," a happy voice said, making Brier spin again.

More energy sparked over her skin, gaining power as it pooled in the empty spot in her chest. A red-haired boy stood no more than two arm's lengths away. The ground rumbled again before she could help herself. "Who are you?"

"Orcus." The boy pointed to his chest happily, showing no concern about the threatening earthquake. "Well, Gil, but Orcus. You're Chaos, of course."

It wasn't a question, but then, after everything that had just happened, no one would have to wonder who she was. Brier fought to gain some control before anger and pain and general *exhaustion* brought the entire city down. "Orcus... god of death?"

The boy, Gil, nodded and opened his mouth. An angry caw cut off his reply, the large raven flapping out of the crater and swooping off toward the edge of town. Brier watched Cerise go and slowly managed to unclench her fits.

"Nankil," Gil said, the name once again a statement rather than a question.

Brier nodded, glancing down at the crater where the dirt path had once been then back at the boy. Thin, gangly, about her height, the boy didn't look much like the wrinkled, thick-robed god of death she had seen depicted in the Augarian temple. Then again, she probably looked about as similar to the statues of Persaea, the Augarian goddess of destruction, as Gil did to Orcus.

"What are you doing here?"

"I was looking for you, yeah?" Gil said as though the answer should have been obvious. "Kosmos said you were here, so—"

"Kosmos." All the energy building in Brier's chest left in a gust, nearly taking her legs out from under her. "You saw Palmer?"

Gil nodded, seeming as blissfully unaware that he'd deflated her as he had about the near earthquake. "He was with Astarte. Both of them got picked up. Or died. Who knows? Shame if they did, though. Us versus them? War'd be over before sunset."

"You don't know if he died?"

"I got out of there." Gil shrugged. "Didn't *feel* like anyone died, but something happened."

"There *where*?" Brier pressed.

"Bit south of here." Gil pointed off before he looked around. "So what are we doing here?"

Brier shifted between her feet, ignoring the question. She could go south and try to find him. If the god of death wasn't certain anyone had died, there was some small chance... the emptiness in her chest didn't let that hope fully take hold. She'd felt Palmer's loss. Still felt it.

But his body... The thought sent a stab through her and made her eyes sting, but he deserved a proper burial. He had done so much for her. She couldn't just leave him lying somewhere—

"You have cultists?" Gil had abandoned their conversation and was standing on top of a nearby boulder. He looked from where he was staring down the hill back to Brier. "Can I play with them?"

Gil looked twelve or thirteen—far too old to be asking for play dates. Brier didn't have the energy to think about it. She gave him an odd half-hearted flap of her hand of assent, and with a smile, he dissolved into a black mist before shooting off down the hill.

"That's... different," Brier mumbled to herself before she sat in a heap at the edge of the crater. She needed Palmer. He would know what she should do. Or he would at least believe he knew what she should do. Either way, there'd be a plan of action. And all she could think to do was find a way to *force* her body to get back into that wine store—even if just the idea of it made her want to vomit—and remain drunk until she finally went numb for good.

THE WORLD SWAM, PALMER'S head feeling as though it were full of sloshing water. He groaned, trying to get the world to focus.

"*Bravissimo.*" Carmella's distorted voice filtered through the sloshing. "Really. Brilliant plan. Went exactly as you wanted, I take it?"

Palmer rolled to his side, fixing Carmella with as dark a look as he could muster before he pushed himself the rest of the way to sitting. He rested his heavy head in his hands, trying to push away the rest of the groggy feeling. Slowly, his senses came back to something close to normal, and he recognized the soft-pattering part of the watery sound as rain.

"They have Rosette. They've done something to her."

"Done what?" Carmella asked.

The feral, desperate thrashing went through Palmer's mind, and his stomach soured. "I don't know." He forced himself to look up. He was back in the original tent with Carmella and Vito—and both of them were staring at him. Palmer closed his eyes, sucked in a final breath to pull himself together, then opened them again. "We need to get her and get out of here."

"Right," Carmella said, lifting her chained wrist. "How?"

The fabric toward the back of the tent rustled, and everyone went silent. After another shuffling sound, a familiar face came into view.

"Peony?" Palmer blinked, half wondering if he was seeing things.

The woman motioned for quiet, glancing over her shoulder before she slid under the fabric side inside. "I had to wait until they were distracted, but I don't know how long..."

"What are you doing here?" Palmer watched her as she moved to his chained wrist.

"You came for me..." She glanced up then down shyly. "Jac taught me to pick locks. I should be able to—"

"Fabulous. Do mine." Carmella shoved her way closer and jabbed her wrist forward.

Peony sent Carmella a look normally reserved for Brier then pulled out two little pieces of metal and set to work on Palmer's restraint.

"What are we supposed to do once we're free?" Vito finally said, motioning toward the wall of the tent. "We're in the middle of an Osamli camp. With these." He held up the other cuff. The *kirilbilzik*.

The lock on the restraint clicked and fell open. Palmer smiled, rubbing his now free wrist. "Brilliant."

Peony offered a weak smile back before moving to Vito, seeming to purposefully bypass Carmella. "The camp broke up last night. After Palmer..." She glanced at him then away. "Part went north. More are packing up now. We might be able to sneak away..."

"We still need to get Rosette," Palmer said.

"Because last time went so well?" Carmella gave one of her pouty frowns.

"Rosette's here?" Peony's eyebrows furrowed.

"The doctor's the one who likely has something to get these off, anyway." Palmer ignored both women as he motioned to his own *kirilbilzik*. "We need to go to that tent."

Vito shook his head, pausing to give Peony a nod of thanks as his restraint came off before he went back to frowning at Palmer. "I'm not going anywhere Discordia is."

"You're welcome to go wherever you want," Palmer said. "We're not forcing you to come."

"No good will come from you helping *anyone* on that side."

"There is no *that side*." Palmer shook his head and stood, ready to check the front of the tent.

"Go out the side," Peony said. "That's where they've packed up most of the tents."

Palmer didn't argue, heading in the opposite direction.

"Soon as I get this off, I'm out." Vito lifted his wrist.

"Noted." Palmer pulled up the fabric and looked out. The entire camp was dreary—gray clouds and a steady rain coming down—but Peony hadn't been kidding. At least a third of the tents from the day before had been pulled up and were nowhere in sight. He could only hope the doctor's tent was where it had been. He turned back to the three behind him. "Ready?"

"Shouldn't I just wait somewhere out of the way?" Carmella crossed her arms.

"Not sure there is anywhere out of the way." Palmer lifted the fabric enough to slide under. "Let's go."

The cold rain came down hard enough that the drops stung. Palmer didn't dare wait. Gods knew how long their luck would last. He heard Peony slip out behind him, and he had to assume Carmella and Vito would follow soon after, if only because they had few better options. Palmer wasn't certain if the guards were busy packing up what was left of the camp or the rain had simply driven everyone inside. Either way, they managed to make it to the doctor's tent without being seen. Palmer slipped under the fabric and looked around the room he had been in the night before.

"Look through there." He pointed Peony—then Carmella and Vito as they appeared—toward the doctor's chests. "Try to find something that will get these off." He pointed toward the small dent in the *kirilbilzik*. "I'll be right back."

If anyone still had an issue with Palmer's plan, they didn't object. He turned toward the part of the tent where they'd been keeping Rosette, grabbing the rag and a bottle of what seemed to be the liquid they'd used to put him and Rosette out the previous night. He hoped there was still enough of the bright little girl he had known that he'd be able to talk reason into her, but in the middle of an Osamli force, they couldn't take any chances.

As quickly as he dared, Palmer pushed his way into the back space... and found nothing. Though the fabric was still set up as it had been the night before, the back of the tent had been entirely cleared away, including the carpet, leaving quickly dampening trampled grass as the only sign that anything had been back there at all. Palmer cursed under his breath, eyes moving back and forth as though he would find some clue as to where they had taken Rosette if he only looked hard enough.

A crash and a cry from the front of the tent made Palmer jump. Spinning on his heel, he rushed back toward the others. A man shouting in angry Osamli had a thrashing Peony by the arm and was attempting to grab Carmella as well. Somewhere in the back of his mind, Palmer realized Vito was gone. There wasn't time to wonder about that. Palmer felt the rag and bottle still in his hand. He rushed forward and clamped the cloth over the larger man's mouth. The man shouted something else, his hand moving toward the rag. Peony twisted, using her entire body weight to keep the man's arms away until he slowly stopped struggling then slumped to the carpeted ground.

Palmer relaxed his arm, breathing heavily.

"What is that?" Peony asked, panting.

Palmer shook his head, hearing more approaching voices. "You find anything?"

Peony shook her head, and Carmella wasn't any more helpful.

"Grab what you can." Palmer shoved the bottle under his arm and went to pack what he could into one of the smaller chests. "We need to leave. We'll just have to see what we have after we go."

"I'm supposed to carry those things?" Carmella wrinkled her nose but set about grabbing as Palmer sent her a dark look.

The voices came too close for comfort. Time was up.

"Out the back." Palmer had to hope somewhere in the chest he held was what they needed. "Run."

In just the few minutes that they had been inside, the rain had turned harder, turning the ground to mud. They slid, the bulky chests throwing everyone off balance, but somehow—gods knew how—they reached the edge of the tents and broke through the faint blue shimmer that made everything behind them invisible once again. Palmer still didn't dare stop until they reached a jagged hill that offered some little protection. He looked between the two women with him—both as drenched and muddy as he was—trying to catch his breath.

"Vito?" he finally asked.

Peony shook her head, still clenching the chest she had grabbed, while Carmella unceremoniously dropped hers to focus on wringing out her hair.

"He must have gone when the guard came in." Carmella somehow managed to sound indignant even in present circumstances. Palmer couldn't worry about Vito. He already had too many other things on his plate.

"Rosette?" Peony asked softly.

Palmer's stomach sank. "They already moved her."

"So we're going, then." Carmella's honey-brown eyes hit him, her statement sounding more like an order than a question.

They needed to get back to Venchia—Palmer felt that in his gut—but he had to imagine Brier was doing better by herself than Rosette was with that doctor. Then again, they weren't going to do anyone any good if they rushed back in with no way to fight and no idea where Rosette even was.

He put down his chest, much more carefully than Carmella had with hers, and undid the latches. "First things first. Let's try to get these cuffs off."

Chapter Fourteen

"**Y**ou've been in here a lot."

Brier paused in her half-hearted examination of the piece of dried meat in her hand but didn't look up at Leone. "Is that an issue?"

"Do I get to take issue with anything around here?"

"Probably wiser if you don't." Brier bit off a part of the jerky, the meat tough enough that it hurt her teeth. "You know, since I'm the one feeding you and all."

"Among other reasons." He picked up his cup as Brier finally slid her eyes up to him.

In the past two days since Gil, little god of death, had arrived, Brier had taken to spending most of her time in the prison-cave with Leone. Cerise did nothing but snip at her—"People die. Get yourself together"—and Gil only wanted to see things destroyed. Both of the gods wanted her to be Chaos. She preferred being Brier and pretending the rest of the world didn't exist.

"What do you do up here, anyway, when I'm not around?" she asked.

"Honestly?" Leone took a healthy drink. "Try to stay drunk and pretend the last year never happened."

"Same as when I'm here, then." Brier picked up her own cup. "*Salute.*"

Leone tapped his wooden cup to Brier's and drank again. He lowered it and looked Brier over. "You found a proper dress."

"When I was looking for more wine." Brier looked down. Though laced as tightly as Brier could manage, the dress gaped a few inches around her chest, and the smooth blue fabric made it much too fine for walking around the ruins, but at least she felt a little more *normal,* no longer wandering town in her shift.

"So it is Catarina's."

"I have to assume. It's old enough." She flicked one of the ties at her shoulder that had once been used to attach different sleeves but hadn't been in fashion for as long as she'd been done with short dresses. Without an extra set of hands, Brier hadn't bothered to take out the sleeves at all. She certainly wasn't attempting to impress any-one and even more certainly wasn't going to ask anyone in town to help her dress.

"Suits you."

"Are you saying I'm old?" Brier cocked an eyebrow.

Leone tossed her a *not amused* look, as though her question did not merit a response. "I mean, it's good to see you looking more like yourself."

A chill swept over the room a second before Gil materialized from his dark cloud, cutting off whatever response Brier could have thought of. Leone's hand tensed around his cup—understandably, as Gil tended to look at the man like he was some tempting dessert—but Gil kept his eyes on Brier this time. Nearly bouncing on his toes, he looked excited enough to make Brier nervous. After Cerise had stopped him from tormenting the cultists his first day, Gil had only ever seemed excited about the idea of destroying things, as though he were a child who had never outgrown wanting to kick down building blocks.

"What?" Brier asked, tossing back another gulp of wine. It wasn't reaching her head as quickly as she would have liked. *Two days, and I'm already getting my tolerance back?* There wasn't enough wine among Orris Adessi's things to support a heavy wine habit.

"There are men," Gil said, as unfazed by Brier's displeasure as ever. "Can we kill them?"

Brier frowned. "Men?"

"Coming toward town. Few dozen of them. Wouldn't be hard for us to blast—"

"I don't think Mommy would be very happy with you killing boyfriend one." Cerise lingered at the mouth of the cave, looking into the dim space. "Lucky you, Cay. Sat up here long enough that you got Nicolas back to handle all the bad things for you. No need to handle yourself at all."

Brier pushed herself up to standing, ignoring the jab in light of the other information. "Nico? Nico's back?"

"And apparently brought friends."

Gil's face fell, the bouncing stopping. "You know them?"

"Oh, they're *special* friends, you could say," Cerise said.

Brier flashed her a glare.

"You tell him I'm here, he's going to kill me." Leone shuffled as though he wanted to stand, but he still couldn't manage it.

"Please." Cerise shook her head. "You're alive as long as Mommy wants you alive."

"You can stop calling me that," Brier snapped as annoyance began to bubble over, even if that would likely only encourage Cerise to continue with the nickname. She turned to Leone. "I won't tell him yet."

Leone didn't look any more at ease, but Brier gave him the rest of the jerky in her hand before brushing past Gil and Cerise to get outside. As Gil had reported, thirty or forty men approached—some on horseback and some walking—carrying a banner. Brier squinted to make it out in the bright sunlight and tried to call up some little-used knowledge from her childhood to place where the two jagged chevrons on a blue shield hailed from, but she couldn't find the answer.

"Not much of an army." Cerise came up beside her.

"Better than you did." Brier didn't bother to look at the woman before starting down the hill.

The first of the horsemen were dismounting by the time Brier made it to the edge of the ruins. He turned back to talk to some of his comrades, and Brier took the chance to size them up. The men were dressed as soldiers, or at least guards, though she couldn't quite place the clothing either. Quickly enough, her eyes found Nico, and she froze. The urge to run up and throw her arms around him battled with the hurt she'd been happily nursing and the awareness that others were watching. The conflict kept her feet stuck where she'd planted them.

As though he felt her eyes on him, Nico looked up, and their gazes locked. Her breath caught in her throat, but she could take some solace in the fact that he seemed just as unable to move. *Serves him right.*

A woman with a thick dark braid dismounted her horse. Nico's head turned to look at her, breaking the stare, and Brier could breathe again. Pulling herself up to her full height, she stepped away from the buildings. Eyes turned toward her, and Brier was suddenly very glad she had found a proper dress. The woman with a braid said something quickly to Nico then started forward when he nodded. Surprise flashed over Nico's face for a split-second before he hopstepped after her.

The woman still reached Brier first, sweeping her gray skirts out of the way and kneeling. "The forces of Ouene to serve you."

The white chevrons on blue clicked into place—the port city of Ouene. A long, long way from the ruins of Venchia. She looked over the woman's head at Nico, forcing her face to remain impassive as she met his eyes again. "You came back."

"I said I would," Nico said, tension visible in his shoulders. "Tash didn't tell you?"

Brier ignored the stab that went through her at Palmer's name. He didn't need to know what she'd gone through. He didn't *deserve* to know what she'd gone through after leaving without so much as a word to her. "I didn't believe him." She dropped her eyes to the woman again, vaguely realizing the men behind her were kneeling as well.

"Suora Lauretta," Nico supplied before Brier could ask. "Anchoress from the Temple of Isnotra."

Brier frowned, not taking her eyes off the woman. The great dress did look like an anchoress's, now that Nico mentioned it, but nothing else about Suora Lauretta said *religious woman*. "Don't anchoresses normally remain at their temples?"

"The oracle said I was meant to come." Lauretta looked up at Brier.

"Oracle?"

"Ouene has an oracle," Nico said. "She's the one who apparently had these men ready for me. She told them to follow me, and I've told them to protect you."

"How kind of you," Brier's voice came out cooler than was perhaps warranted. She couldn't bring herself to retract it.

One of the guards a little farther off stood and moved forward. Brier only noticed at the last moment that it was a woman dressed like the men. "I believe we may have a problem though, s-signora... santità... benedetta...?"

"Signorina is fine." Brier waved for the woman to remain standing as she started to kneel next to Lauretta. Brier didn't feel holy or blessed enough to demand either of the other two forms of address. "And Signorina...?"

"Comandante," the woman said as she and Lauretta stood. "Comandante Lais, signorina."

So she wasn't just dressed as a soldier—she was a captain. Brier refrained from asking about it. "What problem is there?"

"There are Osamli troops about," Nico answered before the comandante could. "We ran across one on our way here."

"*Osamli* troops?" Brier furrowed her eyebrows, turning to him in surprise. "Are you certain?"

"Very." Nico nodded.

"There would have been news if the Osamli Empire were invading." She shook her head.

"Not when they have these." Nico pulled something oval and shiny out of his purse.

Brier gave him a questioning look

"Is there somewhere we can go to explain?" Nico glanced at the rest of the men behind him.

Brier nodded, running her eyes over the men as well. "You might as well tell them to get settled—pick some of the houses or set up tents or whatever they intend to do. Then you can explain." She let sarcasm tint the last four words. She doubted he would explain even half of what he should.

SOMETHING WAS WRONG. Exactly what, Nico hadn't been able to work out since they had arrived that afternoon, but something about the town was putting him on edge. He scanned the dark buildings surrounding the fire the Ouenen guards had built. He needed to find Palmer at some point. Palmer Tash would at least be more forthcoming than Brier. Even walking to Ouene and back to find *Brier's* forsaken town an army apparently hadn't been enough to thaw whatever had frozen between them. If anything, the looks Brier had been giving him were harder. Colder.

His eyes caught on where Brier was standing, speaking with the boy. She had briefly explained that he was Gil, the god of death, before sending him off in an odd cloud to circle the town and watch for approaching troops. The boy hadn't said more than two words to him, yet Nico didn't feel great about another god loitering around when Palmer was nowhere to be seen—not when prophesies about gods' wars were trying to find purchase in the back of his mind.

"Damned oracles..." he mumbled before standing. Gods knew why Palmer Tash was keeping his distance, but the buildings higher up on the hill had to be the first place to look for him.

Nico had barely made it past the first row of houses before the telltale sound of flapping made his jaw clench.

"Brought back a new girlfriend, have you?" Cerise's very unwelcome voice sounded behind him.

Nico made sure his face was entirely blank before he turned to face the raven-woman. The only way to deal with Cerise was to avoid showing any reaction whatsoever. "I've brought more men than you managed."

"A whole handful who can stand around before being mowed down by those troops you saw coming. Bravo." Cerise cocked an eyebrow at him from where she stood, leaning against a cracked plaster wall.

Nico didn't bother to engage. "Have you seen Tash?"

Cerise stared at him for a few seconds, uncharacteristically quiet, before she spoke. "Mommy hasn't told you?"

"Told me what?"

"He's gone."

Nico's eyebrows pulled together in surprise before he could stop the reaction. "Gone? What do you mean *gone*?"

"Just what I said, Nicolas." Cerise straightened, still using the wrong name in a way he had quickly learned was deliberate rather than based on ignorance. "He took off. Before I got back, even. That was something I never saw coming, I must say—you both leaving our girl here all alone."

"Tash wouldn't have left her." Nico shook his head. *Certainly not alone.* For whatever problems Nico had with the man, he at least could respect the way Palmer saw Brier taken care of. "Not alone."

"Don't know what to tell you. He left and never came back." Cerise crossed her arms. "Got himself killed for it, best we can figure."

Nico's mind raced. Palmer simply leaving... that was impossible. Even if he'd had some sort of argument with Brier, that wouldn't have sent Palmer out of the city. And Brier might have twitched when Nico had said Palmer's name earlier, but she would have shown more of a reaction if Palmer were actually dead. She might have been doing her best to freeze *Nico* out, but she wasn't that callous.

This is Cerise. Nico wouldn't have put it past the woman to lie simply to stir up trouble, though claiming someone was dead was low, even for her.

A pained shout echoed from farther uphill, and Cerise's posture went stiff. "Goebel..." she murmured before swearing under her breath and transforming back into her raven self without so much as a glance back.

Tash gone, the half man awake... what else has happened? Nico only realized his fists were clenched when his nails began to cut into his palms. He forced his hands to release, as little as they wanted to, and turned back to look toward the fire. The Ouenen men were still there, but Brier and the little god of death had left. Nico felt the tension in his body pull tighter. If—and it was a large *if*—Cerise was telling the truth, there was more wrong in Venchia than he'd expected. He couldn't imagine what sort of fight would send Palmer from the city, but no matter how bad it was, the thought of him being dead was worse. Angry enough to leave or not, Palmer never would have done a thing to hurt Brier. Nico would stake his life and entire inheritance on that. Some other cretin who suddenly found himself with those powers wandering around somewhere out there? *He* would be an unknown quantity, and with possibly invisible Osamli troops circling, *that* was the last thing they needed—forthcoming gods' war or no. Finding Brier and convincing her to run, or even knocking her out and kidnapping her again, was quickly sounding like their best option.

Nico swore and stalked back toward the fire.

Chapter Fifteen

"It's hard to tell with their shimmer things," Gil said, shifting between his feet as though he were only just putting up with asking for a report, "but it looks like some guys are heading here. The rest are spreading out around."

"Around Venchia?"

Without moving her head, Brier slid her eyes to where Nico was standing off to the side. Either he didn't notice, or he didn't want to look at her, since he continued to stand, arms crossed, waiting for Gil to answer.

"I guess." Gil shrugged, slurring the words together as though he couldn't bring himself to care enough to speak them.

Nico looked at the Ouenen captain. "We barely have the men to face a frontal attack. If they're closing us in—"

"I'll talk to the men." The female captain, Captain Lais, gave a curt nod and turned to go.

Gil asked Brier, "Can I go now?"

At least someone's *talking to me.* Brier nodded for Gil to leave, and the boy was a blur of black shooting away before she had finished the movement. She glanced at Nico again, but he was deep in discussion with the remaining Ouenen guards, his back solidly to her. Releasing a sharp breath through her nose, Brier turned in the opposite direction only to find herself face-to-face with Cerise.

"What?" she snapped.

"Goebel." Cerise motioned for Brier to follow and turned back into the ruins as though that was all that needed to be said. And technically, it was. Brier wasn't certain draining the energy was actually doing any good, but at least doing so was keeping some manner of peace with Cerise—and that was better than nothing. Brier had at least refrained from blowing anything else up since the Ouenen men had arrived.

Before they had even reached the little house, Brier could hear the low, awful keening, which sounded like a horse slowly dying. "Is he awake?"

"I don't have anything else to give him," Cerise said.

Brier slowed to a stop. Dealing with the energy was one thing. It stung, but in a way, it had started to feel good, filling the empty part of her chest. Having to look at a man writhing in pain while doing so, though... "There's a bottle of wine up in the cave." It seemed safer to direct Cerise up there than down to where Orris Adessi's trunks were still stacked. "That might help."

"*You* will help." Cerise frowned.

"I'll help *more* if he's not thrashing." Brier held Cerise's unnaturally black eyes.

Cerise glared back before she gave a nearly imperceptible nod and flapped away off toward the hill. Brier could only hope being on a mission would keep the woman from bothering Leone too much. He was starting to get stronger, even managing to stand the previous day, with Brier's help, but that was because having to hide away or risk running into Nico was beginning to rub Leone's nerves raw. He certainly didn't need Cerise's particular brand of needling any more than Brier did.

Releasing a tense breath, Brier looked back at the little house. The keening had turned to lower moans, but that didn't make it sound any better. She debated waiting until Cerise came back with something that would at least help to take the edge off, but as good as Orris Adessi's wine was, Brier had to doubt it would do much for someone in *that* much pain. With difficulty, she forced her feet forward and stepped into the oppressive little house.

Goebel's eyelids fluttered as he struggled to focus on Brier, but she couldn't stop looking at his hips. Or what was left of his hips. The swirling energy there had turned angry, black mixing with the purple, and it was moving faster, Goebel's body entirely missing up to his hipbone.

"Please..." he whimpered.

Brier swallowed as she lifted her eyes to his. "I don't know what I can—"

"Kill me."

Brier felt the words like a punch to the stomach, a shiver moving through her even as warm as the day was. "What?"

"Please." His eyes screwed shut as another wave of pain rolled through his body.

Brier glanced at the doorway, half hoping Cerise would be back already to save her from having to answer. There was no way Cerise would allow a mercy killing. Not with as much effort as she had already put into saving Goebel.

But... Brier's eyes drifted back to the energy eating away at him. Without Palmer, without *someone* who could properly stop the energy, there was no saving Goebel. Cerise perhaps wasn't ready to admit it, but Brier could see the only two options left—awful pain as Goebel's life dragged out for another few days or a quick death now. Brier knew which one she would choose were she in his position.

But me?

You've killed people before, a voice at the back of her skull reminded her. In the Augarian battle, she had killed men, sliced them completely in half with some power she still wasn't quite sure how to call on outside of the chaos of battle. Still, she hadn't known any of them. And they had all been at a distance, bodies added to an ever-growing pile from all manner of fighting. This was different. Intense. Personal.

Gil. She considered. The boy would no doubt be overjoyed at the chance to kill someone. But who knew how his powers would deal with the angry mess that was at the bottom of what had once been Goebel's body? And Brier wasn't certain she could take *joy* in the current circumstances.

"It must... be you," Goebel murmured as though he had read her thoughts.

"Do... do you want to wait?" Brier glanced at the door. "Say something to—"

"Now." He moaned again. "Please."

There was no one else she could rely on to get her out of this decision. Putting him out of his misery was exactly what Cerise had been pushing, though she surely would have strong opinions about what Brier should and shouldn't do when it came down to it.

Kill him, or leave him to suffer. The two options rattled around Brier's mind, but she knew what she had to do.

Carefully, Brier knelt by the little pallet, staying as far away from the energy at the bottom as she could. "Thank you," she said, though it felt weak. "For... everything."

Goebel's eyes managed to meet hers, something like gratitude behind them, before pain made them shut again. With little time left before Cerise returned, Brier placed her hand lightly on Goebel's forehead and let her own powers begin to grow. The last thing he needed was another slow burn. With one good jolt, it would all be over. Brier took a final shaky breath and let the bolt shoot through him, his body disappearing in one long stretch before energy hit energy with a resounding crash. The power rebounded, making Brier's ears ring and her vision blur. Glass shattered somewhere behind her.

"What did you do?"

Brier barely registered Cerise's shriek past the heady buzz moving through her.

"What did you do?" the shriek repeated as Cerise scrambled onto the floor next to Brier.

"What I had to," Brier murmured.

"What you... what you...?" Cerise's mouth worked as though she were a fish out of water as she turned from the empty pallet toward Brier. "How could you—"

"That's what you wanted, wasn't it? For me to do things myself?"

"You—" Cerise reached for Brier's arm.

With the slightest twitch, Brier sent Cerise flying back hard enough that the woman hit the wall with a hollow thud. The reaction was stronger than she'd intended, but it worked. Brier stood, her legs a little weak as she tried to get them under her. "I've said, don't grab me."

Cerise looked up across the room, either too dazed or too angry to speak, as Brier moved for the doorway. The already uneven cobblestones of the ancient street felt as if they were moving under Brier's feet as she made her way aimlessly forward, the daze helping to keep the building sorrow and guilt from taking hold. But it didn't dampen the building exhilaration. Something about the daze felt frighteningly good, as though she were drunk on something so much better than wine.

And then came the crushing fear. She'd killed a man. A friend. Wiped him from existence. Whatever she *should* have been feeling, it wasn't glee. The pleasant rocking under her turned to spinning as an awful feeling began to take hold in the middle of the elation. Brier's stomach roiled, energy bubbling higher and higher through her body.

With a shout, she aimed it all toward one of the buildings on the street, trying to force everything out of herself at once. She waited for the explosion, but a soft sound, like cloth ripping, floated back to her as the energy pooled in the air in front of her, spinning and expanding until the circle was big enough for her to see through. Her eyebrows furrowed. On the other side of the purple circle was a long stone hallway—nothing like the crumbling plaster building that had been in front of her. Leaning to the side slightly, Brier looked around the edge of the circle. The building was still there, simply blocked from view by the circle. Wise or not, Brier moved forward, reaching through the middle, half expecting to hit something solid like a painted canvas, but her hand passed right through, and when she stepped over the bottom curve, she stood in the center of the stone hallway. Recognition hit her a second later.

Ruhegipfel. She was standing in one of the hallways of the old mountain castle where she had first met Goebel and Cerise, who were now looking at the ruins through the glowing circle. Awareness making her skin tingle, she stepped back out into the ruins and turned toward the circle, the portal. As she faced front, the energy snapped, and the circle pulled shut, leaving her looking at the ruins once again. Frowning, Brier let power gather once again, building it through her core before she threw her hands out, trying to recreate what she'd first done. This time, the building did explode, throwing up dirt and rubble with a crack that resonated through the entire street. Brier barely managed to think quickly enough to protect herself, throwing her hands up at the last second to dissolve any of the rocks flying at her.

Slowly, everything settled again, becoming even more silent than it had been, as though the explosion had startled the world silent. Brier dropped her hands again and stared.

So you have no idea what you did. No idea how you did it. And the only one who could have told you is dead. You killed him.

The grief and guilt she'd been able to keep at bay swept forward. She crossed her arms around her middle, holding herself tightly, feeling where her ribs still stuck out farther than they should. *Ancient goddess, bringer of death.* And she was still just a frail, sad, scared little girl.

The unwelcome cold gust of Gil's approach moved over her a second before he materialized. "Are we destroying things?"

Brier motioned for him to go ahead, though she didn't know what he would find fun in there with nothing to kill. *I wonder if he gets the same feeling from it*, she thought. It at least would explain a little about why Gil liked it so much.

You liked it. Brier's stomach churned again, and she started off, first toward the cave then toward the villa. They would run out of wine soon, but dear gods, did she need to get drunk.

NICO WATCHED THE MEN he had brought from Ouene drill. They knew what they were doing—he had to admit that. Their movements sure and orderly as only a well-trained force would be able to do. Still, against the forces of the Osamli Empire, there was not much that even forty of the fiercest soldiers could do. They would be trampled into the mud two breaths into a battle.

"We're all going to die," Nico mumbled, not sure if he should be more concerned about that fact or that the thought of death barely worried him at all.

"You think so?"

Nico started. "How long have you been there?" He should have known Lauretta would be nearby. She was taking the oracle's instructions to remain with him very seriously. *That's anchoresses for you. If anyone is going to cling to divine instructions...*

"Not long." She nodded toward the men down the hill. "You aren't impressed with our training?"

"I'm not impressed with our chances up against a full army."

A crash like a cannonball striking stone rattled the town behind them. Nico spun, hand going to the blade at his hip as he watched the cloud of dust plume far up on the hill. Instinctively, he took off toward it. Even with him running as quickly as he could, the dust had fully settled by the time he reached the house that had exploded—though *house* was an even more generous term than it had been in the ruins with the little hints of wall surrounding what was otherwise a crater. Even a cannonball would have had trouble being *that* thorough in its destruction.

Nico looked down at a jagged piece of concrete at his feet before a telltale flash of red hair caught his eye. He tensed. "Did you do this?"

Gil's narrow face appeared from behind a little section of wall that was still standing. "*Me*? I wish."

"Then, what happened?" Nico asked, doing his best to bite down the wave of annoyance as he heard Lauretta come up behind him.

Gil shrugged. "Cerise probably. She's who got Brier mad last time things exploded."

Nico frowned down at the crater. "Brier did that?"

"It's not as big as the last one." Gil went back to playing with the rubble. "Course, Cerise isn't lying at the bottom of it either. *That* time was awesome."

Brier randomly blowing things up *only* seemed bad.

"Where did she go?" Nico asked. "Brier."

"Dunno." Gil slurred the word, not looking away from his little project.

Nico's hand tightened around the hilt of his sword, but he held back. Attacking the god of death was likely one of the stupider actions to take, no matter how much of a brat the kid was. Spinning on his heel, Nico headed for the little house Brier and Palmer had taken up. Even if she didn't want to talk to him, if Brier was starting to blow the town apart, it was time for them to speak. He made it over the two streets quickly, but though the house was in one piece, it was empty. He cursed under his breath, realizing that he had no idea where she might otherwise go.

"What's the matter?"

Nico bit down more language he shouldn't use in front of an anchoress. "Nothing."

"Delphi left me here to help you, you know. You just have to let me," Lauretta said.

"I don't need your help." Nico spun on her. "I don't need your oracle. I don't need some doomsday prophecy laying out my importance in the universe. Right now, I just need to find Brier."

"I can help you look."

"What part of 'I don't need your help' did you find unclear?"

Lauretta cocked her head, starting to look annoyed for the first time Nico could remember. "I didn't say you needed it. Things just tend to go more quickly when you don't insist on doing everything yourself for no reason. Just because you *can* do something alone doesn't mean you have to."

Nico exhaled through his nose but forced himself to say, "Fine." He turned out the door again. "I'm not slowing down for you."

"Didn't expect you would."

Chapter Sixteen

"How long are we going to do this?"

Palmer ignored Carmella, as he had been doing for most of the past three days. He was actually getting quite good at it. Unfortunately, the only other thing he'd gotten good at was hovering just outside the blue-tinged veil of the Osamli camp, watching and waiting. For what, exactly, he wasn't certain. While there had been plenty of bits and bobs in the doctor's things, none of them would remove the cuffs on their wrists. With those still firmly in place, there was nothing they could do but continue to follow along, just out of reach.

"We should just go south," Carmella said, continuing the argument she had given at least a dozen times since they'd left the camp, no more deterred by Palmer's silence this time than any other. "We can find some blacksmith to knock these things off, then we can go about our lives. That little girl's dead, as far as we know, and I doubt you're going to be any help to Signorina Chastain if you just get us caught again trying to go north. The way's *blocked*."

Palmer sent Carmella a dark look.

"It's *true*," she insisted. "And I'm sorry, I'm not risking my life for some feral child or Brier blasted Chastain."

"Rosette deserves help," Peony said softly from where she was sitting against one of the trees in the little cropping they had found to rest in. She pulled her knees to her chest. "I'd agree with the second part."

Palmer shook his head, looking back at the blue shimmer that marked the edge of the camp as though staring would give him some new plan he'd simply missed over the past few days.

"Really," Carmella started again. "I'm just saying—"

A shape slipped through the blue shimmer, and Palmer motioned sharply for quiet. By some miracle, Carmella actually cut off. Palmer's eyes followed the shape, what appeared to be a woman in a long gray skirt, though her hair looked as though it had been cropped close to her skull and was only starting to grow back.

"Who is that?" Carmella peeked over Palmer's shoulder.

Palmer sent her an annoyed look.

"I'm just saying, she doesn't look Osamli." Carmella huffed.

What she'd said was true. Though the woman's short hair was as tightly curled as any of the Osamli men Palmer had seen in the camp, her skin was far darker. *Perhaps someone from the far reaches of the empire?* The woman gave a glance over her shoulder and sped up, heading straight for the cropping of trees.

"Hide," Palmer ordered on instinct, slipping behind a tree trunk farther back as Carmella and Peony did the same. The furtive glances at the camp said the woman was running away from the soldiers, not running toward Palmer and the girls, but after the past few days, the last thing Palmer wanted to do was take chances.

The footsteps slowed as they reached the trees, but other than a quick pause and shuffling, the woman didn't stop, continuing on her way south without so much as a glance toward where the rest of them were hiding.

All three of them waited another minute as the woman disappeared down the other side of a hill before Carmella mumbled, "*She* has the right idea."

Palmer allowed himself to roll his eyes before he stepped back around the tree. Something glinting on the ground made him freeze. After sending a final glance in the direction the woman had gone, Palmer moved toward the gleaming object. A flat piece of metal with a gentle curve on one side sat where the doctor's things had previously been. The woman had apparently stolen the pack, but she'd dropped... Palmer carefully picked up the smooth pale-silver hook.

"What's that?" Carmella asked.

Palmer held it for a long moment, frozen.

"Is that...?" Peony trailed off.

Scarcely daring to hope their luck was that good, Palmer lined the curved end up with the dent of his cuff. With a snap, the cuff opened and fell to the ground. Everything came back to Palmer in a rush, all of his senses blotting out as visions and voices flooded his mind at once. Squeezing his eyes shut, he fought to force them all down at least enough to get his own senses back.

"Oh, I'll do it." Carmella snatched the odd key, suddenly in front of him, apparently tired of waiting. Palmer blinked, the world coming into greater focus as Carmella's cuff hit the ground as well. She released a pleased breath as she rolled her wrist. "*Much* better."

"Who was that?" Peony still stood where she had been, looking toward where the woman had gone.

Palmer attempted to call up the information, but the blue-tinged visions only rushed back in, causing his head to feel close to splitting. He pressed the heel of his palm between his eyes. "I'll figure it out later. For now, I say don't question our luck."

"Fine with me," Carmella said. "Now *I* say let's get out of here."

Palmer chanced diving into a little more of his visions and managed to pull out clips of what they really needed—nothing solid but close enough. He looked at Peony. "I know where Rosette is. Not far from here."

Peony's face pinched, but she nodded.

"You can't *seriously* be considering going back in there." Carmella's voice had turned into a whine, though it had mellowed now that the cuff was off.

"You don't have to come." Palmer took the key from her and slid it into his pocket. "Head south if you want."

"By myself? I can't go by myself."

"Whoever that was is by herself," Palmer said.

"She obviously wasn't a *lady*."

Peony swung Carmella a look heavy with judgment.

Palmer stopped himself from rolling his eyes a second time. "Well, *Signorina* Carmella, your options are come along to help or head off. Your choice."

Carmella puffed up, jaw moving indignantly as she started to say at least three different sentences, before she finally stopped and huffed. "Fine. But if we get captured again, I'm killing you myself."

"Noted." Palmer scanned the shimmering blue line. The veil still wreaked havoc on both his eyes and visions, but at least he could somewhat pinpoint where they needed to go. "This way."

BRIER LIFTED THE BOTTLE to her lips once again only to find it empty. She stared at it as though it had only been playing a trick on her before it registered that she had actually finished the bottle. Frowning, she sent a jolt of energy out through her palm, and the glass shattered, spraying across the room. Brier had to admit *that* made her feel a little better.

If she had finished off a full bottle and still didn't feel drunk, her tolerance was getting far too high. Waving her hand, she dissolved the broken glass around her in an arc and moved back to the trunks lining the wall. She lifted the lid of the closest and found it empty. Brier groaned. It certainly wasn't the time to run out of wine. She moved to the next chest to search.

The stack of books looked back at her. Her father's books. Her chest clenched. The buzz in her palms said she half wanted to blast that chest across the room as well, but no matter how bad a mood she was in, she couldn't bring herself to destroy books. Pressing her lips tightly together, Brier picked up the leather-bound tome on top and ran her fingers over the embossed cover. The faint smell of smoke clung to it, saying the book was either old enough to have survived the first library burning, had been taken just before the second burning, or both.

Slowly, Brier cracked the cover and flipped through it, finding careful hand-printed block letters and symbols, all speaking of magic and alchemy. She set it aside and pulled out another. This one contained more of the same, though it had colorful illuminations lining the edges of the pages. She looked at all the drawings, turning the old pages carefully. Just as she went to set it aside, she spotted a silver hoop surrounded by purple lightning. Her eyes slid to the text along the top of the page:

... and with the stolen life, the air itself was ripped in twain, leaving the world open to itself.

Brier flipped to the previous page and read quickly, finding a story that sounded frighteningly similar to what she had just experienced if only she were trying to tell it as something far more legendary than it had been. She went back to the first line she had read.

... and with the stolen life...

So she had found a power she could only use if she killed someone. *Brilliant.* Brier set the book aside a little more roughly than was perhaps warranted and moved to another chest. It contained nothing of interest. In the third chest, she found another half dozen bottles sitting on top of cloth.

Thank you, Orris Adessi. She picked one up gratefully. The man might have been a monster, but he did make sure he had the finer things in life. At the moment, Brier could appreciate him for that. She forced the stopper out with her thumb and went to take a drink, but something stabbed through her chest, feeling like a dozen little needles trying to press out from the center of her diaphragm. She hissed, pressing her fist to it as though that would help the sensation.

The energy that had built up in her chest managed to press down and at least turn the needles into a low burning rather than a shooting pain.

Palmer? The last little hopeful part of her mind tried to reach out, but having Palmer alive had felt warm, solid. It had kept her steady, not stabbed her. If anything, the pain likely meant Kosmos had found a new incarnation. The thought of someone else walking around with Palmer's powers, pretending to be him, was worse than having lost him in the first place. Holding her open bottle and picking up a second, Brier stood and turned for the door. If she had to deal with even more awful thoughts swirling around her mind, drinking alone was no longer an option.

She'd nearly made it up to the cave before she heard a tumbling sound and a string of curses. She stepped inside and let her eyes adjust to see Leone lying in a jumble near the wall. She arched an eyebrow. "Everything all right?"

Leone righted himself, managing to sit upright before he used his hands to move his bad leg into a more comfortable position. "Was trying to get myself up," he grumbled.

"You should have waited for me to get here."

"I'm supposed to rely on you forever?"

"At least until you can manage without nearly breaking your neck, I'd think." Brier moved through the gate that she had long since stopped bothering to close let alone lock and set the bottles down. "I'll try to find you a cane or crutch or something. That should at least help your balance."

"Great. Then I can hobble around like an old man."

"Is that better or worse than having to crawl about like an infant?" Brier sat heavily and went back to her wine.

Leone observed her for a moment before speaking. "You started without me."

"Does it show?"

"You become markedly less genial when you're drunk."

"Or I've just had a bad day and don't feel like pretending I haven't." Brier took a drink. The stopper in the bottle apparently hadn't been placed correctly, because the smooth taste of the wine was tainted with a hint of vinegar. With supplies running low, Brier went with it. The drink was still *more* wine than vinegar.

Leone started to answer before approaching voices cut him off. Brier frowned, trying to place the female voice before she heard the last person she wanted up at the cave. The way Leone tensed said he recognized his cousin's voice too.

Jumping up, she moved toward the mouth of the cave to head Nico off. He and the supposed anchoress who had been following him appeared at the mouth and stopped dead.

The slight flash of surprise on Nico's face fell back off as the hard expression he'd had for a month returned. "We need to speak."

"Do we?" Brier shifted so that she had the best chance of blocking Leone from view, though as tall as Nico was, he wouldn't have any trouble seeing past her if he wanted.

"You blew up a building."

Brier lifted her eyebrows. Nico's tone said that he meant more than he was saying. "That needs discussing?"

"That isn't like you."

"What would you know what's *like me*?" The words came out far more bitterly than Brier had meant them to. It wasn't the time to get into whatever had happened between them. Getting Nico out of the cave before he noticed Leone was far more important.

"Hello." Lauretta spoke before Brier could think of something else to say, her eyes focused on the back wall before she looked at Brier. "Were you busy?"

Nico glanced at Lauretta then over Brier's head, and the hard look turned into something plainly murderous. "You."

"Nic—" Leone's voice squeaked.

"Nico, back down." Brier moved in front of Nico as he stepped toward Leone.

"You knew he was here?" Nico's eyes swung back to her as he jabbed a finger toward Leone.

"Since I brought him here, yes."

"You *know* what he did?"

"I've been told."

"Then what, in the name of all that is holy, is he doing here?"

"He's here for the same reason anyone else is." Brier kept her voice level but with a hard enough tint that it could give Nico's murderous expression a run for its money. "Because I wish for it to be so."

"You want that *thing* here?"

"He's been a better friend than *some* people lately."

Brier had never seen Nico's face turn so red, the color darkening until it nearly looked purple as he fought to get words out. "I... I walked to *Ouene* and back because you wanted to stay in this forsaken town."

"You walked to Ouene and back because you couldn't stand being near me anymore," Brier snapped.

Confusion attempted to break through the rage on his face. "*What?*"

"This is the longest you've looked at me in *weeks*," Brier said. "You couldn't even gather the courtesy to say goodbye in person before you left."

"I—"

"But that's what you do, isn't it?" Now that she had started, Brier couldn't stop the words from falling out, every awful thing she felt pushing the hurt from her mouth. "I doubt you said goodbye to any of the other girls you took to bed once you were done with them, but then, *they* at least would likely understand why, wouldn't they?"

The color drained from Nico's face in a rush, leaving him deathly pale.

"Were you even going to tell me? Or were you going to leave Palmer to do that along with telling me you'd disappeared?"

Something flashed behind Nico's eyes. "He had no right to tell you any of that."

"I didn't have the right to know what happened to my own body?" Brier felt her palms buzzing as her irritation grew.

"What good would telling you have done?" Nico threw up his hands.

"I *deserved* to know."

"You'd rather be upset like this than just pretending it never happened?"

Brier clenched her fists, the buzzing turning into a burn as the energy reached the surface. If this conversation continued, she couldn't trust herself to remain in control of her actions. Not after earlier. "I've had a very, very bad day, as it seems you've heard, so why don't you go back to *pretending it never happened*, and I can go back to sitting there and getting drunk with someone who at least was honest about screwing me over."

Nico's jaw worked in the way it did when he wanted to say something but wasn't going to. He shot another murderous look over Brier's shoulder at Leone then turned on his heel and stormed away.

The anchoress looked after him, met Brier's eyes quickly enough to say, "I hope your day gets better," then turned and left as well, continuing her apparent mission to follow Nico everywhere he went.

As the cave went silent once again, Brier finally released her clenched fists—the power had abated for the time being—and moved back to her spot on the back wall.

Leone watched her as she took a healthy swig of the slightly off wine. "Should I ask—"

"Not if you value your life," Brier said, though at least her tone was less threatening than it had been.

"Noted." Leone picked up his own bottle and popped the stopper out of it. "*Salute.*"

"*Salute*," Brier returned, hoping two bottles would be enough to do the trick.

Chapter Seventeen

Nico's mind spun so quickly he couldn't fully form a thought. At least he knew he was angry. Or mostly angry. Angry, guilty, hurting... he turned and swung at the closest wall, more than happy to focus on the anger. The plaster broke, letting his fist hit rough stone.

Nico hissed as the skin of his knuckles split, and he pulled back. *Stupid...* He began that train of thought, though the pain was something else he could focus on.

"Trying to blow up a building yourself?"

Nico sent Lauretta a glare but didn't have the energy to start another fight.

"Feel better?" she asked with surprisingly little judgment in her tone. That had to be the result of her anchoress training.

Nico shrugged.

"Should likely wash that before you get blood everywhere."

Nico nodded. Silently, he turned for the river running along the edge of town. Of course, Lauretta followed, but Nico was too tired to be annoyed. Reaching the bank at one of the shallower parts of the little river, he knelt and started washing off the blood.

"You know," Lauretta said, sitting somewhere farther back, "I didn't think anyone could beat Delphi and me for having *complicated* relationships."

Nico snorted. "Unless your father set up an engagement, tried to kill her, and set the stage for dual possession, we have you beat."

"You likely do," Lauretta agreed. "Possession? That's what she was talking about up there, I take it?"

Nico's jaw locked as he fought down his first instinct, which was either to tell her it was none of her damned business or simply not answer, but after everything Brier had said, he supposed he at least should give his side. "Some... old version of her managed to possess her one night, and I should have known. It wasn't at all like her. But I'd been drinking too. I didn't catch it. Or didn't want to catch it. I don't know. I let things happen I shouldn't have."

"That's awful."

"I didn't know." He shot her a look over his shoulder.

"That's what I meant," Lauretta said, voice still entirely free of judgment. "It's awful for her, of course, not having any say over what happened to her body, but it's just as awful for you, I would think. You were tricked as well."

Nico scoffed, turning back to the river. "I knew what I was doing."

"But not whom you were doing it with. That must feel..." Lauretta seemed to search for the right word. "Well, violating."

Nico pressed his lips together, not truly sure what he felt about the night he had spent with Brier when she *hadn't* been Brier but certain he didn't want to spend any more time thinking about it. With most of the blood off the back of his hand, he used the bottom of his shirt to apply pressure to his bleeding knuckles. The fabric was already stained enough that a little blood wouldn't hurt it.

He shook his head. "Tash shouldn't have told her. She never would have had to know."

Lauretta hummed. "*That* might be where you were in the wrong, honestly."

Nico sent her another look over his shoulder.

"I doubt anyone would have assumed possession in that situation, especially if you weren't entirely sober yourself, so you're arguably as much a victim as anyone else in that situation. Keeping something like that from her, though, especially if the guilt made you act differently around her without her having any clue why... I could see being rightfully hurt over that."

Nico pointed up the hill toward the cave. "She's up there drinking with a man who kidnapped her and turned her over to my psychotic mess of a father. She's *apparently* forgiven him. You don't think she could forgive me for trying to protect her?"

"Sometimes it's easier to forgive people you don't care about, because they don't have the same power to hurt you as the ones you do."

Nico tossed his hands up. "Aren't you supposed to be on my side, trying to convince me to kill her and all?"

"I'm supposed to be helping you. That doesn't always mean saying what people want to hear."

"So you're anchoress-ing me."

"What can I say?" Lauretta gave a good-natured shrug. "It's what I do."

Nico went back to applying pressure to his damaged hand. "So what would you suggest if I were some unknown person who came strolling into your temple?"

Lauretta smiled. "Well, first, I would suggest you try your best to forgive yourself. No rational person would have immediately thought *possessed* in that situation, and even if you should have known—which is a big *if*—mistakes happen. Punishing yourself in perpetuity doesn't help anyone. All it will do is keep you caught in the past."

Nico struggled to think of an answer. He finally shrugged off the whole dilemma. "I suppose it doesn't really matter, since we're all likely to be dead in a few days."

"We do have a woman who can destroy buildings supposedly on our side."

"And they have who knows how many little devices that apparently mimic gods' powers. *I'd* suggest each of us make peace with our own favorite god."

"We'll see." Lauretta didn't look any more worried than she had back in Ouene.

PALMER'S HEART POUNDED in his ears as he crouched behind one of the canvas tents. Taking a deep breath, he tried to get ahold of himself. With his powers somewhat working, he had managed to get everyone back into the tents without being recaptured, but they weren't strong enough to overcome his nerves, which made it hard to hear whether someone was approaching.

"Are we going to stand here all day?" Carmella hissed over Palmer's shoulder.

Palmer sent her a glare before he returned to scanning the space out in front of them. The camp was quiet, only a few Osamli men wandering about, but that didn't mean there wasn't a force out there just waiting to march back in. He forced his breath out in a sharp puff and nodded. "Peony, keep watch. If you see anyone coming—"

She sent him a vaguely annoyed look, as though insulted that he felt the need to instruct her beyond *keep watch*, but quickly moved to a place that would give her a good view of the tents around them without being out in the open.

Their own guard set, Palmer turned back to Carmella. "Ready?"

"If we must..." she mumbled, honey-brown eyes scanning the tents as well.

With another nod, more to make him feel certain than for Carmella's benefit, Palmer started toward where he hoped Rosette was. As he reached the right tent, a pair of deep voices made him pause.

"If it's so safe, you do it."

"The doctor said her *kirilbilzik* is holding."

"Brat still claws like an animal."

Something about the way the nearly garbled word *brat* felt—as though Palmer's mind wasn't certain it was correct—made him realize the men were speaking in Osamli. His powers were apparently translating. "Something useful for once," he mumbled.

"What?" Carmella whispered.

"Nothing." He shook it off. *Just would have been helpful to know a year ago.* He could have taken Brier and Rosette north when they'd left Ruhegipfel and stayed far away from everything happening back in Latysia, had he known he'd be able to understand people wherever they went. *Then maybe none of this ever would have happened...*

"Stop being a coward and do it already," the second man's voice said. "She needs to be out before we can move her."

Palmer pursed his lips. He didn't love the idea of poor Rosette being put under the way he had, but after her fit the last time Palmer had seen her, the man likely had a point. It would be far easier to get Rosette out of camp unconscious than drag her out kicking and screaming. He likely wouldn't have the time to convince her to come quietly or heal her enough to fix whatever the doctor had done to her.

The one who Palmer assumed was the second man came striding out of the tent. Palmer pulled back, but the man was so intent on wherever he was going that he didn't so much as glance toward the side of the tent. Everything went silent again for a moment before shuffling started inside the tent. *The first man getting ready to face Rosette, no doubt.*

Palmer pressed his lips together and looked at Carmella. "You can compel people to do things, right? That's one of your powers?"

"Yes..." Carmella gave him a suspicious look.

"There's one man still in there. Once he has Rosette unconscious, I need you to get him to leave while I get her out."

"What? No way!" Carmella recoiled. "They'll just slap another one of those birky things on me, and then I'm right back where I started!"

"It's one man. Didn't you just have an entire town worshipping you?"

"I... but..." Carmella fumbled for an argument before she harrumphed and pointed at him sharply. "If they catch us again, I'm dedicating the rest of my *life* to making you miserable."

"Why stop now?" He lifted the back of the tent enough to peek inside. His stomach twisted as he saw the little blond girl once again sitting in the cage, silently picking at her wrist. Heavy footsteps moved across the carpeted ground, and the Osamli soldier appeared, pouring something from a bottle onto a cloth. Palmer let the side of the tent drop and turned to Carmella. "Go around the front, and do whatever is necessary to get that guard out of the way."

"I hate you." Carmella wrinkled her nose, but she still did as directed.

Leaning back slightly, Palmer spotted Peony still positioned as lookout, so they should have some warning before any more guards arrived. A piercing scream went up—the Osamli man must have reached Rosette's cage—before it went muffled, rising and falling in waves. The guard was struggling to keep his grip, if the low stream of curses was anything to judge by. Palmer's fists clenched. If he were Brier, he would have been tempted to blast that man into the mountains for what had happened to Rosette, but having no offensive powers, Palmer forced himself to wait. *Get in, grab Rosette, disappear.* No one would benefit from him getting into a fight he couldn't hope to win.

Slowly, the screaming became weaker and then finally tapered off. Palmer gripped the fabric of the tent, ready to climb under it as soon as the coast was clear.

"Excuse me." Carmella's lilting voice filtered into the silence a moment before the warm, pink-tinted energy Palmer had felt the first time they'd been in Elatita began to fill the air. He pulled the fabric up to look. Though the energy hadn't affected Palmer or Nico when it had been directed at them, the Osamli guard wasn't so lucky. Even from a bad angle, Palmer could see the dazed, besotted look on the man's face as he slowly wandered away from the cage.

Palmer glanced at Rosette, who was now slumped against one side of the bars, and spotted a key sitting abandoned in the lock. "Good work, Carmella," Palmer mumbled.

The guard wandered out of sight before he scrambled under the fabric and into the tent. Voices drifted through one of the cloths dividing the tent inside, the seemingly separate conversations indicating that neither Carmella nor the guard understood each other, but as long as the man was distracted, Palmer supposed he couldn't complain. He'd just have to be quiet.

The key turned easily in the lock, and the cage opened with a quiet squeak. Sending a glance toward the voices—Carmella's getting more and more annoyed as the guard still sounded blithely besotted—Palmer slid Rosette out of the cage and gathered her to him. Palmer frowned at just how light she was. Rosette had always been small for her age, but since the fall of the Augarian, she had been gaining weight. Now she felt lighter than ever—a little pile of bird bones. Palmer felt the anger already in his stomach churn.

"Palmer." Peony's hushed voice took him out of his thoughts.

Palmer glanced over his shoulder to see her face peeking under the tent.

"More men are coming."

Time to go. Palmer moved to the edge of the tent and passed Rosette under the fabric. "Take her and head back for those trees."

"You're not coming?" Peony's dark eyebrows rose.

"I'll be right behind you. You have her?" As light as Rosette was, Palmer had to imagine the girl wouldn't give Peony trouble, but she was still dead weight.

Peony nodded. "But, Pa—"

"I'm right behind you."

Peony didn't look any happier, but she shifted her hold on Rosette to be able to stand, and she disappeared. Palmer released a breath. He didn't like the idea of leaving Peony to deal for herself, especially with Rosette unconscious. But Peony had managed to keep herself in one piece this long, so he had to trust she'd be able to handle things at least long enough for him to get Carmella.

Moving quietly across the carpets, Palmer stopped against one of the sheets dividing the tent and poked his head around the edge. Warm pink energy was still radiating off Carmella, making the other side of the tent hazy as she motioned toward the flap with annoyance, trying to direct the guard to leave. The man, however, seemed in no hurry to go, kneeling in front of Carmella, professing his undying love in sweeping poetic terms that either didn't translate well in Palmer's mind or were just ham-fisted.

Carmella looked over and caught Palmer's eye, and he motioned toward the door with his head. She gave him a look that said, *I'm trying* as loudly as if she had spoken. Palmer gritted his teeth. And then he spotted the cloth the man had no doubt used on Rosette. Palmer hesitated. It wasn't a perfect plan. There was no way he would be able to take the much larger man in a fight, but as long as Carmella kept the guard distracted, there was a chance.

Moving slowly, as though that would make him invisible, Palmer inched forward. Wrapped up in yet another poetic stanza about Carmella's beauty, the guard didn't so much as glance at Palmer as he slipped the cloth away from the man's side. A second before Palmer clamped the cloth over the man's mouth, Carmella caught on to the plan and sent out another wave of energy.

The cloth came down, and the guard jerked, whether in surprise or because of the energy, Palmer didn't know. Either way, the large man didn't fight, his eyes slowly drifting closed before he slumped to the floor.

"About time." The pink energy cut off with a snap. "Where is she?"

"Out with Peony," Palmer said. "It's time to go, unless you want to face more of him."

Carmella huffed, not otherwise dignifying the statement with a response as she strode back into the tent.

Palmer tossed the cloth to the side, pausing for a second as a piece of gauzy gray material near the wall of the tent caught his eye. It seemed out of place. It nearly looked like an Augarian anchoress's veil, but the blue shimmer said the Osamli had done something to it, like what they had done to the air around the camp. He took a half step toward it before a mess of voices reached him.

No time. He turned after Carmella. He'd see if he could divine anything about it once they were out of the camp and Rosette was taken care of. For the moment, it was time to get as far away as they possibly could.

Chapter Eighteen

Brier pressed her fist under her breastbone, trying to force down the upset. Whether it was from that day's nearly constant diet of wine and nothing else or the energy that was trying to force its way back inside her, she wasn't certain. Either way, the nausea made it difficult to focus.

"I don't know." Gil sighed dramatically in response to whatever one of the Ouenen captains had asked. "Ten? Twenty miles out? Far enough it was annoying to ghost to."

"Which is it?" Captain Lais crossed her arms. "Ten or twenty?"

Gil shrugged, staring off past the woman's shoulder as though he couldn't quite manage to give her his full attention.

"Either way, it's within a day's walk," Nico said. "We should up the patrol with our other flyer missing."

Brier made a face. Cerise had given Brier a lot of grief over her reaction to Palmer's death, but at least Brier hadn't dropped out of existence as Cerise had done when Goebel died.

Dropping her fist, Brier focused on Gil. "Have you tried just killing them?" She felt Nico's eyes sliding to her, surprised, but she didn't look away from Gil.

"They have those things." Gil made a vague hand gesture. "I mean, *I'd* do better than Kosmos or Astarte, obviously, but I can't just swoop down like I normally would."

"Astarte?" Brier frowned.

"She was in Elatita too."

"You mean Carmella?" Nico straightened, and Brier finally turned her head to look at him.

"Carmella?" Brier asked. "Carmella Huerta?"

Nico gave a half-hearted nod. "We saw her on the way north. She was living in the temple at Elatita."

"Of course she was," Brier grumbled. She had no idea what Palmer would have been doing with Carmella, but whatever the answer was, Brier would add it to the list of reasons she loathed the woman. *Well, maybe she's dead too.*

"We could retreat," Captain Lais said, bringing the conversation back to what were arguably more important matters. "Some of the hill towns near here would be easier to defend."

"There's no saying we could get to any of them." Nico crossed his arms, settling back into his earlier stance now that the news of Carmella Huerta had passed. "If they're circling us, we are as likely to meet them on the open plain that way as to reach another town."

Unless we walked from here straight into Ruhegipfel. The thought filtered through Brier's mind. With her bad mood, she was half-willing to see what she could do against whatever devices the Osamli Empire had developed. The worst that could happen was she'd be killed.

Worst that happens is they get your powers and take over the entire world, a voice at the back of her mind corrected.

Is that my problem? she asked. The unhelpful inner voice didn't answer.

With the rest of the war council busy discussing strategy, Brier stood, getting ready to leave.

"Brier?" Nico asked, but she didn't turn to look at him.

She heard footsteps behind her, but it was only Gil. The boy jogged a few steps to catch up with her. "What's happening?"

Brier didn't speak until they had made it a street over, away from the rest of the men—and women—talking battle. "Do you think we could take these men? Just us?"

Excitement flashed over Gil's face before it fell off again. "Normally, no problem. But with the stuff they have... would be easier if we got rid of that."

"So we'd need enough men to go in and destroy whatever they're using on us, then we could wipe out the lot."

"Oh, definitely." Gil nodded eagerly then motioned toward where they'd left. "Are we going to send them in?"

"There's no way they'd last long enough against an Osamli force." Brier shook her head. "We'd need more men."

Gil's mouth pinched. "How do we do that?"

Brier let the thoughts churn before making a decision. "I think I have a solution. I need to test something."

"Can I help?"

With the excited glint back in Gil's eyes, Brier didn't think she could handle having him with her when what was left of her conscience was already niggling, begging her to reconsider. She kept her voice hard. "I'll let you know. For now, keep watch and let me know if you find wherever the hell Cerise went."

Gil frowned at the order, but obediently, he nodded and disappeared into his cloud. Lingering longer than she needed to, Brier watched him fly off.

Oh, just do it already, she told herself, forcing down the squirming in her stomach. *They're doomsday cultists. They're all looking to die anyway.* Nodding once, Brier pulled her shoulders back and made her way to where the cultists had set themselves up out of town.

Half-starved and huddled, the cultists didn't look much better than skeletons as Brier approached. A wave of guilt passed through her. She hadn't at all wondered what they were doing for food now that she and the others had taken over the storehouse.

As frail as they were, the cultists dropped whatever they were doing the second they saw her. In a wave, they dropped to their knees and pressed their foreheads to the dirt. Brier faltered, not entirely certain what to do at the veneration, before she pulled her shoulders back and hardened herself. *Be a goddess.*

"I need a volunteer." She drew on her new resolution and spoke in a more commanding voice than she would have thought she'd be able to manage. "A sacrifice," she amended as heads lifted to look at her. "The rest of you shall be rewarded for it."

No one moved for several minutes before a frail-looking man with a shock of white hair pushed himself up. "Please, *mia donna*, honor me."

A few other cultists echoed him in soft murmurs, but Brier motioned the man forward. He hobbled toward her then dropped to his knees once again a few feet away, his head lowered respectfully. A wash of second thoughts moved through Brier's mind, but she could see no way to back out now.

"Thank you," Brier said, keeping the same steady, commanding tone to her voice. She forced her hand out and placed her palm on top of the man's soft white hair. The thought that she should ask his name crossed her mind. She was going to take the man's life, for gods' sake. But then, she wasn't certain she'd be able to go through with it if she knew his name.

Instead, she closed her eyes and let the power begin to gather in her hand. She heard the cultists begin to murmur before the man hissed in pain, and she let the energy shoot straight down. Without Marina's powers, there was no snap this time. In a flash, the man was simply gone, and Brier felt the same heady rush of power go through her as before. The murmuring had turned into frenzied prayers. Brier tried to focus, picturing the plaza at the center of the Augarian before she gathered the pulsing energy and sent it out.

A soft ripping sound floated through the new exclamations, and Brier opened her eyes again. The purple circle had opened once again, though this time, it showed a little village in the middle of what looked like wheat fields, not like anything she had seen near Latysia.

"It's Pavv!" one of the younger cultists exclaimed. "Home!"

"Yes..." Brier dropped her hands and attempted to recover. "Your reward for his sacrifice." At least that wasn't turning out to be a complete lie. "The rest of you shall be spared. Go home."

The murmurs kicked up again.

"Go," Brier snapped, not certain how long the portal would stay open.

In a rush, the remaining cultists scrambled to their feet and piled through the portal, a mix of terror, awe, and elation on their bony faces. The last woman stepped through, and Brier watched as the cultists looked around in a collective daze. Finally, the portal snapped in on itself, and Brier was left standing at the edge of town alone. The exhaustion following the elation began to creep up on her, but she ignored it as she released an annoyed breath. So she couldn't direct the portals. Ruhegipfel, Pavv... it seemed the portals opened to wherever the person—the *sacrifice*—called home. And that meant the only way to get back to Latysia was...

Nico? Her stomach bottomed out at the first thought before the second one dawned on her. *Or Leone.*

No matter where they currently stood, Nico couldn't be considered an option. She might want to strangle the man, but she had likely spent a good half of the past fourteen years wanting to do that. The tension between them was so much worse than ever before, but no, she couldn't sacrifice Nico. But would Leone be any better?

"It's nice to be able to save someone for a change." The memory of her own voice taunted her. Forcing a breath through her teeth, Brier turned back toward town, not able to fully work everything through as the exhaustion made its way into her bones. Perhaps if she lay down for just a few minutes, another option would make itself known, and she wouldn't have to keep thinking about it.

NICO LOOKED UP. THE approaching clouds made the day dreary but did not threaten rain. *Couldn't even give us that to slow the Osamli.* He wasn't certain to whom he was directing that thought. If all the stories he had been told about the gods were of people like him who could destroy buildings with their minds, he had to believe there was no one above them planning anything. It didn't rain because it didn't rain. No one was passing judgment. No one was helping or punishing. No one cared.

"There!" one of the Ouenen men shouted.

Nico followed the man's pointing just in time to see a blue shimmer drop away, leaving a stretch of at least fifty Osamli men standing there. *Not as bad as it could be.* Nico scanned them. They still didn't know what kind of devices the Osamli troops had, but as long as Brier or Gil could do *something* against them, the rest of them could take fifty men. It wasn't enough for them to win the war, but they would possibly make it through another night, and that was more than Nico had originally been hoping for.

A smaller group of men stepped forward, holding a white banner.

"They want to parley," Captain Lais said.

Nico watched the men moving into the empty space between the rest of the soldiers and Venchia. "I don't speak Osamli."

"I do." Captain Lais motioned for a few of the other Ouenen men to go with her.

Nico remained where he was, fingering the hilt of the sword at his hip, doing his best not to give in to the urge to pull his bow as Captain Lais and the others stopped several paces away. A few patches of conversation caught the wind blowing toward Venchia, but not enough for Nico to have understood even if he had spoken the language.

After a bit more conversation, the center Osamli man lifted his hand. Nico's fingers clenched the hilt of his sword, and the man's hand dropped. The air shimmered blue in three other places as more men flashed into view. Nico quickly tried to count. There had to be at least two hundred. The chances of everyone in Venchia making it until nightfall had just fallen to zero.

The man who had motioned nodded once and then turned with the others back toward his men. Nico only waited for the Ouenen group to make it within earshot before calling, "Went well, I take it."

Captain Lais gave him an unamused look and came the rest of the way up before answering. "They said we have an hour to give them the woman with powers here, or they will come and take her."

The other men shifted uneasily but remained silent, and they soon turned their eyes back to Nico.

"I'll speak to Brier," he grumbled and turned back into town.

This time, Brier was in her little house, curled onto her side on the pallet, apparently asleep. The annoyance at the thought that he might have to see his cousin again left him, and in its place, unease took hold. Though she had managed to regain some of the weight she'd lost since they had arrived in Venchia, Brier still looked far too small, her face pinched in concern even in her sleep. Memories of sneaking into her room when they had been children—the only two children in the rebuilding palace—wrenched him. Whatever had happened between them in the past year, he had known her for three-fourths of his life—longer than anyone else alive. He hadn't fully appreciated that.

As though she felt him watching, Brier's eyelids fluttered open, and her brown eyes met his. "Nic?" she murmured.

Nico sucked in a breath and forced his shoulders stiff. It wasn't the time for nostalgia. "Osamli forces are here."

Brier started out of her drowsy haze, and she sat up stiffly. "How many?"

"More than we can take. They're demanding we give you over. We have an hour before they attack."

Brier stared at him long enough that Nico began to wonder if she had understood him. Finally she said, "No plan, I take it?"

"Not if you don't think you can take them."

Brier's lips pressed tightly enough together that they nearly disappeared, and something strained passed behind her eyes. Then she stood. "Get everything you want to take with you, then bring everyone to the cave. We'll leave town."

"We've already talked about leaving. If they're circling us—"

"Do as I say, and I will get us out of town."

The instinct to debate rose in Nico's throat, but Brier was already collecting things. Die in town or die just outside of town—Nico supposed it made very little difference. With a silent nod, Nico backed out of the house and left to get the others.

BRIER MOVED AROUND the chests in the villa, trying to pick out what she needed to take as quickly as possible. Once they were gone, there would be no way back—no one had been *from* Venchia for centuries—and gods knew if she would be able to bring herself to use that specific power again after what she was going to have to do. She could feel exhaustion deep down into her bones. Just giving up and letting them do whatever they were planning to do sounded truly appealing.

But she was supposed to be a goddess, and giving up wasn't what goddesses did. Neither was letting a little thing like death get in the way of a grander plan. That was what the Seers at the Augarian Temple had always said. According to them, no one should question the bad that happened in life because it was all part of the gods' greater plan. People died. That was simply what they did. Her own human body had died multiple times. None of that was important. What *was* important, she had yet to work out, but if there was some greater plan, all she could do was keep moving forward and doing what seemed best—or if not best, necessary.

Slipping the rest of the books she could fit into the pack, Brier sent a final look around the villa and supposed it was good enough. There would be wine in Latysia, she had no use for men's clothing, and as much as it hurt to leave them, the remaining books were too large or fragile to make the trip. She lifted her hand, and with a half-hearted wave, the chests were wiped from existence. She'd do the same to the storehouse on her way up to the cave. The less they left to support an invading army, the better. She hadn't taken any of the classes the boys had attended back before the Augarian university had been destroyed, but she knew that much when it came to military tactics. *When all else fails, burn what you can't take with you and retreat until you find relief troops, or your enemies run out of supplies to follow.*

She slung her pack onto her back with a grunt, the books making the pack feel as if it weighed more than she did. She ignored the weight and forced her way north. Even with her stop to destroy the storehouse, Brier was the first one up to the cave other than Gil.

The adolescent straightened with her approach. "What's happening? Are we leaving?"

Brier nodded. "Wait here until the others come. I need to do something." She wasn't certain if it would be good or bad to have a final moment alone with Leone Adessi, but either way, she didn't need Gil there. He'd be too happy when it was all over as it was.

With little hop steps, Leone was making his way along the far wall. He looked up at her as she dropped the heavy pack. "Would you look at that? Seems I can get up by myself."

"That's great." Brier managed a tense smile.

"Might be able to actually get around town one of these days—you know, assuming Nic will someday not want to kill me."

Well, Nic *won't.* Brier tried to keep her face neutral as she detected a new presence. The way Leone slowed to a stop told her she hadn't succeeded in hiding anything.

"Something wrong?" Leone asked.

"Osamli troops are here." Brier wrapped her arms tightly around her middle, dragging the heavy pack with her deeper into the cave as she heard footsteps coming up the hill.

"*Osamli* troops?" Leone's eyebrows rose. "What are they doing here?"

"Looking for me, it seems." Brier twisted and reached the mouth of the cave. She met Nico's eyes. "Is this everyone?"

Nico nodded once. "What are we doing?"

"Leaving," Brier said.

"Carting *him* along?" Nico tossed his head toward Leone.

"No," Brier said, somehow keeping her voice level though she felt the wobble rising from deep inside her. She forced herself to look at Leone.

Horror was dawning in his face. "You're leaving me behind."

"No." Her voice dropped to a whisper. "I'm sorry."

Leone's eyebrows pulled together as she moved closer. "Chas..."

"I wouldn't... believe me I wouldn't if I didn't have to," she said softly as the purple glow began around her hand.

"Chas." Leone recoiled as his eyes went to her hand, the motion throwing him off balance. He tumbled to the ground, his injured leg not strong enough to catch him. The crippled man looked up at her, terrified.

"I'm so sorry," she murmured, fighting back the tears burning at the corners of her eyes. She had no right to feel sorry for herself. And it had to be done. She forced her hand out, clamped it down over Leone's head, and shot the energy straight down. Leone's mouth opened, but he didn't have time to shout, his body disappearing in a silent ripple. Brier breathed in, the exhaustion and tears both gone in a flash as her skin tingled with ecstatic power.

An external buzz hit her, and she spotted Gil in his black cloud, bouncing back and forth as though his own excitement kept him from taking human form. She shook her head quickly and focused. With a rip, the stone wall to the left of her opened into the great hall of the Augarian. The rebuilding was further along than the last time she had seen it. *Gully's been working.*

Brier lifted her hand and shoved at the black cloud that was Gil. "Move."

Still buzzing with excitement, he shot through the portal.

"And you." She turned to the group still standing at the mouth of the cave, pulling her shoulders back tautly. *Be a goddess.*

The entire group stared at her, wide-eyed.

"You want to fight the Osamli by yourself here? Fine. Do so." Brier pointed over their shoulders, having to curl in her fingers again quickly as energy tried to shoot out unbidden. "You want to live, I suggest you move."

Captain Lais shot an uneasy glance at Nico but gave the order for the Ouenen men to advance, picking her way toward Brier carefully. The woman stepped through, her eyes widening as she took in the building on the other side of the portal. Brier watched for a minute until the stream of soldiers stepping through blocked Captain Lais from sight. Brier turned back toward the mouth of the cave, where only Nico and the anchoress remained.

Nico stared at her, his voice soft. "What did you do?"

"What was necessary to get us out of here." Brier pulled up her skirts as she stepped over the rim of the circle, looking at him and Lauretta just past the other side. "I suggest you hurry. These don't stay open long."

Nico's face remained dire, but he at least moved forward, and Brier stepped to the side, keeping the edge of the portal in sight as she looked around the building that had once been her home. She had to admit, Gully and his men had made good progress. Though there were still cracks and chunks missing from the last battle there, the building was in better repair than she likely would have managed to accomplish. She had to assume the walls were doing even better. The place was much easier to defend than the ruins at Venchia.

"Where are we?" one of the Ouene soldiers asked loudly enough for Brier to catch it over the general murmuring.

"Latysia," Brier said, seeing the portal snap closed close enough behind Nico and the anchoress that it nearly caught the long gray skirt. Brier half wondered what would have happened if it had. "The Augarian Palace, to be specific." She caught sight of Gil's black cloud bouncing around the high ceiling. "Gil."

It paused as though looking at her.

"There should be soldiers around. Bring one."

The cloud folded slightly as if nodding before shooting off.

"*What*"—Nico's voice, surprisingly close, made Brier jump—"did you do?"

She turned to face him, puffing up at his dark expression as though that would do anything to lessen the height difference between them. "Fun little thing I learned I could do. I killed someone—ripped open the very fabric of the universe."

"You killed him." Nico over enunciated the words.

"You wanted him dead." Brier shrugged more callously than she felt.

"But *you* killed him."

"The power only gets us to wherever the sacrificed person lived." Brier went back to studying the hall. "I needed you or him to get here. I figured you'd prefer this way."

"We shouldn't be here." The added tension that slipped into his voice at those words made Brier look at Nico again, but the effort to keep the door open kept her from responding.

Gil ran in, looking quite amused, with three soldiers at his heels, all dressed in the red coats of Gully's men. The soldiers skidded to a halt at the sight of the crowd standing in the hall.

The soldier to the right's eyes darted around. "What in the—"

"Ah, good of you to join us." Brier strode forward, the lingering pleasant buzz helping her keep the airy, commanding tone she had heard every ruler use.

"Where did you come from?" The soldier in the center frowned.

"You..." the soldier to the left whispered.

Brier turned up the corners of her mouth in a way she was certain didn't look friendly. "He seems to remember who I am. Do the rest of you need a reminder?"

The soldier on the left murmured something to the other soldiers, and their eyes widened.

"Good," Brier said. "Now, where can I find General Gully?"

The soldier in the center opened his mouth then snapped it shut again and motioned for Brier to follow. After briefly instructing the captains to get the Ouenen men settled, Brier turned to follow the soldiers through the opening. Gil, Nico, and his tagalong anchoress were behind her.

Brier kept her eyes forward, trying not to look around. Being back in the once-familiar halls that now felt so foreign left her feeling dizzy. The last time she had been back home, she'd felt entirely different from the girl who had grown up there. This time, the place didn't even feel like home anymore. She was, yet again, a different woman, and she didn't even entirely feel like *herself*, to be honest.

She didn't have time to stew too long as they turned into one of the wide rooms that had once held important government meetings that Brier certainly had never attended. With its slightly arched ceiling, it had held up better than other parts of the palace. The plaster from the ceiling frescos was still in one piece. The dark wood table in the center, however, looked too rough-hewn to be an original part of the grandly decorated room. It had likely been brought up from the kitchens.

The large bearded bear of a man that was General Gully looked up from whatever paper he had spread out on the table in front of him and blinked. "If it isn't little Miss Chaos."

"I prefer *mia donna* these days." Brier found the words leaving her mouth as she planted herself across the table from the general and the dozen or so red-coated men with him.

"Is that so." Gully straightened. "You've gotten tired of playing war out in the countryside?"

"Can't say I was ever playing." She stared the man down. "It seems you didn't understand that my saying I needed your troops was an order, not a request."

Gully lifted an eyebrow, looking for all the world like a father who wasn't intending to put up with the tantrum his child was threatening. "You give me orders now?"

"I give orders to whomever I so choose. But as it seems you are unable to follow them, I thought I would come and claim my men here instead."

The displeased look turned dangerously dark. "*Your* men?"

"Indeed. *My* men," Brier said in a mocking tone. "My men. My city. Now, either you may agree to help me, or I can make you do it. I don't especially care which way we go about it. One will just be much more pleasant for you."

Nico mumbled, "Brier..." from behind her, but she ignored his warning.

"Now, you listen here, little miss." Gully stalked forward. "I don't know who you think you are—"

Brier flicked her hand, and the wooden table went flying across the room, slamming Gully into the wall before splintering. She saw the dozen men shift, their hands going to their swords but not pulling them out.

She focused on the general sprawled on the floor, feeling the tingle of the energy beginning to build inside her. "I know exactly who I am, General, and it isn't any sort of *little miss*. Do you still wish to do this?"

Gully pushed the chunks of wood off with his broad hands and began to right himself. "I saved this city. I don't have to listen to some little girl—"

Brier flicked her hand again, and the man slid like a tossed rag doll, nearly taking out one of the soldiers closest to him. Out of the corner of her eye, she saw Gil begin to jitter as though he were only just managing to remain solid. The tingle turned to a low burn in Brier's hands, the faintest hint of purple beginning to build.

Nico took a few steps toward her. "Bri—"

She flashed him a dark enough look that he cut off.

"Now, see here!" Gully fought to get his feet under himself.

Brier went to flick the large man again, but this time, the power in the air coalesced, the purple beam shooting out before Brier could catch herself. With a slash, it went straight across the man's shoulders. For an instant, his neck and head floated in the air above what used to be his body, then it fell with a sickening crack on the marble floor, the large torso tumbling after it. The black cloud shot forward, bouncing around the prone body. Brier stared, stunned for a split second before she realized all of the men across the room were watching her.

Putting on as strong a face as she could manage, she let her eyes move over the rest of them. "Anyone else have an issue with my taking charge?"

A few of the men still had their hands on their swords, but no blades were pulled, and a general murmur of assent went through the group.

"Good. You may let the rest of the men out there know." She waited, but no one moved. "I meant *now*."

The men sprang into action, rushing past Brier and the others out into the hallway.

Nico didn't try to speak again, but the silence felt damning.

"Gil," Brier snapped as the cloud continued to bounce around.

The boy turned back into his human form. "That was *terrific*." He grabbed Gully's head by the gray-streaked hair and lifted it. Brier had to fight back a flinch. At least with her powers, there was no blood.

"Can I have this?" Gil turned the dead face toward him.

"Leave it," Brier said.

The boy's face dropped.

"Go with the soldiers," she directed. "Listen to what they're saying. If there's anyone causing problems—"

"Kill them?" The smile hinted at returning.

Brier nodded once, and Gil happily dropped the head back onto the ground. She held her hand out as he began to dissolve again. "Remember, we need them. Only kill enough to stave off any trouble."

Gil nodded quickly and, in a flash, was gone. With Gil's added energy no longer in the room, Brier felt herself deflate. She glanced at Gully's body then turned away.

"You didn't have to kill him," Nico said, his eyes still on the bifurcated man.

"I... didn't mean to necessarily," she admitted before she tried to shrug it off. "It works, though, I imagine. I doubt we'll have much trouble from the men."

Nico's eyes finally met hers. "So that's your plan? Rule by fear?"

"If it works."

"This isn't you, Bri."

That wavery part of her chest that made her feel too close to tears threatened to come back. She pulled herself harder. "Perhaps it is. And who are you to judge? How many men have *you* killed, Nico Adessi?"

"That isn't the point."

"Why? Because you just get to do whatever you want, and I'm supposed to sit there in my room like a good little girl and take it?"

"Because this isn't good for you!"

Brier's jaw locked. "You, of all people, don't get to tell me what's *good* for me. I saved your sorry life today. I got us an army. I got us our city back. Now you can help me plan a way to defeat those Osamli bastards out there—since I imagine they'll be coming as soon as they figure out where we've gone—or you can go off and do whatever the hell you want, but you do *not* get to stand here and lecture me like you're some paragon of virtue. You would have done the same damned thing, were you in my shoes." Dear gods, did she need a drink. She shouldered past him. "Get out of my way."

Part of her wanted him to follow, but the hall remained silent as she stalked off toward the Augarian kitchens. She bit down that last little stab of hurt along with everything else she had to swallow. She was already keeping herself from crying over things far worse than Nico Adessi being emotionally dense. She'd learned as a child not to cry over that, for gods' sake. No, she was going to keep herself together, one way or another, because she shuddered to think about what would happen if everything fell apart.

Chapter Nineteen

Nico glanced at the large man, the large *corpse* at the far side of the room, not liking the twist in his stomach. Brier had been right—at least that Nico had killed enough people that two more wouldn't have likely been a problem for him. He would have gladly killed Leone himself. He couldn't say he would have been quite so quick to kill the general, though. As large as the man was, Nico wasn't certain he would have even been able to kill him. And that was part of the problem, wasn't it? Men died. Men killed other men. It had been the way of the world long before any of them had been alive. But Brier wasn't a man. She wasn't human. The Osamli might have worked out a way to defend themselves, but no one else stood a chance in the face of divine displeasure. If any of them were going to be safe, they needed the old Brier—the one who, even when angry, still truly did care about others. Gods knew what would happen if they had to face a woman who could kill two men with the flick of her wrist and then shrug it off as nothing. They were different from each other. She could destroy the world. He couldn't.

He looked at Lauretta out of the corner of his eye. She was still standing silently by the wall as though she had become part of it. "Aren't you going to say, 'I told you so'?"

Lauretta lifted her eyebrows. "About what?"

"We're in Latysia, aren't we?" He threw up an aggravated hand.

"I don't take any joy in this." She looked at Gully's body as well before meeting Nico's eyes again.

"I can't kill her. I won't." The words came out before Nico could stop them.

Lauretta didn't answer.

"You don't believe me?"

"I believe fate is fate," she said softly.

Nico scoffed. "There's no such thing."

"And yet..." Lauretta lifted her hands, looking around the grand room that was so different from the little shells of buildings they had occupied out in Venchia.

Jaw locking, Nico turned on his heel and left the room.

"Where are you going?" Lauretta followed.

"Leaving. If there's really some second gods' war coming, then I want no part of it."

"If you have no part of it, that will be the end of the world."

"So goes fate." Nico spat the final word, shifting his pack on his back.

He had supplies for another week of travel, gathered on the off chance they didn't immediately run into Osamli troops and die. He could simply go and not look back. Really, the end of the world didn't seem that bad a deal, as long as he could spend the time until then not worrying about anything other than what his next good meal would be. He still had his purse full of Adessi money. He hadn't had a reason to spend it since buying that pastry in Ouene. He likely could make a good dent in it, spending as though the world was ending.

Ingrained familiarity took him through the twisting halls to a side door without issue, and Nico came out to the wide piazza that stretched between the Augarian palace, temple, and university—still cracked from the last time Brier's powers had gone unchecked. He ignored the twinging at the base of his skull and walked around the soldiers, who were cowering from the black cloud circling them all. Nico could only assume Gil had gone straight to work finding someone to get rid of.

Good riddance. Nico turned for the gate out to Latysia. The soft footsteps behind him made him roll his eyes. He turned on the anchoress. "Thanks, but I don't think I've gotten all the help I need. You'd obviously be better suited to dealing with everything here than I would."

"But—"

"Enjoy the rest of the world." He gave a sarcastic salute and turned away again, shouldering past the soldiers at the gate, who seemed far more interested in the god menacing them all than whatever Nico was doing.

PALMER KEPT A CAUTIOUS eye on Rosette as she darted around the deserted buildings that had once been as packed as the river slums of Latysia, sniffing the air like a hound who'd caught scent of some sort of prey. At least, for the moment, she had moved past her screaming and thrashing, so he would take it. Even though she wore the cuff, traveling with a little girl in a perpetual state of tantrum had strained the rest of their already frayed nerves on the trip south.

"Shouldn't she be on a leash?" Carmella eyed Rosette uneasily as she wrung her dark curls out. Carmella was far more preoccupied with washing than the rest of them now that they were by the river.

"I don't think there's much trouble she can get into down here." Palmer shook his head. "Seems everyone's long gone."

"Everyone had moved up closer to the walls, last I was here." Peony looked up the hill toward the Augarian walls. "Was easier to grab things from the supply trains up there."

Palmer nodded, not feeling the need to get into Peony's thieving days with Carmella around. He didn't have to give the women any more reason for animosity. Looking up at the Augarian, he frowned, the sight of the palace not sitting well in his stomach. Something had changed.

"You feel it too?" Peony murmured.

"What?" Palmer brought his eyes back to her.

"The ring's here."

Brier...

The fact that Peony could confirm that the ring was nearby suggested his instinct to go south was right—though how she could have beaten him to Latysia, he wasn't certain. Perhaps she had managed to skirt the Osamli troops while he'd been stalking their edges. Still, something wasn't right.

"We should keep moving th—" Palmer felt the new presence a second before he heard footsteps. There was only a single person, so it couldn't be one of the street gangs that had taken over Latysia after the fall of the Augarian. Still, Palmer motioned for quiet. Remarkably, even Rosette's darting slowed. Palmer moved to a corner of one of the buildings. The sight of the familiar blond head made his eyebrows rise. "Adessi?"

The man spun, his hand going for his sword before the surprise on his face passed into recognition then relief then right back to surprise. "Tash? You're supposed to be dead."

Palmer frowned as he stepped fully around the building, not entirely certain how he was supposed to respond to that. "I am?"

"That's been the word around here."

"Well..." He looked himself over, holding his hands out to show that he was, in fact, alive. He glanced at the pack on Nico's back. "Are you going somewhere?"

A pinched look came over Nico's face. Rosette slipped around Palmer's legs and stared up at Nico, circling him slowly. He tensed but didn't otherwise move, keeping his eyes on Palmer. "You found the kid too."

"The Osamli had her." Palmer watched Rosette, but she didn't seem about to lash out. She actually looked fascinated, as though she couldn't quite figure out why she knew him.

"Great. So they might be able to set off a plague, then?" Nico finally glanced down at Rosette.

"What?" Palmer asked.

"That's what they're doing, right? Stealing your lot's powers?" Nico looked up again, crossing his arms. "That's why we apparently came here rather than staying in Venchia. Brier didn't think she could take them on."

Carmella's dramatic sigh sounded behind Palmer's shoulder. "So I am going to have to see her?"

Nico's eyes flicked to Carmella. "Ella, I heard tell you might be around."

"You heard right." Carmella strode forward, earning an unhappy hiss from Rosette but nothing else. "Though what, may I ask, are you doing down here if Signorina Chastain is up there?"

Nico took a moment before he asked Palmer, "How are your visions working?"

"Better than they were, but not as good as they could be," Palmer said. "Why?"

"I had a supposed oracle give me a prophecy. Was wondering if you agreed with her."

"What prophecy is that?"

Nico seemed to pick his words carefully. "Supposedly, I'm the most important person alive right now, with everything that's happening."

Palmer snorted. "Can't say I've gotten *that*."

Nico paused. "Nothing about me?"

Palmer shook his head.

"Can you check?"

Palmer released an exasperated breath but closed his eyes and searched his mind for anything he could find about Nico Adessi, keeping the blue-tinged parts of his visions pressed down. "You get married, apparently. Have a family." Palmer opened his eyes again. "Seems like a completely ordinary life, from what I can tell."

"And the world doesn't end?"

Palmer frowned at the way the tone of the question tipped up as though Nico was sincerely worried, but he shook his head again. "Not from what I see."

"I think you're *very* important, Nic, if it makes you feel better." Carmella placed a hand on his chest, voice teasing.

Nico rolled his eyes but then nodded once and turned back up the hill. "Why are we waiting around here, then? I think Brier very much needs to see you."

BRIER SAT AT THE LITTLE desk in the bright room that was the new Augarian library. Nico and Palmer had made it for her back when they were pretending that everything would be all right. *When someone actually cared.*

Brier pushed the self-pitying thought aside and pulled out the books she had taken from Orris Adessi's trunks. Instinct honed from growing up with a librarian father made her reach for the little stack of cards she had been using to record what they had saved from the much larger, much grander original Augarian library before she stopped herself. It didn't really matter how she was going to catalogue them—certainly not more than figuring out what else was in them. Going straight for the illuminated manuscript that had gotten them home, she flipped open the old cover and began scanning what was there. She had missed the faces on the opening pages last time she'd thumbed through, the ancient pantheon with the names written under them—some the same as the Augarian pantheon, some markedly different. Why the Augarian had seen fit to change some but not all, Brier would probably never know. It seemed people chose the gods they needed more often than worrying about what was true.

Truth... She studied the two-dimensional faces on the page, all eight of them staring back blankly at her. Kosmos could almost have passed for Palmer, if he had only been twenty years older with a beard, but she certainly looked nothing like the very stern, very *male* Chaos sitting on the opposite side of the page. Then again, her mother had apparently played host to Kosmos as well before the visions had driven her to take her own life. Brier rubbed the stone on her finger. The gods weren't exactly picky about what they looked like. She couldn't say why one had chosen her—the *real* her, some little girl caught in the middle of a battle.

Maybe it was the battle and not me at all. She turned the page as the door to the library opened.

"There you are." Nico's voice made Brier tense.

"Come to lecture some more?" She didn't look away from the book in front of her, letting her voice hold more disdain than she would have thought possible.

"No. I can't promise Tash won't, though."

Anger flared at the sick joke, and Brier snapped her head toward the door only to feel everything freeze as she found herself looking straight at Palmer—deeply tanned, face drawn, but undeniably him. And undeniably alive. She stood sharply enough that the chair overturned behind her, and she instinctively took a step back.

Palmer lifted a sheepish hand in something like a wave. "Hi, Bri."

"H..." She fought to get such a banal word out of her mouth in current circumstances. "Hi? *Hi?*"

Palmer moved a little closer. "I'm sorry. I—"

Brier heard the slap before she realized she had struck him, the contact making her hand sting. She curled it into a fist, feeling nearly as stunned as Palmer looked. "I'm..." *Sorry.* The apology caught in her throat. It felt fragile. Weak. "I thought you were dead." Her voice wobbled dangerously.

Palmer blinked, still looking a little shocked that he'd been slapped. "I... I heard. Gil—"

"I *felt* you die!"

His dark eyebrows furrowed in confusion. "You... what?"

"One second, I could feel you." She pressed her fist into the burning place above her diaphragm. "The next, you were gone. It was like you'd been torn away."

Palmer frowned before realization came over his expression. "The cuffs."

"What?"

"We were captured by some Osamli troops." Palmer motioned for her to follow him. "Adessi said you've seen them about."

Brier nodded, keeping a little more distance than was strictly necessary between her and the men even as she trailed after them, listening to Palmer's explanation of what had happened and the cuffs with some strange name that apparently could cut off their powers. Her mind started to drift as he began talking about the doctor who was the one studying them all. So it had been a good thing that they had left Venchia, if the Osamli not only could protect themselves from attacks but also had the ability to cut off their powers. Her powers had been getting harder to control sometimes, but the idea of being captured by an invading force with no protection whatsoever made her insides squirm.

"She's... not doing well"—the way Palmer glanced back at her made Brier tune back in—"so we left hers on."

She was about to ask who Palmer meant when he opened another door, and her eyes caught on the little blond blur all but throwing herself around the room. "Rosie!"

Rosette spun, staring wild-eyed.

"Brier, she's—" Palmer began before Rosette ran straight for Brier's legs, throwing her arms around Brier's skirts as well as she could manage.

"Oh, *piccola*." Brier crouched awkwardly to get on the girl's level.

Rosette didn't lift her head, mumbling something that was entirely lost in Brier's skirts as she held her tiny wrist out.

"That's one of the cuffs," Palmer explained as though Brier wouldn't have been able to come to that conclusion.

"Why's it still on her?" Brier glanced up as she rubbed the little girl's back.

"I told you, Bri. She isn't doing well. I—"

Rosette pulled back again, tears running down her dirty cheeks as she continued to murmur things Brier couldn't quite make out. Brier's mouth pinched, and she noticed the ugly raised scars running down Rosette's arm, as though she had been cut ritually, with the largest angry red circle in the center of her palm.

"Oh, Rosie." Brier took her hand. "Did they do this to you?"

Rosette nodded with some more mumbling before she fell back into Brier's skirts. Shock and horror morphed into anger, Brier suddenly feeling as though she could strike down the entire Osamli army—the entire Osamli *Empire*—by herself.

"Get it off her," Brier said through a clenched jaw.

"Brier, she can't control her pow—"

"I said, get it off her!" Brier snapped, anger crackling over her skin.

Palmer flinched more than when she had physically slapped him, but he fished some other piece of metal out of his pocket and lined it up with the little cuff on Rosette's wrist. With a snap, the metal fell off.

Rosette screamed into Brier's skirts, a wave of the little girl's energy—red-hot with anger—shooting out. Brier absorbed it all, keeping her arms locked around Rosette's back, rubbing light circles. "It's all right, *piccola*. It will be all right. Those bad men are going to pay. We'll make sure those bad men pay."

Nico finally spoke again. "How are we supposed to attack if they can—"

"I'll open up the ground under them." Brier seethed, lifting Rosette as she straightened, still rubbing comforting circles as though Rosette were a sobbing infant. "I'll crack the earth from here to their damned capital if I have to."

"Brier." Palmer held out a placating hand.

"Find out where they are." She didn't take her eyes off Nico. "Get me some sort of battle plan. I'm done running from them. The next time I see them, they're *going* to die."

Both men started to say something, but Brier couldn't calm the blood pounding in her ears long enough to hear as she swept out into the hallway, bringing with her the poor crying little girl whom she had failed to protect.

PALMER STARED OUT THE door, his skin still twitching at the lingering power in the air. He was somewhat surprised Brier had managed *that* much rage without bringing half the building down around her.

"She's been like that at least since I got back," Nico said.

"She took... all of Rosette's energy straight on." Palmer shook his head, trying to explain what he had just seen. "That's a lot of anger all at once."

"And her slapping you?" Nico crossed his arms, shifting his weight uncomfortably before he shook his head. "She killed two men today—one, apparently, without entirely meaning to. She's been going too far. Refusing to see reason. She's..."

"Out of control?" The familiar voice inside the room made Palmer turn. Cerise sat on the sill of a now-open window, her legs stretched out in front of her and ankles crossed. "Same thing happened with Marina once Goebel couldn't rein her powers in."

Palmer tensed. "She isn't Marina."

"A little more angry than enthusiastic about all that power, perhaps, but looks remarkably similar to me." Cerise kept her arms crossed, not moving.

Nico glowered. "Where the hell have you been?"

"Was going to head back to Ruhegipfel, see if Goebel had anything in his things about what to do if *this* happened." Cerise nodded toward the door Brier had gone through then stood and moved out of the way to show a dark-skinned woman with close-cropped hair standing just outside. "Seems I found myself an oracle instead. Perhaps we should go somewhere to speak, hmm?"

Palmer pressed his lips together but nodded, letting Cerise bring the woman in over the windowsill before leading them to a room farther down the hall. He took a seat at the low table, keeping his eyes on the woman. If he'd had any doubt before, the case in her hand quashed it.

"You're the woman from the Osamli camp. The one who stole that."

The woman cleared her throat as she placed the case on the table. "Yes, sorry. My vision told me it would be there for me to take. It didn't show you all." She took her own seat. "Delphi, by the way."

"Come all the way from Ouene." Cerise remained standing by the door. "Apparently, she and Nicolas have met."

Palmer glanced at Nico long enough to see him send Cerise a withering glare but then turned back to Delphi. "Why did you take our case?"

"Because of these." Delphi carefully took out the little vials of blood one by one. "My vision said we needed them, and I've learned to trust my visions."

Nico grumbled something under his breath.

Palmer kept his eyes on the vials. "Did your vision say why we needed those?"

"Because of this, I imagine." Cerise pulled out a long-bladed knife made of what looked like the same pale-silver metal as the Os-amli devices. She set it on the table.

Palmer studied it without moving to touch it. Slanted script ran up each side, just past the honed edge, before scrolling vines and other decorative designs filled the rest of the flat front. It had to be a ceremonial piece rather than a practical one.

"What's that?" Nico asked before Palmer could, sounding as though he was physically forcing the words out.

"The only thing in the world that can kill a god," Cerise said.

"From experience, I know there are plenty of things that can kill us." Palmer shook his head.

"Not kill the body." Cerise rolled her eyes. "*Obviously*, you can do that. I mean, Cay's been dead...what, three times now? This kills the actual god parts. Stops us from reincarnating. Ever."

Palmer suddenly felt the need to slink farther away from the blade. "How?"

"It's ancient," Delphi took over explaining. "Some say created during the first gods' war by divine instruction. Others say by men who believed the gods had become too powerful. Either way, once anointed, that is how you kill a god."

"We're *not* killing her," Nico groaned as though this were an old argument he'd had a dozen times.

"Her?" The meaning registered in Palmer's mind. "You want to kill Brier?"

"A little slow on the uptake today, are we, Kos?" Cerise cocked an eyebrow.

"Why would we do that?"

"You just saw her." Cerise motioned vaguely. "And that hasn't been the half of it. She's out of control. You leave her like this, the world is going to end."

"Tash is back." Nico motioned. "He'll talk her back down. *He's* not seeing the world ending."

"I mean no disrespect," Delphi said. "It's hardly my place to question a god, but... well, if he were strong enough to deal with all this, it wouldn't be a problem in the first place. He can't control her, can't balance her. And the stronger she becomes, the more his abilities will likely fail."

"Then why are *your* visions so crystal clear?"

"I serve Isnotra," Delphi said simply. "Not Kosmos."

Nico scoffed. "Of course."

"We have most of what we need," Delphi continued, looking back at the vials. "Before the blade will work, it must be anointed with the blood of the other seven gods—supposedly their show of agreement to kill one of their own. From what I can make of these"—she lifted one of the little glass bottles—"the Osamli already had blood from Heke, Discordia, Isnotra, and... well, Kosmos." She glanced at Palmer before motioning to Cerise. "We have Nankil's consent. That only leaves Astarte and Orcus."

"Both conveniently here in Latysia," Cerise added.

Nico snorted. "Even if we did decide we were going to do this, our dear deranged god of death would never agree to anything like this."

Palmer noted Nico didn't apparently see any trouble in bringing Carmella on board.

"It doesn't have to be willing consent," Cerise said. "Just means we need to cut the brat before actually using the blade. As long as they're in the same place, that wouldn't likely be difficult. Slice one. Stab the other."

"This is madness. I'm not listening to it." Nico moved for the door, sending Palmer a hard look. "I'm surprised you are."

Palmer shook his head, standing but not yet moving. "I'm just back. You think I might take the chance to talk to her before we jump right to... deicide?"

Delphi's dark eyes were sympathetic. "I've seen the future, signore. I've seen how all of this plays out."

"If you'd ever been inside my head, you'd know there are a hundred possible futures. Nothing is set in stone."

"As you say." Delphi seemed less than convinced, packing the little vials away as Cerise took the knife.

With that apparently settled for the moment, Palmer released a breath and turned for the hall as well.

Nico attacked before Palmer had gone a dozen steps. "You can't actually be considering any of that."

"No." Palmer sent the taller man a look. "That's why I was planning on talking to Brier now."

"Good. Because I'm having no part in that."

"Noted." Palmer rubbed his temples in an attempt to stave off the headache that was quickly building there. "If you'll excuse me, then..."

Nico looked at Palmer for another long beat before he turned on his heel and stalked off.

"Home sweet home..." Palmer murmured, not feeling any better being inside the Augarian Palace than he had when he'd left it.

Chapter Twenty

Brier's heart pounded in her ears so loudly she could no longer tell if Rosette was crying. She still didn't let the little girl go as she stormed down the hall toward her library. Whether the anger was due to Rosette's power or simply righteous, well-earned rage, Brier wasn't certain. She didn't care. Someone was going to pay. If she could pull on the energy crackling around her to make that happen, all the better.

Stepping through the door, Brier finally set Rosette down. "Wait there, all right, *piccola*? I just need to find something."

Rosette picked at her rough skirt silently.

"Then we'll get you something proper to wear too," Brier added, turning toward the books on her desk. If they had told her how to open the portals to her home, they had to have something she could use against the army out there that their little metal devices wouldn't be able to stop. Ideally, she'd need to do it soon, because the army was days away, and she wasn't in the mood to wait.

She felt the cold gust a moment before Gil materialized inside the room.

"You found Discordia."

She looked at the red-haired boy.

"I felt the blast." Gil smiled at Brier quickly before studying Rosette. "What happened to her?"

"Those Osamli *asini*." Brier flipped the first book cover open to punctuate her insult. "They had her, a *little girl*, tortured, and now they are going to pay."

Gil's hands fluttered with excitement. "Pay how?"

"They're going to die. Can you read?"

195

Gil made a face as though Brier had asked him if he knew how to skin a kitten—though, knowing Gil, he likely would find the latter more to his taste.

With an annoyed grunt, Brier handed him the top book and pulled a different one for herself. "That one has pictures. Tell me if you see anything that looks promising."

"Promising for what?"

"Anything that will kill all of those *asini*."

"Once we have their metal things?"

"Before." Brier flipped the next cover open.

"But—"

"I can rip a hole in reality itself," Brier snapped. "I think I can find a way around some little toys, don't you? Find something for me."

Gil looked at her for a moment before a wide smile broke out. "Will do."

Brier tried sitting at the desk. Agitation made her stand again. She flipped page after page, sending glances over her shoulder at Rosette every minute or so, the little girl's blank, silent staring driving her forward.

After a while, Gil looked up. "How about this?"

"What is it?" Brier moved behind him to look.

"That looks like opening the abyss, yeah?" Gil pointed at a picture of a man standing on a plain, a jagged black crack opening in the sky above him. "That's something that happens in the myths."

Brier knelt next to him and quickly read the text below the picture. The words were as grandiose and legendary as elsewhere, but they did speak about Chaos calling on the abyss in the middle of battle, threatening to send all of reality back into the nothing from whence it had formed. "That would certainly work," Brier murmured, picturing all the little men with their tents outside Venchia being thrown up into nothingness. It was an attractive image. She continued reading and frowned. "It says he used stolen Kosmic powers."

She perhaps could bring Palmer on board, making him truly think about what must have happened to Rosette, but he was always so cautious, so righteous. It wouldn't be easy to get him to agree. *Not easy, but not impossible...*

"Don't you have some?" Gil asked.

Brier turned her frown to him.

"That's what everyone's talking about with that ring, right?" He nodded down at her hand. "From what I've overheard, at least."

Brier looked down at the red-flecked green stone sitting as benignly as ever on her finger. There was Clover somewhere inside it. As a specter of a former Kosmos, she only had a bastardized version of Palmer's powers, perhaps, but Marina's had done just as good a job of signing Goebel's death warrant as Brier's would have managed.

"I'd have to find a way to get to them," she said, thinking out loud.

"Well, you can rip reality itself..." Gil smiled.

Brier nodded slowly. *Definitely an option.*

"Brier?" Palmer's voice made her start.

Her head jerked up to spot him standing in the doorway. She snapped the book shut on instinct. "What?"

"Hey, you're alive," Gil said.

Palmer's face darkened. "No thanks to you."

"I told you to run." Gil shrugged before addressing Brier again. "Are we going to—"

"We'll talk later," she answered though she didn't take her eyes off Palmer.

"But—"

She flicked Gil a glare she had to imagine Cerise would be proud of, daring him to challenge her.

Gil sighed but mumbled, "Fine," and shot off for gods knew where.

Silence fell back over the library as Brier looked up at Palmer from where she was kneeling. She glanced at Rosette to find the little girl still staring blankly at her lap. Brier released a tense breath. "Yes?"

"I... we didn't really get a chance to talk."

"And whose fault is that?" She went back to her books.

"Bri, you know I couldn't just leave Peo—"

"There are more important things to worry about right now than whatever happened with you and that woman, don't you think?"

"Nothing *happened*—"

"Palmer." She finally snapped her eyes to him. "I. Don't. Care. All I care about right now is making those *animals* pay for whatever they did to that poor little girl." She pointed at Rosette.

Palmer glanced where Rosette was sitting, a pained expression moving over his face, before he brought his eyes back to Brier. "I understand, Bri—"

"Do you?"

"Of course I do." An annoying level of sincerity dripped off his words. "How do you think I felt when I saw what they'd done to her? I wanted to blast them myself."

Brier paused. So even if Palmer was being his standard, infuriating level of calm, there was perhaps a chance. He understood what the men out there deserved. "You'll help me, then?"

Palmer shifted awkwardly from foot to foot before he finally stepped forward. "Help how?"

"Help me kill them."

Palmer flinched. "Brier—"

"You don't think they deserve it?"

"Whether or not they do, I don't think you should be the one to do it."

Irritation sparked over her skin. Brier did her best to tamp it down, knowing it wouldn't help her cause at all. Palmer was always so cautious. With the first sign of her powers coming out, he would want to have her sit with him in a room and work out what was happening and what they could do to *fix it*. But caution wasn't what they needed right now, and she certainly didn't need to be *fixed*.

"And why is that?" she asked.

"You aren't a killer."

She pushed herself up off the ground. "How would you know what I am?"

"I know *you*."

"You left me!" All the frustration and anger of the past weeks came rushing out. "You left me and let *that* happen to Rosette, all because you have to be the great savior of humanity. Bunch of street thugs? Better get them fed. Stupid girl throwing a hissy fit? Better go wander off and nearly get myself killed! Are you ever going to do what's best for *us*?"

Palmer gripped the side of his trousers, some cracks satisfyingly beginning to show in his calm exterior. "I've *always* done what's best for us."

"You've always done what you think is *right*. There's a huge difference, especially when you're taking humanity's side over your own."

Palmer released an incredulous breath. "You don't think we're a part of humanity?"

"We're gods," Brier said. "I've had to learn to be one. It's likely time you grew up and did too."

"Learn to be one by killing people, you mean?"

"The ones who deserve it." Brier nodded.

"Like Gully? Did he deserve it?"

The question dug in straight to Brier's stomach. *They've been talking about me.* There had been plenty of people there when Gully died, but she had to assume that Nico had been the one to tell everyone about it. They'd been talking about her for months, after all—having their secret conversations and deciding what was apparently best for her without ever once thinking to bring *her* in on it.

She spoke through a locked jaw. "I gave him the chance to step down."

"And then killed him when he didn't?"

Brier shrugged, keeping her face more indifferent than she felt. "It's one way to get people to listen to you."

"You don't mean listen—you mean make people afraid of you."

"That's not the same thing?"

Palmer held her eyes, shaking his head. "This isn't you, Brier."

"Perhaps it's who I always should have been," Brier returned. "I've done what I've had to. Nothing more. Maybe if I'd started taking care of things myself to start with, we wouldn't be in this mess at all."

"We'd just be surrounded by a pile of bodies."

"Better theirs than ours." She turned back toward the book on the floor.

"Brier." Palmer caught her wrist to stop her.

An unpleasant jolt went through her. Instead of soft and healing, Palmer's power shot straight for her chest as though it were trying to bury itself deep inside her. She jerked away. "Don't touch me."

Palmer glanced from his hand to Brier then back. "Bri—"

"Are you going to help me or not?" She picked up the book and placed it on the desk, careful to keep her eyes in front of her.

"Bri, there's something wrong with—"

"There's nothing wrong with me!" Her voice came out far shriller than intended. She cleared her throat and continued in a much more measured tone. "Now, you can help me or get out of my way. Your choice."

"I'm not going to let you kill people, Bri." Palmer took a few steps closer to her.

Brier's palms tingled as irritated purple energy tried to flare. She clenched her fists. "You think you can stop me?"

He paused before saying, "It's what I'm supposed to do, isn't it? Balance you."

"Because you're so good at that." The swirling purple energy flared to life, and Brier lifted her hands so she wouldn't damage the book.

"Brier, stop." Palmer held his palms out placatingly, his eyes glued to her hands.

"Why?" She turned to face him. "You can do that for me, right?" She let the energy flare brighter. "Go ahead. Stop me."

"Brier," he repeated, warning tone in his voice.

She brought her hand closer to a mostly empty bookshelf. "Go on. You're going to stop me from killing a bunch of animals who deserve it, so certainly you can stop this."

"You're upset. You have a right to be—"

She blasted the top off of the wooden shelf, not willing to hear whatever mind-numbing platitudes he was going to attempt. "That's one. Think you could manage it before two?"

"Bri—" he started before she sent out a second blast.

Gold energy shot through his hands, curling around Brier's like a net. It held for a moment, keeping the purple swirling inside, before the netting snapped. The purple reached the shelf, and wood splintered, the purple dissolving all the small pieces before they could hit anyone in the room.

Brier held Palmer's eyes, finding herself less moved by the confused worry behind them than she would have imagined. "You're not going to stop me," she said, voice level. "So you can either stop prancing around, playing at being humanity's champion, and help me, or you can get out of my way."

"And if I don't?" he asked.

"I'll get you out of my way." The words came out before Brier could think about them. "I'm *finished* letting people use us, capture us, *hurt* us." She pointed at Rosette, who hadn't moved a muscle through it all. "I can end it, and I will."

"The Osamli?"

She nodded, flipping through the book in front of her, though she was careful to stay away from the page Gil had found. "That's what I already should have done, isn't it? All of *this* mess has been to save me from just wiping them off the map. I can still do that."

"Even if you could," Palmer said slowly, in the careful, placating tone that was already quickly beginning to grate on her, "that wouldn't be good for you."

"How would *you* know what's good for me?"

"I know you, Bri. And how you're acting..."

"How am I acting?"

"Honestly?" he said. "A little out of control. You killed someone today?"

A pang of conscience moved through her. She pushed that down as well. "You're sounding like Nico."

"So we're *both* worried about you, then."

"You shouldn't be."

"Are you certain of that?"

"I've done what I need to do!" Brier slammed the book shut and faced him head-on. "You left. You disappeared and left me there to deal with everything alone. I've done what I've had to do. *Only* what I've had to do. And you have no right to judge me for it."

"I'm not judging y—"

"Please," she scoffed. "All you do is judge people." She added a mocking whine to her voice. "That's wrong. We shouldn't do that. We can't..." She shook her head, holding her arms out. "You know what I learned while you were away? We're gods. We can."

"We can't just do *anything*." Palmer moved closer to her. "There has to be some sort of balance."

She flexed her hand, letting the bright-purple energy swirl over it. "Then balance me," she challenged, staring him down. "Can you?"

He looked at her palm warily. "Brier..."

"Go on." She moved her hand over the edge of the desk, palm down, the energy building.

"Brier." He stepped forward and grabbed her wrist.

Gold energy built at the touch, stinging her. She sucked in a breath but pushed through it, sending all of her irritation straight down toward the ground. The edge of the desk exploded with a resounding crack, sending wooden splinters flying through the air.

She pulled her hand free as the heady buzz of energy lingered over the dust floating in the air. "Seems you can't. So help or leave. Your choice."

Palmer looked at her another moment, expression unreadable, before he turned on his heel and left the library. Brier sucked in and exhaled, his departure making it a little easier to breathe. She returned to her desk and opened the book.

The cold cloud flew back in. "You always make me leave before the good stuff," Gil whined, crossing his arms as he looked at the carnage of the shelves.

"Well, you're going to get to help with this one." Brier stood again, pulling the ring off of her finger to study it. "We need to get the power out of here."

Without looking at him, Brier could feel the boy smile.

PALMER RUBBED HIS TEMPLES, trying to ignore the burn in his hand that hadn't faded after nearly an hour. Brier was upset about Rosette. She had every right to be. *He* was upset about Rosette, but never before had she managed to outdo him like that. Even when she had entirely lost control in the first battle they had fought in the Augarian, he had been able to rein her back in. He'd had Goebel's help, but still...

Not only could he not stop her powers, but they had hurt him as well. The Osamli must have done something to him. His powerlessness was the lingering effect of those stupid cuffs, perhaps. But whatever had happened, it wasn't a good sign.

The door to the room opened, and Palmer dropped his hands, finding a dark-haired woman standing there.

"Oh," she said. "I didn't know anyone was here."

Palmer could not find the energy to divine who she was. "Have we been introduced?"

"Not yet. I don't think Nicodemo is ready to see me again yet."

Palmer pulled his eyebrows together, not certain he had ever heard anyone call Nico by his full name, outside of Brier when she was really annoyed at him. "Palmer Tash."

"I know." She moved farther into the room. "I'm Lauretta. Suora Lauretta if you stand on formality."

That didn't clear up Palmer's confusion. "You're an anchoress?"

"I came with Delphi." Lauretta moved to the half-broken step Palmer was sitting on. "May I?"

Palmer nodded, watching the woman closely. There hadn't been any anchoresses at the Augarian temple—as a pantheon, the Seers had seen to the supposed needs of the gods rather than being an order pledged to a specific deity—but Suora Lauretta didn't look like any of the anchoresses he'd seen elsewhere in his life. "You served the Temple of Isnotra?"

She nodded. "Though I have to admit it's nice to have the chance to get away."

Palmer pressed his lips together. He'd be more than happy to have the chance to get away from everything happening in the Augarian. "You're avoiding Adessi?"

"Not avoiding," she said. "Just waiting for him to need me."

"Need you?"

"It's not an easy thing, hearing that you're going to have to kill someone you care about. Delphi asked me to help him through it—or at least do my best."

Palmer felt his face twitch. "So you believe he is going to have to kill her?"

"It's what Delphi says. And I've never known Delphi to be wrong."

"There's no one future." Palmer looked straight ahead, studying the cracked mosaic on the far wall, the tile looking far too new to be so damaged after as long as he had spent in Venchia. "I should never have left—I see that now—but I *know* Brier, and that wasn't her. Once she's calmer, I can find some other way to get through to her."

"You believe we'll have the time? It doesn't sound like the Osamli are far."

There has to be. Palmer kept that thought to himself, forcing his voice to sound more confident than he felt. "I'll be able to."

"By doing what?" Lauretta asked, sounding genuinely curious rather than accusatory.

Palmer released a heavy breath. "I'll work it out once I get rid of this headache."

"Do you get those often?"

Palmer shrugged. "I never really wanted to use my powers much before. It's difficult to at this point, I suppose." He looked at her. "Is there a reason I'm telling you all this?"

"Most people want to talk things out, I find. There are just few friendly ears around to actually listen." Lauretta gave a quick smile.

"I, personally, have had a lot of experience being a friendly ear. It was most of what I did at the temple."

"No star charts?"

"Star charts?" she asked.

"That's what they mostly had me doing as an acolyte."

Lauretta laughed lightly, resting back on her hands. "A god as an acolyte. That seems…"

"Ironic?"

"Ironic yet fitting, I'd say," she said, squeezing his arm lightly. "Gods tend to find their ways into temples one way or another."

"Brier tends to end up destroying temples." The shell of the Augarian temple and rubble of Venchia's temple passed through his mind. Both had been more Orris Adessi's fault than Brier's, of course, but the closest thing Brier ever had to a temple was her library—and even that she was starting to destroy.

A thought came to him. He didn't have Goebel to help train him, but the Augarian library, even just what was left of it, had to have thousands of years of knowledge still in it. If he could just find the right book, it was possible he'd be able to pinpoint something that he could use to help Rosette. And once he did that, he would possibly be able to take Brier off the warpath.

He stood sharply before looking down at where Lauretta was still sitting. "If you'll excuse me, I just realized there's something I need to do."

Lauretta nodded, not seeming in the least bit perturbed at the sudden change. He had to assume the kindly, placid expression was something else she had developed after years at her temple. He left her and strode across the room and out into the hallway.

After months wandering ruins and the countryside, he should have been glad to be back in a real, if damaged, building. As little as he'd wanted his life in the Church, the Augarian had been his home for nearly a decade and a half. As he maneuvered through the palace, though, it felt far from homey. Something in the air felt heavy—not just Brier's powers, but something else as well. Carmella, Cerise, Gil, Rosette, Brier... perhaps there were simply too many deities in one place, too much energy for one little walled city to handle. It certainly hadn't felt that way when just he, Brier, and Rosette were there.

He turned the corner and had to stop short not to collide with Nico. Palmer hesitated for a second before shaking his head and moving forward. "You should probably come with me."

"Why?" Nico shot him a suspicious look.

"I don't know Brier's coding system, so I'll need help finding the books I need."

Nico frowned but followed all the same. "We're in the middle of a war, and you want to go do research?"

"You have a better idea, I'm more than happy to hear it."

Nico didn't look any more pleased, but he remained silent, trailing Palmer through the halls to the little library. From a distance, Palmer didn't feel Brier inside, but he still opened the door carefully and glanced around to make sure that they were alone before stepping through. He couldn't say what exactly he thought he was going to find, but it seemed best to avoid Brier when she was so tightly wound about Rosette.

"So what are we looking...?" Nico stepped in after him, trailing off as his eyes hit the desk. "What the hell happened there?"

"What do you think?" Palmer moved to the little card catalogue Brier had been putting together before everything else happened. He hoped something would pop out at him.

"She..." Nico shook his head before turning away from the desk toward Palmer. "Shouldn't you be stopping that?"

"That's what I'm trying to do." Palmer continued to flick through the little pieces of paper, each with Brier's neat handwriting and numbers that no doubt made sense to her.

"Reading's going to fix your powers?"

The words were sarcastic, but they did make a point. "Maybe," Palmer said. "See if you can find anything about powers and healing or anything like that."

"*Anything like that.* Very specific instructions."

Palmer didn't bother to respond, continuing to look at each little card. Even with everything happening, he had to be a little impressed. Between the fire and dealing with Clover and Marina in her head, Brier had still managed to put together a proper library.

"Should I bother asking how it went?" Nico crouched by the desk, gathering the papers scattered around it.

"She's upset about Rosette."

"She wasn't when she killed Gully."

Palmer shook his head. He'd have to deal with one thing at a time. "Our oracle brought an anchoress."

Nico looked up from his spot near the desk. "You've met Lauretta?"

Palmer nodded, picking out a card that looked promising. "She seemed to know you well."

"I'm surprised I haven't seen her already," he grumbled. "She's barely left me alone since..."

Palmer twisted as Nico trailed off. "What is it?"

Nico stood, looking between an old book and one of the papers he had gathered. "What...?"

Palmer stepped up to him, looking at the foreboding illustration paired with a number of scribbles, nothing like the neat script cataloguing the library. Pain shot across his skull, pounding directly behind his eyes as a vision ripped through him, darker, more powerful than anything he had managed in months. Tents on the hills around Latysia. Brier on the roof, barely looking like herself as purple energy surrounded her, so dark it nearly looked black. The power shooting up until it ripped a jagged crack in the sky—in the universe itself...

the vision was sucked away, leaving Palmer panting, resting against the side of the desk that remained standing.

"What?" Nico watched Palmer cautiously, his eyes sliding up and down as though he were worried Palmer was going to grow a second head—or perhaps explode.

Palmer grabbed for the book, looking at the picture again before reading the text above it. *Chaos calling on the abyss.* He swore under his breath.

"*What?*" Nico repeated, annoyance leaching into the word this time.

Palmer forced himself to swallow, not able to pull his eyes away from the book in front of him. "She's going to destroy the world."

Chapter Twenty-One

Brier picked her way through the dirt and debris, the smell of burned paper still heavy in the air as she made her way through what had once been where Orris Adessi's alchemists had worked. Why Orris had decided to place it under the old Augarian library, other than simply to mock her, Brier had no idea, but with each step kicking up ash from what had once been her father's books, every bad memory she'd ever experienced was trying to emerge. From the way Rosette had pressed herself into Brier's skirts, clutching them as they moved, it seemed the little girl was feeling the same.

"Why are we here?" Gil looked around, as chipper as ever.

"If we're going to find a way to extract power, this is likely the place to do it." Glass crunched under Brier's foot, and she realized she was next to the tube Orris had locked her inside during the last Augarian battle. Her stomach twisted enough that she nearly had to pause, but somehow, she found the motivation to keep going.

"It's all burnt," Gil said, oh so helpfully stating the obvious.

Brier set the book she had taken from Venchia down on a table that had somehow made it through the fire. She pulled the ring back off her finger. "Look for a brace or something that can hold this." She rolled the band of the ring back and forth between her fingers.

Gil nodded and began kicking ash off of things haphazardly. Brier rolled her eyes but turned toward Rosette, gently easing the fabric out of the little girl's hands before kneeling to be on her level. "You wait right here, all right, Rosie? You can let me know if there's any trouble."

Rosette nodded and found a spot along the wall, poking at things along a low table. Brier watched to make sure there was nothing dangerous that Rosette might hurt herself with then started to look around.

"Will this work?" Gil picked up some sort of vise.

It was a little big, but it would work. Brier motioned for Gil to bring the vise to the table in front of her and pinched the band of the ring between the two plates. The setting twisted in a way that said the soft gold couldn't hold up to the clamp, but the gold wasn't the important part.

She let her hand drop from the vise and stared at the green stone staring back at her. The red flecks inside it seemed brighter than normal, glinting in the ash-filled room.

Gil looked at Brier then at the stone then back up again. "Now what?"

Brier chewed on the inside of her cheek. The last little niggling voice, asking if she was doing the right thing, tried to find purchase. She released a sharp breath, forcing the voice away as she flipped the book open, looking for Orris Adessi's writing in the margins of the page. She was *certainly* doing the right thing. Protecting them. Ridding the world of those who hurt them. What true god didn't smite those who wronged her?

"They were trying to pull powers out with some sort of... device in here. We need to find that."

"You don't think it burned?" Gil frowned.

"It was metal. I think." *I hope.* She hadn't been paying the most attention to what Orris Adessi was using when he was trying to steal her powers, since she'd been in the process of... well, dying. But the crude drawing with Orris's notes certainly looked like metal wires connected to a larger box. "It should look like this."

Gil continued to frown as he looked at the page, but then he went back to making his way through the ash, kicking up half-burned book pages as he went. Brier clenched her jaw, doing her best to look around the space without facing any of the memories there.

She had a purpose. It was the only reason she had decided to go through the tunnels back to that place. She wasn't going to give up simply because there were bad thoughts lingering there. She began making her way through the ash, kicking with a bit more finesse than Gil to uncover the bits and baubles on the ground that had survived the fires.

After what had to be a quarter of an hour, Gil released a heavy sigh. "I don't see anything."

Brier pressed her lips together, having to admit she hadn't been any more successful. Perhaps she'd been wrong. Perhaps they hadn't been wires but bits of glass that had cracked or wood or something else that wouldn't have survived everything that had happened to the room. She turned over ideas in her mind, trying to think of what she could do if the device was gone.

A tug on Brier's skirts took her out of her thoughts, and she looked down to meet Rosette's large blue eyes. Silently, the girl lifted a jumble of wires with two flat pads on one end. They were missing the rectangular receptacle from the picture—likely the wooden box that Orris Adessi had brought with him to Venchia, or at least one like it—but that was certainly what they'd been looking for.

"Good job, Rosie." Brier smiled, taking the jumble from the little girl. "Let's get to work."

PALMER LOOKED UP AS the raven flapped in through the window and quickly shifted to human form. The uncharacteristically serious expression on the woman's face gave him the answer before Cerise spoke.

"No sign of Cay, the kid, or the brat as far as I can see. Wherever they've gone, you can't see them by air."

Palmer felt the strong urge to swear. After finding scribblings in the library, they had searched every inch of the palace that was still reachable past rubble and hadn't found Brier, Rosette, or Gil. With Cerise not spotting anything in her search, there was no saying where the three had gone.

"Did you look outside the walls too?"

Cerise nodded. "But there are a lot of buildings out there. Many things I can do, but seeing through walls is not one of them."

Pinching the bridge of his nose, Palmer turned toward the rest of the people in the room—Peony, Carmella, Nico, Delphi, and her anchoress—wishing they would stop looking at him at least long enough for him to think. He addressed Nico. "Is it possible they're in one of the hidden passageways? There are more of those, yes?"

"Half of them are destroyed." Nico shook his head, his expression as dire as everyone else's. "I've gone through the rest that I know of. She's not anywhere we used to hide."

"So you're saying we should have just stabbed her when we had the chance." Carmella continued to pout from her chair, arms crossed.

Palmer sent her a stern look before addressing the rest of the room. "We have at least until the Osamli troops get here. They're the ones she wants to pay."

"By destroying all of us," Carmella interjected.

"If we can just find her before they arrive"—he spoke over her, motioning between Nico and him—"we can talk to her."

"Last time you talked to her, she decided she was going to destroy the world." Carmella stood.

"It's already decided," Delphi said before Palmer could defend Brier or himself. "We don't have another choice than the dagger."

"There's *always* another choice," Palmer snapped.

"Yeah, and ours are: one, we stab her with that thing"—Carmella motioned to the dagger on the table between them—"two, a lot of people die, and *then* we stab her with that thing, or three, we let her do this, and then she's dead anyway along with the rest of us. Great choices."

Palmer released a deep breath through his nose, pretty certain that with the irritation building through his shoulders, he would be close to blasting walls apart if he had the ability. He flexed his hands then looked at the one with which he'd grabbed her, the skin still red and angry. He held it up. "Even if I wanted to—and that is a very large *if*—I can't do anything to her right now. That's what happened the last time I touched her."

"That's why it has to be him." Delphi looked at Nico, her voice calmly matter-of-fact. "That's why I've been saying it has to be him."

Nico's jaw twitched, and he turned for the door. "I'll check the passageways again."

"Nic!" Carmella called after him, looking ready to stamp her foot. Delphi whispered to Lauretta, and the anchoress quietly slipped away after him. Carmella blew out a long breath but re-frained from any foot stomping. "Could we at least get that thing ready just in case? We need all our blood on it, yes?"

"I have the vials," Delphi said, keeping her eyes on Palmer. "But it's up to you."

Palmer wasn't certain if she meant a general "you" or him specif-ically. Either way, he didn't feel any better. Lips pressed into a thin line, he met Delphi's dark eyes. "We'd still need Gil's before it would work at all? Even if the rest of us... did it?"

Delphi nodded, leaning forward to point at the seven circles in the scrollwork along the blade. "All seven of those need to be full be-fore it works. Otherwise, it's just a knife. It would kill a human—a host—but not a god."

Palmer stared at it for what felt like an eternity, the entire room remarkably silent for once as he worked everything out in his mind. No matter how many times he tried to play out options, the only image that returned to him was the vision from the library. The crack in the universe. The death of everything *he* was supposed to protect. *Just because we have it doesn't mean we'll have to use it,* he argued with himself, though the justification didn't make the churning in his stomach retreat. It was a step toward the worse, a step toward killing a woman he would certainly have died for, and no weak justification would make that any better. He still forced himself to nod.

"Finally!" Carmella exclaimed, stepping forward and offering her left hand. "You need my finger or something?"

Delphi nodded, more fittingly somber than Carmella. Picking up the dagger, the oracle took Carmella's hand in hers and pricked Carmella's finger with the tip. As the blood touched metal, a wave of rosy light climbed up the scrollwork, flowing into the first little circle on the side before it died off, leaving what looked like a pink-enamel dot.

Delphi looked at Palmer, but he shook his head. "Do the others first."

Delphi didn't argue, turning to Cerise instead. Her face still hard and serious, Cerise held her hand out. With another prick of the finger, a silver dot climbed into the next circle. Delphi took the little vials from the pack and silently added them one by one. Heke, green. Isnotra, blue. Discordia, red.

With five of the seven circles full, she looked up at Palmer again, holding his vial. "I can do it with this. You don't have to—"

"No," he said. If he was the one condoning this, he couldn't attempt to salve his own guilt by pretending that vial would make him innocent of it. He could perhaps find some other way than having to use the blasted dagger, but if not, he was still signing her death warrant. He would have to live with that, whatever way his blood hit that dagger. He held out his good hand. "Do it."

Giving him a sickeningly apologetic look, Delphi moved up to him and lowed the blade to his pointer finger. The metal stung, feeling like ice shooting down into his veils for a split second before the flow of gold energy made its way up the scrollwork to take the sixth spot. Once Gil—Orcus—was added, it would be done. Palmer dropped his hand, the cut already healed by the time it reached his side.

Delphi looked at the side of the blade, something sadly resigned passing over her face before she carefully took hold of the blade and turned it so Palmer could take the handle. "It does have to be him." She nodded toward the door Nico had exited. "None of us will be able to get close enough to her... when it happens."

Palmer still had no idea how he would convince Nico to actually go through with it, but he took the handle and slid the blade into his belt with a nod.

Chapter Twenty-Two

Brier adjusted the pads on the stone, the connections big enough to cover the entire thing.

"Are you done?" Gil asked.

She hissed for him to be quiet.

"I just—"

"What part of 'Shh' was unclear?" Brier snapped, shooting him a glare before she stepped back and released a tense breath.

With only the scant guidance from the margins of the book, she was as much guessing what to do as following instructions—though perhaps that was for the best. Orris Adessi had gotten himself killed messing around with these things. She certainly didn't intend to let the same thing happen to her. She double-checked that the wires were secure in the glass cylinder she and Gil had found—hoping, since Orris had used a larger version to successfully hold her, it would work as well as a box—and then released a tense breath. It was now or never.

She nodded to Gil. "All right. Go."

Gil grabbed the metal handle of the crank and began to turn it. Slowly, energy began to crackle in the air, the vise shaking slightly before a mix of gold and purple light began to build in the cylinder.

Brier smiled. "It's work—"

The glass shattered, the energy shooting out with a loud crack. Rosette straightened from her place in the corner, and Gil jumped back with a mumbled exclamation. Brier frowned, looking around the room for something else that could work as a container.

Two more glass vials suffered the same fate, and anything else she brought close to the light dissolved. Brier bit down a more colorful curse than she should say with Rosette in the room. She pressed the heels of her palms into her temples.

"Should we try putting it in you?" Gil still studied the wires.

"What?" Brier said, dropping her hands again.

"You can hold onto stronger power than that. If you just need some Kosmic power..."

Brier exhaled sharply. "I've had both of them in my head before. I don't need that again." And everyone who'd had Clover and Marina in their heads had died before they managed to get in there—Brier in that tube and Orris after he had used that box in Venchia. The thought registered. *Except Peony.* Peony had only been unconscious when Clover had been inside her head, and even Palmer had said Peony had a connection to the ring. "Maybe she actually could be useful," Brier mumbled, more to herself than anyone else.

"Who?" Gil asked.

A loud boom rumbled through the ground, for once not Brier's doing. She looked up at the hole that still led into the shell of the old library above them.

"What was that?" Gil frowned.

She glanced at Rosette. Though the girl was tense, she hadn't moved from her spot. Brier turned back to Gil. "Go find out. I'll meet you back in the palace."

Gil lifted his eyebrows, questioning, but when she didn't offer more of an explanation, he dissolved into his dark cloud and shot off through the open ceiling.

At least he's obedient. Brier pursed her lips before she undid the vise and gathered up the misshapen ring and wires. "Come on, Rosie. We're going to go find our good friend Peony." She offered her free hand, and Rosette took it, letting Brier lead her back out into the tunnels.

PALMER TAPPED HIS HAND on his thigh, the dagger at his hip feeling heavier and heavier each moment he wore it. Just as he was considering taking it off and leaving it somewhere to come back for later, he heard Nico's voice down the hall. A jolt of hope shot through Palmer's chest, and he half jogged to the doorway down the hall, but it wasn't Brier. Nico and the anchoress were talking, calm sympathy on Lauretta's face as Nico glared. Palmer's hope sputtered out.

"No luck?" Palmer couldn't bring himself to care if he was interrupting. Two pairs of brown eyes turned toward him.

"A moment maybe?" Nico grumbled at Lauretta when she didn't move.

She sent him a sympathetic look that only seemed to annoy him further and slipped out into the hall.

Palmer watched her until she was out of sight then looked back at Nico. "Everything all right?"

"Just her talking about my destiny. Again." Nico shook his head. "The oracle apparently made me her project, and she takes that annoyingly seriously."

"Your destiny is killing...?"

Nico's eyes narrowed as though he were daring Palmer to finish that sentence.

Palmer pulled the dagger from his belt and held it out. "You should still probably have this."

Nico glanced at it but made no move to take it before his narrowed eyes came back up to Palmer.

"I don't intend to use it," Palmer said. "But if worse comes to worst..."

"You're actually considering it?"

"I'm saying we need to find her *now* so we don't have to consider it, but... it's my job to protect the world. As much as I want to keep ignoring that, I can't."

Nico continued to glare at him.

"It just needs Gil's blood." Palmer forced himself to keep the dagger held out. "Just in case."

Nico's eyes slid back down to the blade, staring at it as though he was half hoping he could set it on fire with his mind. He looked up again. "Could you do it? Kill her?"

Palmer's jaw locked, making him fight to speak. "I don't think we'll have to."

"But you have that ready."

Palmer couldn't argue with that.

"So could you do it—not just hand that thing off but actually kill her, all powers aside?"

"No," Palmer admitted. "I couldn't."

"Then how do you expect me to?"

All of the arguments Palmer could think of were insultingly trite compared to that question. He ended up with, "You said you were done before you left Venchia."

"Because that's what she wanted." Nico shook his head as if he couldn't believe he had to explain it. "*Because* I care about her. Not because I don't. Everything I've done has been to do what's best for her. Can you say the same thing?"

The fight they'd had before he'd left flashed through his mind. Brier wanting him to stay. Him insisting on going. The weight in his stomach grew at the thought that everything wouldn't have gone quite so wrong if he'd listened to her, yet he knew he couldn't have. As awful as everything had turned out, going after Peony was still the right thing to do. He couldn't have given up on her any more than he could have given up on the universe. And as much as he had always pushed that part of his powers away, as much as he wanted the world to just be him and Brier and Rosette, he couldn't. He was Kosmos, and for the moment, that took precedence. Perhaps it always had, and he had simply been lucky that what was best for Brier had been what was best for the world—keeping her happy, settled...

"No." He forced the word out. "No, I can't."

Nico scoffed, turning away but not yet moving for the door.

"You have to take it," Palmer said, the weight only growing heavier, the dread in the pit of his stomach harder, the longer they talked. "I'm not giving up on her—you know I'm not—but you have to."

Nico's back rose and fell as he sucked in a breath then released it, but he otherwise didn't move.

"Ades—"

A loud rumble cut Palmer off before he could finish the name. He looked off in the direction it seemed to come from.

"Brier?" Nico finally turned to look in the same direction.

Palmer's eyebrows pulled in. Something about the sound was not quite right. "I don't think so..."

He heard the flapping before he saw Cerise take form by the door. She moved across the space with quick, determined steps. "You know how you said we didn't really have to worry until those troops got here, Kos?"

The weight in his stomach turned into a full churning.

"Well, look outside. I think we really have to worry."

Chapter Twenty-Three

"How could they have gotten here so quickly?" Palmer hurried up the staircase after Cerise, heading for the roof.

"Same way they could be invisible, I'd guess," Nico grumbled, a step behind them.

"Don't know what to tell you, Kos," Cerise said at the same time, speaking over Nico, as she threw the door open and stepped onto the roof.

Palmer glanced around the space, half expecting to see Brier already standing there as she had in his vision, but other than Nico, Cerise, Delphi, Lauretta, and him, the roof was empty. The flat blocks around the edge were still the way they had been the night he'd saved Brier from falling over... he forced his thoughts back to what was most important at that moment.

Palmer moved to where Delphi and Lauretta were looking out over the Augarian walls. "What are they doing?"

"Nothing so far," Lauretta said, pointing out at the tents scattered along the hills outside of Latysia. "A few appeared, there was that sound, and now they're sitting there."

"Do we know if there are any more under those veil things?" Nico's eyes moved over the visible tents as though he were already working out some strategy.

"I don't think there's a way to," Lauretta said.

"They could be waiting for their friends up north," Cerise said.

"Why show their positions, then?" Nico shook his head. "They wouldn't be popping up if they didn't want us to know they're there for some reason."

"Maybe they're trying to get us to send out soldiers," Lauretta suggested.

"Whatever it is, we need to find Brier. Now." Palmer addressed Delphi. "No helpful visions, I take it."

She shook her head. "You?"

He didn't bother to answer that as he turned away from the edge. "Cerise, see what you can find from the air."

She raised an eyebrow.

"Try again," Palmer said.

Her expression didn't change, but she turned away and once again became the familiar raven.

"She was on the roof in my vision, so I'll stay here, try to keep her from coming up, and watch those tents." Palmer attempted to make a plan even as he spoke. "Adessi, check anywhere you think she could be, even the places you've looked before. I think Rosette had a hiding place in the throne room. They might be there."

Nico nodded and turned for the stairs, likely more than happy to get away before Palmer could argue for him to take the dagger again.

Palmer looked between Lauretta and Delphi before settling on the latter. "You have anything close to a vision, come tell me. Otherwise..." He tried to think of something more helpful they could do but ended up simply motioning after Nico. "Help him look."

The pair nodded and started for the stairs.

"If you see her"—Palmer held up his hand with a grimace—"don't try to talk to her. Just... get one of us." He motioned between himself and where Nico had gone. Brier might be angry with either of them, but their chances against her were higher than those of some women Brier didn't know.

They nodded again then disappeared back into the palace. Tapping his fingers irritably on his thigh, Palmer did his best to relax at least a little. There weren't as many tents on the horizon as there had been in his vision, but that was weak comfort. From what he could tell, the camp had been moving north toward Venchia when he'd gotten away, not south toward Latysia. Yet there the Osamli were, as if they'd simply been waiting for Palmer to reach the palace before making their presence known.

You're missing something, a little voice at the back of his skull said.

Then why don't you tell me what?

Nothing answered him. Annoyed, Palmer tried to pull up any vision other than the one he'd had about Brier, but nothing but blue-tinged pain shot behind his eyes.

Of course. Why be helpful now? Palmer pinched the bridge of his nose until the pain passed then began pacing, moving to the walls to look at the tents then back to the door. He both wanted to see Brier and desperately hoped she wouldn't appear. Whatever was going to happen—or whatever *was* happening—Palmer couldn't imagine it was going to be good.

BRIER STOOD BY SOME of the scaffolding still in the grand hall, watching carefully as Peony wandered along the surrounding hallways. She appeared to be looking for someone—Palmer more than likely, if Brier knew Peony. Brier stroked Rosette's hair absentmindedly, taking comfort in the fact that Palmer seemed to have forgotten the woman yet again. It truly was remarkable that Peony hadn't said to hell with it and left. She'd managed to grow enough of a backbone once. Brier could only imagine what Palmer had said to get Peony back once again, but whatever it had been, it must have suited her purposes. Peony might actually turn out to be important after all.

The black cloud circled before landing at Brier's side. Checking to make sure Peony hadn't noticed, Brier grabbed Gil's arm as he rematerialized and pulled him deeper into the scaffolding.

"Did you find out what that sound was?" She spoke in a low whisper.

"There are tents out there. Like the ones that tried to catch me."

Already? A jolt went through her. She'd certainly thought that before the Osamli arrived, she would have more time to work out exactly how to do what she needed to do. But if they were in such a rush to die, she couldn't disappoint them.

She leaned forward enough to see where Peony had gone before addressing Gil. "Do you think you could knock her out without killing her?"

Gil's eyebrows furrowed. "I can't just kill her?"

Brier vaguely considered it, but that seemed foolhardy when she didn't know if the plan would work at all. And Palmer would no doubt *truly* lose his head if she did that. Even if he barely seemed to remember the woman existed a majority of the time, he wouldn't likely accept another death. Since those would be *wrong.*

Brier shook her head. "I just need her unconscious. Can you do that?"

"I don't know." Gil's mouth pursed. "I've never tried."

Rosette tugged at Brier's skirt, and Brier looked down to see the little girl pointing at herself.

Brier frowned. "You want to try something?"

Rosette nodded. Brier hesitated. She didn't care for the idea of Rosette getting more involved than was absolutely necessary.

Gil looked the girl over, his head cocked. "Let's see it, then."

Before Brier could speak, Rosette dashed out from their hiding place and ran forward. Peony started, turning toward the sudden movement. She began to say something, but before she managed a syllable, Rosette threw her arms around Peony's legs. A jolt moved up Peony's body, her eyes rolling back into her head as she crumpled, convulsing. Stepping back, Rosette turned to look at Brier and Gil.

"Good job, little sister," Gil murmured.

"I suppose that'll work." Brier moved out of the scaffolding before calling back to Gil, "Watch for anyone coming." She touched Rosette's shoulder with a quick smile. "You too, *piccola*. Let me know if you see anyone."

Rosette nodded quickly and rushed off to the entrance of another hallway that led into the great hall. Brier pursed her lips. She should have thought things through a little better and tried to get Peony an easier place to hide in, but with time being of the essence, *good enough* was going to have to do on all accounts today.

Peony's eyelids were still fluttering, but she otherwise seemed dead to the world. Whatever the Osamli animals outside the city had done to Rosette, the girl was obviously still in control of her own powers. Brier could take a little comfort in that.

Kneeling, she quickly set to work, placing the wires meant for a receptacle at Peony's temples before making sure the pads were where they were still supposed to be on the ring. She had no idea if the wires were meant to connect directly to a human body, but the alchemists had twice tried to suck her powers out with them. Of course, the act had killed her both times and killed Orris Adessi as well when he had tried moving the powers the opposite way, but again, it had to be good enough.

Focus on what's important, Brier told herself as she turned the little crank. The wires buzzed, Peony's body jerking slightly, though Brier couldn't see any of the purple or gold light. She kept turning, waiting for something to happen. Just as she began to think it wasn't working, Peony's nose wrinkled, her face moving as though she were trying to get used to it before her eyelids fluttered open.

"Ugh, this entire place feels like Clover..." She sat up, rubbing the wires away.

Brier hesitated, the irritated prickle at the back of her neck confirming her question before she asked it. "Marina?"

Peony's dark eyes snapped to Brier's face, narrowing venomously. "You never seem to die, do you? Boyfriend's been bringing you back still?"

"*You* never managed to kill me," Brier returned. "Is Clover in there?"

"Who wants to know?" Marina looked down over herself. "I have to say, much better body this time. Though..." She sighed heavily. "Really? You have us sharing three-ways again?"

So Peony was still alive.

"Clover is in there," Brier said.

"Of course she is." Marina shook her head to the side as though trying to clear water from her ear. "That's my punishment, isn't it? Always dealing with that righteous—"

Rosette's dramatic waving caught Brier's attention a moment before she heard Nico's and Lauretta's voices. Brier pushed herself up and grabbed Peony's thin arm. "Time to go."

"Who says I want to go anywhere with you?" Marina stumbled to her feet.

"Who says you have a choice?" Brier nodded for Rosette and Gil to follow, dragging Marina opposite from the direction of the voices.

For all the talk, Marina didn't fight Brier but let her lead. "Are you *still* avoiding Nico? Really, I tried to help you—"

"Nothing to do with that." Wherever she and Nico stood after Marina's *involvement* was yet another thing that didn't matter nearly enough to waste time with today.

"So you aren't running away from him right now?"

"Just avoiding unnecessary complications." Brier motioned for Rosette to pull open one of the secret passages in the wall to get out of sight. "He already thinks I'm going too far. I don't think he or Palmer would agree with what I'm doing."

Marina arched an eyebrow, the defiantly curious expression looking entirely wrong for normally mousy Peony. "And what is that, pray tell?"

"Ripping a hole in the universe to throw an army into."

Her other eyebrow lifted to join the first. "Well, listen to that. Seems I rubbed off more on you than I thought."

Gods, I hope not. Brier pushed away Marina's words before she could consider them. Rubble narrowed the passageway as she climbed, part of the stairs looking entirely impenetrable. With a quick wave, Brier cleared them and continued forward. "You wouldn't be here if I had any other choice."

Marina smiled. "You need my help?"

Brier scoffed. "Hardly. I need Kosmic power to do it, and Palmer isn't going to help me."

"You think Clover is? My Kosmos is as self-righteous as yours, just so much more incredibly whiny about it."

"I don't need her to agree," Brier said. In fact, she didn't need anyone to agree. "I just need her in there."

Marina studied the side of Brier's face much more closely than Brier was comfortable with. "Are you going to let me keep the body if I help you suck her out or whatever you plan on doing?"

"I don't need your help." Brier shook her head.

"But I imagine it would be a lot easier for you if I didn't let Clover up right now to stop you or run away to *your* Kosmos or what have you, wouldn't it?"

"I'm stronger than either than you."

Marina made a face that said she couldn't argue with that statement. "But all I'm asking for is the body. And from what I'm seeing up here, it doesn't like you very much—though it has had some *thoughts* about your boyfriend."

They hadn't made it halfway across the palace, and already, Brier was ready to blast Marina back to where she'd come from. "I don't need to hear those."

"*I* don't need to see them. Honestly, I truly don't see the appeal. Like I said, I *tried* to give you a push in the right direction, but—"

"Does she always talk this much?" Gil asked from farther back.

"You could have met a *very* different Chaos," Brier replied.

"Are you certain about that?" Marina cocked her head. "Ripping open a hole in the universe... sounds just like something I would have tried if I'd thought of it. Though Goebel's family didn't think to tell me about that power, for some reason."

An unhelpful pang of conscience went through her at Goebel's name. "He's dead, you know."

"Dominik?" Marina used his first name, which made sense. They had supposedly been in love at one point. Or at least, he had been in love with Marina. "Well, I assumed. Even he wouldn't have survived a straight hit like that."

"And that doesn't bother you at all?" Brier glanced back.

"Should it?"

"All right, I like parts of her," Gil said good-naturedly.

The entire exchange made Brier's insides start twisting, all the little niggling doubts emerging from the recesses of her mind. She wasn't Marina. She had never wanted to be Marina. And she certainly didn't want to be Gil. The callousness it took to end so many lives all in one pass—that wasn't who she used to be. Then Rosette nudged her way past Marina's legs so she could press herself into Brier's skirts—not at all like the freedom-loving little girl they'd once had to make sure didn't stray too far from them—and the anger all came rushing back full force. Was there another way to destroy the army out there without getting their little metal bracelets away from them? Possibly. Did she have time to figure one out? Not in the slightest. They'd made sure they were there to meet their fates. It was only fair that she oblige them.

With a few more waves to clear rubble, Brier made it to the hatch that led to the room. She pushed the panel up and stuck her head out for a second before ducking down again.

"What is it?" Gil asked.

"Palmer." Brier released a heavy breath. He would manage to be exactly where she didn't need him. She looked down at Rosette. "Do you think you could distract him, *piccola*?"

Rosette's frowning face tilted out of Brier's skirts.

"Just for a little bit? Long enough to get him off the roof?"

"Can't you just... knock him off the roof or something?" Gil shook his head. "There's no way he could stop you."

"We're not trying to kill *him*." Brier sent Gil a look before turning back to Rosette.

Rosette's frown had turned into an unhappy pout, as though she were loath to leave Brier's side, but she peeled away and slipped up through the hatch.

Marina watched for a moment before looking back at Brier. "Didn't she use to be more talkative?"

A rush of anger made Brier's skin tingle, but she forced it back down, doing her best to remind herself that she needed Marina—or needed Clover, which meant that Marina was part of the package—at least a while longer. Another rattling *boom* shook through the ground, making Brier question the integrity of the hidden stairwell.

"Is that our cue to go?" Marina asked.

Now or never. Brier nodded and pushed up the panel once again.

Chapter Twenty-Four

Another rattling boom echoed through the air, and Palmer froze then spun back around to look over the Augarian walls. More tents had appeared, popping up in little blue waves across the landscape as though they were forming out of thin air. Palmer gnashed his teeth. The scene looked more and more like his vision by the moment.

Scrubbing his face with a hand, Palmer tried to keep himself calm. It would all work out. It had to. Today was not the day the world was going to end, and if he had anything to say about it, it wouldn't be the day anyone died either.

Movement out of the corner of his eye made Palmer start. His head snapped toward it, and he frowned. "Rosie?"

Rosette stood a few steps away at the roof edge, staring at the tents.

"Rosie." Palmer walked toward her slowly. He wasn't certain where she'd come from, but that wasn't the most important thing at the moment. He held a hand out as he worked his way closer, as though she were a horse that was going to spook—or make half the city deathly ill—if he moved too quickly. "You shouldn't be up here. It's dangerous."

Rosette looked at him, her face impassive, before she turned back toward the tents. Her little shoulders tensed, and the energy in the air shifted.

"Rosie, no." Palmer felt his own powers try to flare to counteract Rosette's. "We're not doing that."

Rosette glared, the look dark enough that Palmer could believe that she wanted him in the ground. Holding his eyes, she slowly lifted her hand as though daring him to try to stop her.

"Rosie." He reached out to grab her.

She ducked, leaving Palmer grasping air as she ran for the stairs that led into the palace.

"Rosette!" Palmer turned and headed after her down the stairs. He made it to the first landing before he felt energy above him shift. He slowed. No one had passed them on the stairs...

He closed his eyes realizing what an idiot he was. Rosette had appeared from nowhere. There was another entrance to the roof... and he'd just left it. Sending a last look down after where Rosette had gone, he grimaced and turned back around. Rosette could start some serious havoc if she wanted, but she couldn't end the world. He ran back up the staircase.

Panting more from alarm than exertion, Palmer threw the door at the top of the stairs back open and saw Brier, Gil, and Peony standing by the far wall, which hadn't entirely been completed. He frowned at the odd grouping before calling, "Brier."

Three pairs of eyes turned toward him, Gil's glaring as darkly as Rosette's but Brier's and Peony's simply annoyed.

"Whatever you're planning," Palmer continued, moving toward them, "there's still time to stop it."

"That suggests anyone would want me to stop it," Brier scoffed.

"We shouldn't want to stop you destroying the world?"

"Not the world. Just them." Brier made a wide gesture toward the Osamli troops.

"You don't have to do this."

"You saw what they did to her. You can't tell me they don't deserve whatever is coming to them. And truly, it solves our problem. We've been hiding, trying to get people to ignore us long enough for us to disappear. Cerise is right. We're *gods*. They"—she motioned again with a jerky movement—"don't get to decide what we do. After this, no one will *dare* do anything like this to us ever again."

Cerise... "Cerise is a trickster goddess." Palmer shook his head. "No good is going to come from listening to her."

"She's been much more helpful to me than you lately." Brier's eyes moved over him derisively. "You're not stopping me, Palmer, so I told you before, you can help me, or you can leave. Your choice."

Palmer opened his mouth to answer, but Peony cut him off with a scoff. She tilted her head, placing a hand on her hip in a very un-Peony-like motion. "You know he isn't going to help you. Can we skip all of this and get on with it?"

Palmer stared at her for a moment before it clicked. "Marina."

She wiggled her fingers in a sarcastic wave.

"What happened to Peony?" Palmer's eyes snapped to Brier. "Why is *she* here?"

"I needed some help, and you said yourself that Peony was connected to the ring. She seemed like the best place to put them."

He released a breath, shaking his head slowly. "Brier, you have to see this is madness."

"This is what's necessary. Now, get off my rooftop."

"No." He continued toward her.

She sighed, looking at him as though he were a gnat buzzing around her ear. "I really don't want to have to force you, Palmer, but I will."

"If you do this, you're *going* to destroy the world."

"Can you for *once* pretend you *think* you know what I'm doing?" Her voice tipped up dangerously.

"Not when you *don't*."

Brier's face went hard, and she glanced at Gil. "Keep him out of the way."

Gil smiled. "Gladly."

"Dear..." Palmer cursed under his breath for what felt like the twentieth time in the past hour and watched as Gil dissolved into a dark cloud. As though she couldn't be bothered with him anymore, Brier turned toward Peony, saying something Palmer couldn't make out before the dark cloud swooped at him.

On instinct, Palmer pulled the dagger from his belt, though what good it would do against a cloud, he had no idea. If he was going to get Gil's blood on it, he needed to force the boy back into human form—and pray he didn't die first. Palmer ducked the first pass, managing to gather enough energy to throw up a net before Gil could swoop again. The cloud thrashed, anger radiating out of it as it found itself caught. Perhaps Palmer didn't have enough energy to take on Brier, but it seemed he could manage Gil.

The cloud jerked to one side and then the other, finally pulling hard enough that it spun Palmer on his heels. With all its force, the cloud tugged, and Palmer realized it was dragging him toward the side of the roof that hadn't yet been completed. The edge led to a five-story drop straight onto the marble of the piazza.

Hissing with frustration, Palmer dropped the net, only to have the cloud swoop right back toward him again. This time, Palmer sent up little bursts, deflecting Gil at the last second with every swoop. The strategy seemed to be working for the moment, but whoever ran out of energy first would ultimately lose that fight. And with the dangerous energy already in the air above them, Palmer didn't like his chances. He sent a glance toward Brier just in time to see her clamp her hand down on Peony's head and close her eyes. A mass of purple and gold energy flowed up her arm, turning into an unearthly glow as though purple and gold flames were licking up around her feet.

"Brier!" he tried calling.

She didn't bother to look at him before Gil swooped again. A little too slow this time, the cloud hit, sending Palmer skidding back across the roof. He groaned, making sure he hadn't lost the dagger before going to push himself up.

Gil materialized just past Palmer's sprawled legs, face pinched. "If you were normal, you'd be dead right now."

"Good thing I'm not, I suppose, then." Palmer stood.

"Other ways to do it." Gil shrugged then rushed forward. His shoulder hit Palmer straight in the stomach.

The air in Palmer's lungs left in a puff as they both tumbled backward. They skidded to a halt too close to the edge for comfort. Palmer turned his head toward Brier. The flames were more purple than gold now, with Peony in a slumped pile on the ground.

"She just said to keep you out of the way." Gil straddled Palmer's chest, keeping him pinned. "Doesn't seem she cares how right now."

With as much of an arc as Palmer could manage, he swung the dagger forward. It connected squarely in the middle of Gil's thigh, slicing deep. Gil exclaimed, reeling back as black began to climb up the scrollwork. Palmer did his best to sit up, his head beginning to spin from the energy in the air.

"You'll pay for that!" Gil screeched, lunging forward.

Not certain he had the energy to do anything else, Palmer rolled to the side. It was enough. Midair, Gil couldn't change directions. The rage on his face turned to surprise as he sailed past Palmer's side then shock as the momentum outlasted the edge of the roof.

"Gil." Palmer turned, reaching out a hand to help, but he felt as though he were moving through sand. His fingers brushed the boy's trouser leg but couldn't get a full grip, and Gil flew over the edge. Palmer scrambled to look. The black cloud began to form but only reached midthigh, as though Gil's body had forgotten how to change above the cut. A second later, the boy hit the ground with a thud.

Palmer grimaced, watching to see if Gil moved, but then the energy shifted again. He took as deep a breath as he could manage and forced himself up onto his feet, though he staggered as if he'd suddenly become drunk.

"Brier!" He forced his voice to be as loud as he could manage. Between the crackling in the air and the energy encasing her body, which was so thick he could barely make out her shape in the middle of it all, he had no idea if she could hear him. "Brier!"

Her head turned, her voice carrying too loudly above everything. "Do you just not *stop*?"

"Not as long as you're like this."

"There's nothing you can do to stop it now." She turned back to face him, a shadowy face visible past the purple flames. "It's almost there. I can feel it."

"You do this, you know I have to stop you."

"You can't."

"I can." He lifted the dagger, already knowing it was partially a bluff. There was a chance he would be able to get close enough to cut her, but it was so infinitesimally small that he wasn't certain it truly counted as a chance. Not with her energy so charged. Not with how dizzy he felt.

"And how would you do that?" Her voice turned mocking. "With that little—" She cut off, the shadowy face tilting as its eyebrows pulled together. "You think you're going to kill me?"

"What?" He fought to get the word out, his breathing already turning labored.

"There's some of Clover in here. I can *see* it. You think that thing is going to kill me!"

"You know I don't want to," he said. "But—"

"Good thing you can't, then." The words felt more whispered in his mind than said out loud. Her arm lifted, and a wave of purple energy shot across the roof, throwing him almost the entire way back toward the stairs before he hit the raised edge with a slam. Palmer attempted to lift his head again, but it was all too much. The world turned gray, and everything went dark.

Chapter Twenty-Five

Nico opened the door to the library, looking around the space for what had to be the fourth time. As always, it was empty, but with none of the other places turning up anything better, the library was still most likely where Brier would be. At least, that was true of the old Brier. The new hard, angry Brier he'd seen over the past couple of days—he couldn't begin to say where she would be. Sure, he'd seen her angry—he'd been the *cause* of her anger plenty of times—but he couldn't begin to imagine what had happened while he was away to turn her into the woman he'd found when he returned. Something had gone horribly wrong. Though she looked like Brier, she certainly wasn't acting like her. Even Palmer Tash had decided to turn on her. Nico never would have thought he'd see the day—not after everything *both* of them had done to save her over the past year.

He knocked a few smaller books off one of the shelves in frustration but then returned to the front, shaking his head, to tell Lauretta and Delphi to move on. He hadn't had the energy to try to get them to leave him alone after Palmer sicced them on him, but blissfully, both women had remained mostly quiet, only asking where to look when they entered a bigger room. After Lauretta's insistence on *talking* over the past weeks, Nico was more than happy to accept that.

They stepped into the hallway, and Nico hesitated. He could keep running circles around the palace, checking all the places he had checked before on the off chance that Brier had moved in the time he'd been looking elsewhere, but there had to be a better way to look. Even half-destroyed, the Augarian Palace was massive. And if Brier didn't want to be found—

"Where to now?" Lauretta asked as they continued to stand in the hall.

Before Nico could think of a properly sarcastic response—or any response at all—Delphi's eyes fluttered. Squeezing them shut, she pressed her fingers to her temples. Lauretta's attention was off Nico in a flash.

"Are you having a vision?"

Delphi nodded slowly, her eyes moving under the closed lids before she opened them to look at Nico. "Is there a small staircase somewhere? Looks like stone. Goes toward the roof."

Nico ran through all of the stairways, trying to think of one that would match that description. "There used to be. I think rubble has blocked it off, though."

"She can dissolve whatever she wants, can't she?"

The words bounced around Nico's mind before he cursed under his breath. He hadn't bothered to open any of the old passageways that he knew were blocked. Most had enough rubble in them that it would have taken several days for workmen to clear the space for them to walk through them again. But Brier wasn't some workman. Nico had seen her dissolve an entire building with a wave of her hand in Venchia, solely because she didn't want to deal with anything that happened inside of it. She would have been able to clear enough space to use those passages if she wanted to.

"I'm an idiot," he mumbled before meeting Delphi's eyes again. "Stairs, you said?"

Delphi nodded. "That's what I saw."

"This way." Nico motioned for them to follow him to the only passage he could think of that matched Delphi's description.

After turning down what he thought was the right hallway, he ran his hand along the wall and found the little catch about where he remembered it being. The door pulled open without complaint, showing the bottom of the stairs he and Brier had used now and again when running about unsupervised—which was more often than not when they were children. Thoughts of happier times only made his shoulders tense. He did his best to ignore them and started up the stairs.

With the cracks and loose stones scattered over the stairs, Nico had serious doubts about their integrity, especially as the deep rumbles started coming louder and faster. From the piles of rubble that looked as if they'd been sloppily erased in places, though, he had to assume that Brier had come this way. He approached the hatch at the top of the stairs far sooner than he wanted, and the odd crackling sound outside didn't make him feel any better. Brier was likely out on the roof, and something was happening.

"You think that thing is going to kill me!" The shriek joined the crackling as Nico pushed the hatch open.

"You know I don't want to. But—" Before Palmer could finish, a wave of purple energy shot across the roof and tossed him like a little girl's poppet, sending him halfway across the length and into the raised edge. The dagger in his hand went skidding as he went limp.

"It's full," Delphi said quietly. "He got Orcus's blood."

Nico's body still revolted against the idea of picking the thing up. His eyes swung from it to Brier, and everything went silent. She was barely recognizable behind the mass of purple, the light from the undulating energy so bright it was nearly flame. Yet Brier herself was in shadow, patches of black swirling in front of her face quickly enough that Nico wasn't certain she could see. He crept to the side, picking up the blade carefully before looking at her again, barely certain what he might be facing once she noticed him.

The purple flames swelled, and Brier thrust up a hand, the crackling energy shooting straight into the sky. The entire day dimmed as though a shadow was moving in front of the sun, but instead of another eclipse, a dark, jagged line opened up over Latysia, slowly revealing a black so deep, so absolute that it nearly hurt to look into it.

Wind kicked up strongly enough that Nico nearly lost his footing. He readjusted just in time to see the buildings along the far edge of Latysia beginning to break apart, little chunks floating up into the abyss.

Nico's grip tightened on the dagger instinctively. He raised his voice, not certain he would be heard above the building wind. "Brier!"

Her hand dropped as her head snapped toward him, the crack not closing but at least not growing either. The shadows around her face lifted enough for him to see the tense glare. "Will you both just leave me alone?" Her voice reverberated, though from the energy or the wind, Nico couldn't tell.

"You need to stop this," Nico yelled from his spot across the roof.

"They deserve it." She looked out toward the men gathered around their tents, the crack seeming to shift toward them as she stared.

"You're going to destroy the world!"

"Dear gods, you sound like Palmer!" Her entire body jerked toward him in one unnatural movement. "I know what I'm doing!"

"You obviously don't." He moved the dagger behind his leg to hide it from view, though with Brier moving in a supernaturally monstrous way, she might not notice it at all. "Stop this now." He tried to keep his voice commanding and level.

"You don't get to tell me what to do anymore, Nic. No one does. You'll all see that's for the best once I'm done." She jerked back toward the horizon and lifted her hand, the crack growing larger with each moment. The wind roared. Entire buildings from what had once been the slums along the river left their foundations as the little men by the tents began to panic, running even as the wind began to drag them backward.

Nico glanced at the hatch and saw Lauretta staring at him, wide-eyed, while Delphi just looked sadly resigned. He moved forward, having to lean against the wind. "Brier."

"Leave. Me. Alone!" Her other hand flew out, a stream of purple flying at him as it had at Palmer.

Nico grunted as the energy hit like a punch to the gut, but it glanced off him, scattering to either side. Brier's other hand dropped, confusion playing over her shadowy face as he continued to move forward. Another beam of energy shot out, hitting even harder than the first but still not knocking him down.

He tried again. "Brier."

"Leave me..." She trailed off, sounding more human in her confusion even as she continued to strike him. Maybe he still had a chance. He reached the flames. Even they didn't harm him.

With the wind whipping so badly he could barely hear himself, Nico yelled, "Stop this!"

"No!" Brier yelled, a thousand years of pure rage mixing with the frustration in her voice. The energy shot straight up to join the abyss. The sky ripped, pulling up buildings, dirt, and men indiscriminately.

"Brier!" he tried a final time, but he couldn't hear his own voice against the chaos. There was nothing left to try. He would do what he'd been trying so hard to escape doing, or he would embrace the end of the world. There was no control left. There barely seemed a Brier left either. Forcing his fist to rise, he whispered, "I'm sorry," though the words were torn away before he could fully form them. With more effort than he'd ever felt in his life, he drove the blade forward into her side.

Everything went silent, entirely frozen for a split second. Brier's mouth opened, pure shock rising above everything else. The purple light flickered behind her eyes and in her open mouth as the flames diminished. Her hand dropped to her side, the wind dying down as she looked at him, her expression more confused than angry. "You... stabbed me."

Her legs gave out. Nico released his hold on the knife to catch her, carefully lowering her to the ground as her head fell back. He knelt, barely registering the light returning as the sky slowly healed, no more power feeding into it.

"Bri...?" He touched her face. Her skin was still warm though she didn't move. "Brier."

A hand touched his shoulder—Lauretta or Delphi.

He shook it off. "Don't you *dare* speak to me right now."

Lauretta knelt beside him, pulling the dagger free before bunching up fabric to press to Brier's side. "If you work fast, you may still be able to save her."

Nico's eyebrows pulled together. "*What*?" Whatever sick joke the woman was playing at after weeks of trying to convince him to do exactly what he had just done, she deserved to be stabbed as well.

"Look around you." Lauretta continued to press the fabric to Brier's side as she fumbled for something at her waist. She glanced up when Nico didn't stop staring at her. "Go ahead. Look."

Nico did as directed, seeing Palmer still collapsed by the wall and Peony slumped by Brier's opposite side. They'd been previously hidden by the flames. He turned his head enough to look back toward the hatch and saw Delphi slumped as well. His mind tried to take it all in. "What...?"

A gold glow brought his attention back to Lauretta, and he looked down just in time to see a small device pressed against Brier's side—something shiny, shaped similarly to the veiling device they had taken off the soldier what felt like a lifetime ago.

"It won't have power for long," she explained. "All their powers will be gone soon, but Delphi made sure it had Palmer's blood on it before all of this. It may still not do any good, but it's a chance."

"A chance for *what*?" Out of all the emotions fighting for space inside him, anger was quickly beginning to win.

"You needed to kill the god." Lauretta pulled the device back with a pinched look. "Not necessarily the body. Delphi couldn't see anything past you doing it—killing them. But she said there was a chance."

"Killing *them*," Nico said.

Lauretta released a heavy breath and sat back on her heels, nearly close to tears as she met his eyes. "She wasn't exactly an *oracle*, if you hadn't figured that out."

Nico's mind turned over, attempting to keep up with everything. Something clicked into place. "Isnot..."

Lauretta nodded even though he couldn't complete the goddess's name. "She truly felt... awful that this was the way everything had to happen. She couldn't just come out and say it, but he was right." She glanced at Palmer before bringing her eyes back to Nico. "There's no one future, and this was the only path that led us here."

"To Brier *dead*?"

"To all of them dead." Lauretta sucked in a shaky breath. "Remember what I told you about the first gods' war? The world almost ended then, so Isnotra did the only thing she could do: she scattered them all. When she started having visions about this place, about how many were gathering once again, she began planning how to scatter everyone again, but none of those futures worked. They all ended with... that." She motioned up to the once again blue sky. "The abyss opening. The world ending. The only option was for them—all of them, the entire pantheon—to die. The blood on that dagger wasn't *permission*. Driving their energies into Chaos... that's the only way to end it all."

"To kill the gods?"

Laurette shrugged. "The world is changing. There are fewer believers. More and more don't believe in the pantheon. The Osamli don't. It's why she started working with them. She said it was time to let all the old gods die. All the magic and powers... the world will go on without them. It just wouldn't have gone on with them."

Nico looked down at Brier, still limp in his arms. "She may not die?"

"I don't know. Delphi couldn't see it, so I certainly couldn't."

He narrowed his eyes.

"You could just do *that* because her powers rubbed off on you," Laurette said. "I knew Delphi as well as you knew Brier. Can't say I ever saw the future, but I sometimes knew things. That should be gone now, though."

Nico released a breath through his teeth. "You knew she may not die, and you still let me believe—"

"The *only way*," Lauretta said. "You have no idea how many futures Delphi looked through. This was the only one that brought us here, at least by the time she caught what was happening and Kosmos had already let himself be outpaced. He'd weakened himself enough that she had to keep blocking his visions, only giving him these ones."

"She engineered *all* of this."

"She was the goddess of wisdom, the only one to keep her memories after the first gods' war. She's been watching out for all of us far longer than any of us have been alive. With each new reincarnation, she made sure no other god became too powerful, trying to keep a balance when no one else would. Perhaps it's the Ouenen in me, but I do think we always had the best patroness."

A groan from Peony made Nico start. She stirred then sat up, rubbing the side of her head. "What happened?"

"Do you want the long or the short version?" Nico grumbled as she looked around the rooftop, eyes going wide.

Standing, Lauretta brushed her skirt off and studied the mix of people around the space with a sigh. "We should get them all downstairs. Like I said, Delphi wasn't able to see beyond right here, so I can't say when or if they're all going to wake up, but the deal was they would stay out of the city until I signaled."

"They?" Peony asked.

"The troops out there." Lauretta motioned vaguely toward the horizon before turning to gather Delphi up. "It's all rather complicated, and Delphi knows it better than I do, but I'll do my best to explain inside."

Chapter Twenty-Six

Palmer slowly blinked, trying to get his eyes to focus. The ceiling above him looked familiar, though he couldn't place why. Then it all came rushing back to him. The roof. The dagger. He sat up with a jolt and looked around the room. First things first: it *was* a room, so the universe hadn't ended. What had happened, though, he wasn't certain he wanted to know.

Placing his feet on the floor, he listened. Though he was alone in the room, there were voices out in the hall. By instinct, he attempted to pull on his powers to see who it might be, but of course, nothing came to him.

So that hasn't changed. He pushed himself off the soft mattress, frowning. His entire body ached. He pulled up the side of his shirt and saw the deep-purple bruise splayed across his ribs. Grimacing, he glanced at his wrists and made sure that he didn't have one of the cuffs on. It seemed something else was causing issues with his powers this time.

"Something else to deal with," he mumbled before moving carefully toward the door.

"Delphi's coming around." Lauretta's voice floated down the hall. "She's just a little confused. Like I said, she's always had her memories, so without Isnotra... it may be a while before she's fully back to herself. If there will be a *back to herself* after all of this."

Palmer left the little room and started down the hall.

"Anything with...?" Lauretta trailed off.

"Still asleep," Nico's low grumble answered. "Though her heart's beating, which is more than can be said about some of the times I've found her after these sorts of things."

A little tingle of hope tried to take hold. The world was, as far as Palmer could tell, in one piece, and Brier was possibly still alive. He had no idea how that could have happened, but if that was where they were, he was more than happy to take it. Favoring his hurt side, Palmer moved toward the voices and turned the corner.

Face-to-face with Palmer, Nico cut off mid-word as their eyes met.

Lauretta twisted to look at Nico and offered Palmer a quick smile. "Hey. How are you feeling?"

"Fine," Palmer said, feeling no need to get into any of his current complaints. "What happened?"

They were silent for a moment before Nico said, "You've been turned human."

Palmer pulled his eyebrows together. "What?"

"You'd better come with me," Nico said before addressing Lauretta again. "You'll check on Carmella? She was throwing a fit last I saw her. Maybe with your anchoress training, you can talk her down."

As sarcastic as Nico made the final sentence sound, Lauretta still smiled and moved off. Nico motioned Palmer forward and turned into the room behind him. Palmer followed, a sense of trepidation forming low in his stomach as he walked into the darkened space. With the curtains drawn on the far side, most of the room was shadows, but his eyes quickly found the shape lying in the center of the bed, chest rising and falling. The urge to rush forward moved through him, but his feet suddenly felt frozen to the tile floor.

He swallowed, trying to dislodge the lump in his throat. His voice still came out strained. "She's not...?"

"Dead?" Nico completed. "Doesn't seem that way."

"But you stopped her."

"We all did exactly what we were supposed to, apparently."

Palmer continued to give him the same confused look. With a heavy sigh, Nico laid out the full story—who Delphi actually was, how he'd been pulling strings to see all the gods dead...

Palmer pressed a hand to his bruised side. "That's why I'm not healing?"

"Your powers should be gone. For all of you. Lauretta used the last bit to heal Brier's side"—Nico's eyes went to the bed—"but there's no saying that it was enough. Everyone whose body could take what happened has slowly been waking up. We don't know about her."

Whose body could take what happened? The phrasing didn't make Palmer feel any better.

"Gil didn't survive the fall he took."

Guilt joined the trepidation in Palmer's stomach. He should have been able to stop that—grab the boy or not stop him from transforming with that stupid dagger. But what was done was done. And without powers, there was certainly no hope of bringing him back.

Nico continued. "We found him out on the piazza with... well, Lauretta believes it's Cerise."

"*Believes*?" Palmer repeated, not certain he wanted to know what that meant.

Nico opened his mouth but then nodded for Palmer to follow him into a nearby room. He moved to a desk, looked at a box, then pulled the sheet off the top. He motioned Palmer to join him.

Stepping forward cautiously, Palmer peered over the edge to see what he first thought was a remarkably large dove before realizing it was a raven with gray and white feathers.

"Cerise could keep shifting younger, apparently," Nico related as though he barely believed it himself, "and she hadn't been killed, so *that's* her original form. Without her powers, she was just too old."

"She was *literally* a raven."

"So says Lauretta. Or so says Delphi, I suppose. It's what Delphi told Lauretta before everything got wiped away." He shook his head and moved back to Brier's room. "So we're waiting to see..."

"If Brier wakes up."

Nico nodded, crossing his arms as he stood against one of the walls.

Palmer released a tense breath, staring at the still body in the bed before him. "Rosette?"

"Still not talking but awake. We found her at the bottom of the main stairwell. Lauretta found her a doll from somewhere, and she seems perfectly happy entertaining herself, even if she won't look at anyone."

Palmer nodded and added seeing Rosette to his list of things to do now that he was awake. The world he'd woken to didn't entirely make sense. He took a seat at the edge of the bed. Brier's face was entirely placid and innocent, nothing like the near monster that had been standing on the roof. But if she did wake up, would she even be the old Brier? How much of that anger had been hers and how much simply the energy inside of her? Marina had gone power mad without a Kosmos to balance her and gotten herself killed by running into battle simply to fight. He'd let his powers get taken away, and the same thing had happened to the woman in front of him—the woman he had to admit he still loved, powers or no.

"And we have to decide where we're going," Nico said.

Palmer tore his eyes away from Brier's sleeping form to look back at Nico. "Going?"

"Delphi was working with the Osamli to have all of this happen. Her blood is what gave them the ability to use those veil devices. She's the reason so many were already here. They've apparently been waiting for weeks for everything else that was supposed to happen."

Palmer continued to stare, his anger beginning to bubble up at the thought of what Delphi had allowed to happen to Rosette—to *him*—in the name of this grand orchestration.

"She offered them Latysia for their help."

"Because it's hers to give?" Palmer shook his head.

"They're the Osamli Empire. They could just take it if they wanted to at this point, so I don't think it's worth arguing about. They've already started sending Gully's men home—most of whom seemed more than happy to be out of here, between Brier's little show earlier and the number of Osamli troops that came knocking on the gate—and we don't exactly have any giant cracks in the sky that are going to keep them out."

"The sky cracked open?"

"You missed the whole show." Nico shook his head, his eyes drifting to Brier. A twitch of pain moved over his face as he looked at her before it turned back into his normal stoic mask. "If she wakes up, do you think...?"

He didn't finish the sentence. Palmer didn't need him to. What would be waiting for them when everything was completely said and done, he didn't know. And with a world without gods or oracles, no one could know.

Palmer gave a lackluster shrug. "We'll just have to wait to see."

Chapter Twenty-Seven

Rosette poked her head out of the little room the nice lady, Suora Lauretta, had left her in. All day, there'd been men walking up and down the halls, talking in a funny language that made her nervous for some reason she didn't really understand, but now everything had gone quiet. No one was in sight, so with her doll tucked under her arm, she ducked out into the hall. Her mind felt a little fuzzy, memories not having settled quite right, but for the first time in her life, she felt light. Free.

Finding one of the secret passageways along the hallway, she pulled the small door open and followed it toward Brier's room. Men were talking by the other end of the passage, but it was Palmer and Nico, and Rosette could understand what they were saying. And even if Nico could be a mean bully, he didn't make Rosette scared. If he was mean again, she could always just kick him like last time. She smiled. *That* memory was entirely clear. The way he'd doubled, and the slight smirk Brier had given after it had happened... Rosette *liked* that memory.

"Lauretta's taking Delphi back to Ouene, unsurprisingly," Nico was saying, "and Peony's already agreed to go as well. I think she's had enough of all of this, and I can't say I blame her. Carmella has family up north if she wants to go there. That just leaves the rest of us."

"There are plenty of Adessis around," Palmer said.

"I'll land on my feet, I'm sure."

Not caring what they were talking about, Rosette ducked through a side passage that would take her into the hallway on the other side—as long as she ducked over some bigger rocks that had fallen—and slipped into Brier's room.

252

Brier was asleep in the middle of her bed, so Rosette climbed up on the side and picked up the silver hairbrush on the table next to the bed so she could fix the doll's hair.

The mattress behind her shifted. "Rosie?"

Rosette turned around, holding out the doll. "She lost her friend. She's lonely."

The corner of Brier's mouth turned up. "That's okay, *piccola*. We'll find her another friend. I'm sure there are plenty buried somewhere around here."

"She doesn't *want* another friend." Rosette pouted. "I think she needs a family."

"Well, maybe we can find her one of those too." Brier smiled before grimacing as she tried to sit up.

"Are you hurt?"

"I'm fine, *piccola*," Brier said, even though her face said she was fibbing. Adults always did that.

The voices in the hall cut off, and the door was pushed open in a rush. Both Palmer and Nico were there.

"Brier." Palmer's eyes moved between Brier and Rosette, almost as if *he* was scared of them.

"Rosie lost her other doll." Brier pet Rosette's hair, her other hand holding her side. "Gods, what happened?"

"What do you remember?" Nico moved farther into the room.

Brier's face scrunched up in concentration, but she just ended up shaking her head. "Not a lot. But... we weren't here, were we? There were... ruins?"

The tension on Palmer's face lessened, and he moved forward as well. "There's a lot happening. It's messed with some people's memories, but... you feel like you?"

"Should I feel like someone else?" She lifted an eyebrow.

A full smile broke out on Palmer's face, and he bent down to kiss her.

"Ew!" Rosette wedged herself between them. "Don't be gross!"

Palmer pulled back as though he was shocked Rosette had said something.

"Well..." Brier gave a weak smile, still holding her side. "Someone is going to have to tell me why I feel like I just fell down a flight of stairs, but I think food is in order first. Don't you, *piccola*? A family dinner so your doll isn't lonely?"

Rosette looked around the room. If Brier and Palmer were her mom and dad, she supposed she would take Nico if she had to—a *really* old brother who was *really* annoying. Or... something. She'd figure it out later.

She held up the little doll. "She'd like that."

Also by Jessica Dall

Beyond the Style Manual
Building the Bones: Outlining Your Novel

Order and Chaos
Raining Embers
Graven Idols
Shattered Tempests

Watch for more at jessicadall.com.

About the Author

Jessica Dall finished her first novel at the age of fifteen and has been hooked on writing ever since. In the past few years, she has published two novels, *The Copper Witch* and *The Porcelain Child,* along with a number of short stories that have appeared in both magazines and anthologies.

In college, Jessica interned at a publishing house, where her "writing hobby" slowly turned into a variety of writing careers. She currently works as both as an editor and creative writing teacher in Washington, DC.

When not busy editing, writing, or teaching, Jessica enjoys crafting and piano, and spending time with her friends and family. She can most often be found at her home in Maryland with a notebook and her much-loved, sometimes-neglected husband.

Read more at jessicadall.com.

About the Publisher

Dear Reader,

We hope you enjoyed this book. Please consider leaving a review on your favorite book site.

Visit https://RedAdeptPublishing.com to see our entire catalogue.

Don't forget to subscribe to our monthly newsletter to be notified of future releases and special sales.